continued . . .

BARBARA METZGER

Father Christmas

A SIGNET BOOK

SIGNET
Published by New American Library, a division of
Penguin Group (USA) Inc., 375 Hudson Street,
New York, New York 10014, USA
Penguin Group (Canada), 90 Eglinton Avenue East, Suite 700, Toronto,
Ontario M4P 2Y3, Canada (a division of Pearson Penguin Canada Inc.)
Penguin Books Ltd., 80 Strand, London WC2R 0RL, England
Penguin Ireland, 25 St. Stephen's Green, Dublin 2,
Ireland (a division of Penguin Books Ltd.)
Penguin Group (Australia), 250 Camberwell Road, Camberwell, Victoria 3124,
Australia (a division of Pearson Australia Group Pty. Ltd.)
Penguin Books India Pvt. Ltd., 11 Community Centre, Panchsheel Park,
New Delhi - 110 017, India
Penguin Group (NZ), 67 Apollo Drive, Rosedale, North Shore 0632,
New Zealand (a division of Pearson New Zealand Ltd.)
Penguin Books (South Africa) (Pty.) Ltd., 24 Sturdee Avenue,
Rosebank, Johannesburg 2196, South Africa

Penguin Books Ltd., Registered Offices:
80 Strand, London WC2R 0RL, England

Published by Signet, an imprint of New American Library, a division of
Penguin Group (USA) Inc. Previously published in a Ballantine Books edition and in a Signet double edition with *Christmas Wishes*.

First Signet Printing (Double Edition), November 2004
First Signet Printing ($6.99 Edition), October 2008
10 9 8 7 6 5 4 3

Copyright © Barbara Metzger, 1995
All rights reserved

Dedicated to Peace on Earth,
Goodwill to All Mankind.
Soon.

Chapter One

The Duke of Ware needed an heir. Like a schoolyard taunt, the gruesome refrain floated in his mind, bobbing to the surface on a current of brandy. Usually a temperate man, His Grace was just a shade on the go. It was going to take more than a shade to get him to go to Almack's.

"Hell and blast!" Leland Warrington, fifth and at this point possibly last Duke of Ware, consulted his watch again. Ten o'clock, and everyone knew Almack's patronesses barred its doors at eleven. Not even London's premier *parti*, wealth, title, and looks notwithstanding, could gain admittance after the witching hour. "Blasted witches," Ware cursed once more, slamming his glass down on the table that stood so conveniently near his so-comfortable leather armchair at White's. "Damnation."

His companion snapped up straighter in his facing seat. "What's that? The wine gone off?" The Honorable Crosby Fanshaw sipped cautiously at his own drink. "Seems fine to me." He called for another bottle.

Fondly known as Crow for his anything-but-somber style of dress, the baronet was a studied contrast to his longtime friend. The duke was the one wearing the stark black and white of Weston's finest evening wear, spread over broad shoulders and well-muscled thighs, while Crow Fanshaw's spindly frame was draped in magenta pantaloons, saffron waistcoat, lime green wasp-waisted coat. The duke looked away. Fanshaw would never get into Almack's in that outfit. Then again, Fanshaw didn't need to get into Almack's.

"No, it's not the wine, Crow. It's a wife. I need one."

The baronet slipped one manicured finger under his elaborate neckcloth to loosen the noose conjured up by the very thought of matrimony. He shuddered. "Devilish things, wives."

"I'll drink to that," Ware said, and did. "But I need one nevertheless if I'm to beget the next duke."

"Ah." Crow nodded sagely, careful not to disturb his pomaded curls. "Noblesse oblige and all that. The sacred duty of the peerage: to beget more little aristocratic blue bloods to carry on the name. I thank heaven m'brother holds the title. Let Virgil worry about the succession and estates."

"With you as heir, he'd need to." Crow Fanshaw wouldn't know a mangel-wurzel from manure, and they both knew it.

The baronet didn't take offense. "What, ruin m'boots in dirt? M'valet would give notice, then where would I be? 'Sides, Virgil's managing to fill his nursery nicely, two boys and a girl. Then there are m'cousin's parcel of brats if he needs extras. I'm safe." He raised his glass in a toast. "Condolences, old friend."

Ware frowned, lowering thick dark brows over his

hazel eyes. Easy for Crow to laugh, his very soul wasn't engraved with the Ware family motto: *Semper servimus.* We serve forever. Forever, dash it, the duke unnecessarily reminded himself. His heritage, everything he was born and bred to be and to believe, demanded an heir. Posterity demanded it, all those acres and people dependent upon him demanded it, Aunt Eudora demanded it! God, King, and Country, that's what the Wares served, she insisted. Well, Leland made his donations to the church, he took his tedious seat in Parliament, and he served as a diplomat when the Foreign Office needed him. That was not enough. The Bible said be fruitful and multiply, quoted his childless aunt. The King, bless his mad soul, needed more loyal peers to advise and direct his outrageous progeny. And the entire country, according to Eudora Warrington, would go to rack and ruin without a bunch of little Warringtons trained to manage Ware's vast estates and investments. At the very least, her annuity might be in danger.

Leland checked his watch again. Ten-ten. He felt as if he were going to the tooth-drawer, dreading the moment yet wishing it were over. "What time do you have, Crow?"

Crosby fumbled at the various chains crisscrossing his narrow chest. "I say, you must have an important appointment, the way you keep eyeing your timepiece. Which is it, that new red-haired dancer at the opera or the dashing widow you had up in your phaeton yesterday?" While the duke sat glaring, Fanshaw pulled out his quizzing glass, then a seal with his family crest before finally retrieving his watch fob. "Fifteen minutes past the hour."

Ware groaned. "Almack's" was all he could manage to say. It was enough.

Fanshaw dropped his watch and grabbed up the looking glass by its gem-studded handle, tangling ribbons and chains as he surveyed his friend for signs of dementia. "I thought you said Almack's."

"I did. I told you, I need an heir."

"But Almack's, Lee? Gads, you must be dicked in the nob. Castaway, that's it." He pushed the bottle out of the duke's reach.

"Not nearly enough," His Grace replied, pulling the decanter back and refilling his glass. "I promised Aunt Eudora I'd look over the latest crop of dewy-eyed debs."

Crosby downed a glass in commiseration. "I understand about the heir and all, but there must be an easier way, by Jupiter. I mean, m'brother's girl is making her come-out this year. She's got spots. And her friends giggle. Think on it, man, they are, what? Seventeen? Eighteen? And you're thirty-one!"

"Thirty-two," His Grace growled, "as my aunt keeps reminding me."

"Even worse. What in the world do you have in common with one of those empty-headed infants?"

"What do I have in common with that redhead from the opera? She's only eighteen, and the only problem you have with that is she's in my bed, not yours."

"But she's a ladybird! You don't have to talk to them, not like a wife!"

The duke stood as if to go. "Trust me, I don't intend to have anything more to do with this female I'll marry than it takes to get me a son."

"If a son is all you want, why don't you just adopt one? Be easier in the long run, more comfortable, too. M'sister's got a surplus. I'm sure she'd be glad to get rid of one or two, the way she's always trying to pawn them off on m'mother so she can go to some house party or other."

The duke ignored his friend's suggestion that the next Duke of Ware be anything less than a Warrington, but he did sit down. "That's another thing: No son of mine is going to be raised up by nannies and tutors and underpaid schoolmasters."

"Why not? That's the way we were brought up, and we didn't turn out half bad, did we?"

Leland picked a bit of imaginary fluff off his superfine sleeve. Not half bad? Not half good, either, he reflected. Crow was an amiable fribble, while he himself was a libertine, a pleasure-seeker, an ornament of society. Oh, he was a conscientious landowner, for a mostly absentee landlord, and he did manage to appear at the House for important votes. Otherwise his own entertainment—women, gaming, sporting—was his primary goal. There was nothing of value in his life. He intended to do better by his son. "I mean to be a good father to the boy, a guide, a teacher, a friend."

"A Bedlamite, that's what. Try being a friend to some runny-nosed brat with scraped knees and a pocketful of worms." Crosby shivered. "I know just the ticket to cure you of such bubble-brained notions: Why don't you come down to Fanshaw Hall with me for the holidays? Virgil'd be happy to have you for the cards and hunting, and m'sister-in-law would be in alt to have such a nonpareil as houseguest. That niece who's being fired off this season will be there, so you can see how hopeless young chits are, all airs and affectations one minute, tears and tantrums the next. Why, if you can get Rosalie to talk of anything but gewgaws and gossip, I'll eat my hat. Best of all, m'sister will be at the Hall with her nursery brood.

No, best of all is if the entire horde gets the mumps and stays home. But, 'struth, you'd change your tune about this fatherhood gammon if you just spent a day with the little savages."

Ware smiled. "I don't mean to insult your family, but your sister's ill-behaved brats only prove my point that this whole child-rearing thing could be improved upon with a little careful study."

"Trust me, Lee, infants ain't like those new farming machines you can read up on. Come down and see. At least I can promise you a good wine cellar at the Hall."

The duke shook his head. "Thank you, Crow, but I have to refuse. You see, I really am tired of spending the holidays with other people's families."

"What I see is you've been bitten bad by this new bug of yours. Carrying on the line. Littering the countryside with butterstamps. Next thing you know, you'll be pushing a pram instead of racing a phaeton. I'll miss you, Lee." He flicked a lacy handkerchief from his sleeve and dabbed at his eyes while the duke grinned at the performance. Fanshaw's next words changed that grin into so fierce a scowl that a lesser man, or a less loyal friend, would have been tempted to bolt: "Don't mean to be indelicate, but you know getting leg-shackled isn't any guarantee of getting heirs."

"Of course I know that, blast it! I ought to. I've already been married." The duke finished his drink. "Twice." He tossed back another glassful to emphasize the point. "And all for nothing."

Fanshaw wasn't one to let a friend drink alone, even if his words were getting slurred and his thoughts muddled. He refilled his own glass. Twice.

"Not for nothing. Got a handsome dowry both times."

"Which I didn't need," His Grace muttered into his drink.

"And got the matchmaking mamas off your back until you learned to depress their ambitions with one of your famous setdowns."

"Which if I'd learned earlier, I wouldn't be in this hobble today."

The duke's first marriage had been a love match: He was in love with the season's reigning Toast, Carissa was in love with his wealth and title. Her mother made sure he never saw past the Diamond's beauty to the cold, rock-hard shrew beneath who didn't want to be his wife, she wanted to be a duchess. There wasn't one extravagance she didn't indulge, not one risqué pleasure she didn't gratify, not one mad romp she didn't join. Until she broke her beautiful neck in a curricle race.

Ware's second marriage was one of convenience, except that it wasn't. He carefully selected a quiet, retiring sort of girl whose pale loveliness was as different from Carissa's flamboyance as night from day. *Her* noble parents had managed to conceal, while they were dickering over the settlements, that Lady Floris was a sickly child, that her waiflike appeal had more to do with a weak constitution than any gentle beauty. Floris was content to stay in the shadows after their wedding, until she became a shadow. Then she faded away altogether. Ware was twice a widower, never a father. To his knowledge, he'd never even sired a bastard on one of his mistresses, but he didn't want to think about the implications of that.

"What time do you have?"

Crosby peered owl-eyed at his watch, blinked, then turned it right side up. "Ten-thirty. Time for another drink." He raised his glass, spilling only a drop on the froth of lace at his shirtsleeve. "To your bride."

Leland couldn't do it. The wine would turn to vinegar on his tongue. Instead, he proposed a toast of his own. "To my cousin Tony, the bastard to blame for this whole deuced coil."

Crosby drank, but reflected, "If he was a bastard, then it wouldn't have mattered if the nodcock went and got himself killed. He couldn't have been your heir anyway."

His Grace waved that aside with one elegant if unsteady hand. "Tony was a true Warrington all right, my father's only brother's only son. My heir. So *he* got to go fight against Boney when the War Office turned me down."

"Protective of their dukes, those chaps."

"And *he* got to be a hero, the lucky clunch."

"Uh, not to be overparticular, but live heroes are lucky, dead ones ain't."

Leland went on as though his friend hadn't spoken: "And he was a fertile hero to boot. Old Tony didn't have to worry about shuffling off this mortal coil without a trace. He left twins, twin boys, no less, the bounder, and he didn't even have a title to bequeath them or an acre of land!"

"Twin boys, you say? Tony's get? There's your answer, Lee, not some flibbertigibbet young miss. Go gather the sprigs and have the raising of 'em your way if that's what you want to do. With any luck they'll be out of nappies and you can send 'em off to school as soon as you get tired of 'em. Should take about a month, I'd guess."

Ware frowned. "I can't go snabble my cousin's

sons, Crow. Tony's widow just brought them back
to her parents' house from the Peninsula.''

Fanshaw thought on it a minute, chewing his
lower lip. ''Then marry that chit, I say. You get your
heirs with Warrington blood, your brats to try to
make into proper English gentlemen, and a proven
breeder into the bargain. 'Sides, she can't be an antidote; Tony Warrington had taste.''

The duke merely looked down his slightly aquiline
nose and stood up to leave. ''She's a local vicar's
daughter.''

''Good enough to be Mrs. Major Warrington, eh,
but not the Duchess of Ware?'' The baronet nodded,
not noticing that his starched shirtpoints disarranged
his artful curls. ''Then you'd best toddle off to King
Street, where the *ton* displays its merchandise.
Unless . . .''

Ware turned back like a drowning man hearing
the splash of a tossed rope. ''Unless . . . ?''

''Unless you ask the widow for just one of the
bantlings. She might just go for it. I mean, how many
men are going to take on a wife with *two* tokens of
her dead husband's devotion to support? There's not
much space in any vicarage I know of, and you said
yourself Tony didn't leave much behind for them to
live on. 'Sides, you can appeal to her sense of fair-
ness. She has two sons and you have none.''

Leland removed the bottle and glass from his
friend's vicinity on his way out of the room. ''You
have definitely had too much to drink, my tulip.
Your wits have gone begging for dry land.''

And the Duke of Ware still needed an heir.

Heaving breasts, fluttering eyelashes, gushing sim-
pers, blushing whimpers—and those were the hope-

ful mamas. The daughters were worse. Aunt Eudora could ice-skate in Hades before her nephew returned to Almack's.

Ware had thought he'd observe the crop of debutantes from a discreet, unobtrusive distance. Sally Jersey thought differently. With pointed fingernails fastened to his wrist like the talons of a raptor, she dragged her quarry from brazen belle to arrogant heiress to wilting wallflower. At the end of each painful, endless dance, when he had, perforce, to return his partner to her chaperone, there was *la* Jersey waiting in prey with the next willing sacrificial virgin.

The Duke of Ware needed some air.

He told the porter at the door he was going to blow a cloud, but he didn't care if the fellow let him back in or not. Leland didn't smoke. He never had, but he thought he might take it up now. Perhaps the foul odor, yellowed fingers, and stained teeth could discourage some of these harpies, but he doubted it.

Despite the damp chill in the air, the duke was not alone on the outer steps of the marriage mart. At first all he could see in the gloomy night was the glow from a sulphurous cigar. Then another, younger gentleman stepped out of the fog.

"Is that you, Ware? Here at Almack's? I cannot believe it," exclaimed Nigel, the scion of the House of Ellerby which, according to rumors, was more than a tad dilapidated. Hence the young baron's appearance at Almack's, Leland concluded. "Dash it! I wish I'd been in on the bet." Which propensity to gamble likely accounted for the Ellerbys' crumbling coffers.

"Bet? What bet?"

"The one that got you to Almack's, Duke. By Zeus, it must have been a famous wager! Who challenged you? How long must you stay before you can collect? How much—"

"There was no wager," Ware quietly inserted into the youth's enthusiastic litany.

The cigar dropped from Ellerby's fingers. His mouth fell open. "No wager? You mean . . . ?"

"I came on my own. As a favor to my aunt, if you must know."

Ellerby added two plus two and, to the duke's surprise, came up with the correct, dismaying answer. "B'gad, wait till the sharks smell fresh blood in the water." He jerked his head, weak chin and all, toward the stately portals behind them.

Leland grimaced. "Too late, they've already got the scent."

"Lud, there will be females swooning in your arms and chits falling off horses on your doorstep. I'd get out of town if I were you. Then again, word gets out you're in the market for a new bride, you won't be safe anywhere. With all those holiday house parties coming up, you'll be showered with invitations."

The duke could only agree. That was the way of the world.

"Please, Your Grace," Ellerby whined, "don't accept Lady Carstaire's invite. I'll be seated below the salt if you accept."

No slowtop either, Leland nodded toward the closed doors. "Tell me which one is Miss Carstaire, so I can sidestep the introduction."

"She's the one in puce tulle with mouse brown sausage curls and a squint." At Ware's look of disbelief, the lordling added, "And ten thousand pounds a year."

"I think I can manage not to succumb to the lady's

charms," Ware commented dryly, then had to listen to the coxcomb's gratitude.

"And I'll give you fair warning, Duke. If you do accept for any of those house parties, lock your door and never go anywhere alone. The misses and their mamas will be quicker to yell 'compromise' than you can say 'Jack Rabbit.' "

Leland gravely thanked Lord Ellerby for the advice, hoping the baron wasn't such an expert on compromising situations from trying to nab a rich wife the cad's way. Fortune hunting was bad enough. He wished him good luck with Miss Carstaire, but declined Ellerby's suggestion that they return inside together. His Grace had had enough. And no, he assured the baron, he was not going to accept any of the holiday invitations. The Duke of Ware was going to spend Christmas right where he belonged, at Ware Hold in Warefield, Warwickshire, with his own family: one elderly aunt, two infant cousins.

Before going to bed that night, Leland had another brandy to ease the headache he already had. He sat down to write his agent in Warefield to notify the household of his plans, then he started to write to Tony's widow, inviting her to the castle. Before he got too far past the salutation, however, Crow Fanshaw's final, foxed suggestion kept echoing in his mind: The Duke of Ware should get a fair share.

Chapter Two

"Of all the outrageous, high-handed, arrogant—"

Vicar Beckwith cleared his throat. "That is enough, Graceanne."

"No, Papa, it is not nearly enough! That . . . that bounder thinks he can simply appear in Warefield village and claim Willy! What am I, then, his liege vassal from the feudal days, that some dirty-dish duke can demand my firstborn son? By Heaven, I am not!"

"I said that is enough, Graceanne," the vicar firmly declared. "I shall not have blasphemy at the dinner table, nor such disrespect for your betters poured into Prudence's innocent ears."

Better? Graceanne fumed, but she looked across the table to where her younger sister sat. Pru's blond head was deferentially lowered, but not enough that Graceanne couldn't see the smirk on her lips or the malicious gleam in her eye. If there was innocence at this table, the overcooked capon they were about to eat held more of it than seventeen-year-old Prudence.

When Graceanne would have continued to argue—indeed, she was so angry she would have thrown crockery had she still been in Portugal—her mother begged, "Please, dear, my nerves." Mrs. Beckwith, in her Bath chair at the other end of the sparsely filled table, dabbed at her forehead with a wisp of cloth.

Graceanne subsided, and addressed herself to decapitating a boiled parsnip. She had to choke back her ire when her father smoothed out the embossed page of Ware's letter—a letter she couldn't help but notice was addressed to herself, Mrs. Anthony Warrington—and stated, "His Grace's claim to Wellesley is not entirely out of bounds, daughter. I'll have to think on it."

Graceanne put down her knife and fork. She loathed parsnips and the capon tasted like sawdust. As calmly as she could, choking on the urge to scream, she said, "There is nothing to think about, Papa. Wellesley—Willy—is my son the same as Leslie. I shall never let anyone else have the raising of either of them, duke or not."

"You are being overhasty and emotional, daughter." The vicar managed to express his disapproval around a mouthful of green beans. Then again, the vicar never had trouble expressing his disapproval. "And selfish. Think of the advantages young Wellesley would have."

Graceanne knew her father was thinking of the advantages *he* would gain by letting Ware have Willy: the gratitude of a wealthy patron, and one less little boy creating noise and mess and expense in his frugal household. Furthermore, she suspected her father considered the identical twins to be freaks of nature, somehow unholy. He'd be relieved to have the taint of the diabolical removed from his hearth.

Beckwith was warming to his theme: "I shouldn't have to remind you that what I can provide on a parson's income can never come close to what Ware can offer. Think of Wellesley's education, the career opportunities, the chance to better himself in the world."

"The chance to become a care-for-naught wastrel like his noble benefactor? An opportunity to become a libertine? Or perhaps you think three-year-old Willy needs lessons in arrogance? Is that what you want for your grandson?"

Beckwith paid her objections as much notice as he would have the capon's protests over being eaten. "I am certain that on reflection you wouldn't wish to hold the boy back with your foolish prejudices and idle gossip. Think how much further our limited resources could stretch in Leslie's direction if the duke takes over Wellesley's upbringing. Yes, a proper mother would set aside her own whims for the best interests of her child."

"Whims? Why, I—"

"Cook tells me that May Turner is ailing, Graceanne dear," Mrs. Beckwith interrupted in quavering tones. "Perhaps you would go visit her this afternoon? I would, naturally, but . . ."

"Of course, Mother." Graceanne returned to pushing the parsnips around on her dish, despite her father's glower. At least her twenty-three years, motherhood, and widowed status gave her the privilege of leaving food on her plate. Heaven knew she had to fight for every other right. But her children? No one could steal them from her.

"I agree with Papa, Grace," Prudence was saying although no one had asked her opinion. "I think you should at least consider the duke's offer to take

Willy. After all, it's not as if you'll never see him again. He'll be just next door at Ware Hold. You can visit anytime."

"And take my little sister to cheer him up, especially when the duke is in residence, or happens to have guests? In particular, young bachelor guests who are well-to-pass?" Graceanne couldn't keep the sarcasm from her voice; Prudence had never had an unselfish motive yet. Willy's well-being was so far from being Pru's major consideration that the little baggage had managed to misplace both twins just last week when she found a handsome Irishman to flirt with. Graceanne couldn't blame her entirely, since Warefield was practically devoid of both personable young men and lively entertainments the vicar deemed suitable for his offspring. Graceanne wished she might brighten the younger girl's life, sure that would sweeten her disposition, but not at Willy's expense.

"What's so wrong with wanting to visit at the castle?" Pru wanted to know. "Why, His Grace might even invite us to stay so Willy doesn't get homesick."

Graceanne had to smile at the thought of Willy being consoled by the doting aunt who threatened him with her hairbrush just the previous day for laying jam-sticky fingers on her muslin gown. Graceanne stopped smiling when her father told Prudence to stop her foolish air-dreaming. He'd never allow her to put one foot over Ware's threshold when the duke had his rakish friends visiting, nor let her stay overnight there no matter how many widowed sisters chaperoned. "Never."

"Your reputation, dear," Mrs. Beckwith murmured, hoping to avoid another angry outburst as

Prudence pursed her lips. She should have looked at her other daughter.

"What do you mean, Pru cannot stay there?" Graceanne raged. "Ware's company is fit for your grandson but not your daughter? If her good name cannot survive the rakehell's very presence, how can poor little Willy's moral character?"

"Quiet!" Mr. Beckwith thundered back. "I will not have this brangling at my dinner table. Apologize to your mother, Graceanne, and strive to show more respect for your elders. The discussion is finished."

"I am sorry, Mother. I did not mean to overset your nerves. Shall I wheel you into the parlor until tea is brought? Perhaps Pru will play for us. You know how that always soothes you."

Mrs. Beckwith managed to doze off by the fireplace despite Prudence thumping out her discontent on the pianoforte. Graceanne took up her knitting, colorful scarves and mittens for the needy parish children, including her own.

Too short a while later Prudence swiveled on her stool and snarled, "It is not fair," low enough to let her mother go on sleeping. "I never get to go anywhere or do anything!"

"But, Pru, you're only seventeen." Graceanne tried to be sympathetic.

"All the other girls get to go to the assemblies and parties. Lucy Maxton is already engaged, and she's no older than I am! Now the most dashing gentleman in the whole county is coming for the holidays, and I'll barely get to meet him if Papa has his way. They say Ware is a regular out-and-outer."

Graceanne looked up from her knitting. "I daresay a dashing out-and-outer is not what careful parents seek for their young daughters." She scowled at the mittens in her lap. "But you will get to meet him nevertheless. He's bound to call, the maw worm."

"And I suppose you'll give him a regular bear-garden jawing," Pru said with a giggle. "I hope I'm around to hear it, although I don't know how you'll dare. I mean, a real duke, Gracie."

"He's just a man, Pru, even if he is more pig-headed and obnoxious than most."

"Nevertheless, I admire your courage. You even stand up to Papa. I remember when he didn't want you to marry Tony, but you insisted on having the man you loved. It was the most romantical thing I ever heard. Why, all the time you were gone I dreamed of a handsome soldier coming to steal me away."

"Papa gave in because he is dependent on Tony's cousin Ware for his living," Graceanne pointed out. "Besides, my marriage wasn't all romance. Portugal was awful, and Tony was always miles away in danger."

"Still, you had your grand passion despite Papa." She sighed and went back to plunking at the keys. "He won't even let me invite Liam to tea."

"Mr. Hallorahan is Irish, Pru. You know Papa won't approve."

"But that's so unreasonable! Why, Papa calls Liam a jumped-up groom just because he's helping Squire set up a stable. Papa won't even listen when I tell him that Liam's father owns one of the finest race-horse breeding farms in all of Ireland."

"Pru, racehorses are for gambling, and you know Papa doesn't approve of that any more than he does of heretics."

"Liam isn't a heretic!" Prudence insisted. "Besides,

Papa doesn't approve of anything! Did you know that ours is the only house in the whole village without a single Christmas decoration? The vicarage! We're like the cobbler's children going barefoot. Even the poorest cottage has a sprig of holly on the door!"

"Papa says that's a pagan tradition to ward off evil, and has nothing to do with the real Christmas celebration, no more than wassailing does or wishing on a Christmas pudding."

"Oh, I know all that," Prudence complained. " 'Yule logs are from Roman Saturnalia, and mistletoe is just an excuse for loose morals,' " she recited in her father's stentorian tones.

Neither girl heard their father's approach over their laughter until he slammed his hand down on the side table. "I shall have respect in this house!" he shouted, startling his wife awake to ask if it was teatime yet.

"Yes, Papa." Prudence jumped up and bobbed a hasty curtsy. "I'll go help Cook with the tray."

And "Yes, Papa," Graceanne murmured. "I'll go check on the boys."

"Yes, Papa." How many times in her life had Graceanne said those same two words, tiny words that yet robbed her of her opinions, her desires, her very selfhood?

She stood in her sons' bedroom, the tiny room under the eaves next to the servants' quarters, where the children's play couldn't disturb the vicar or his delicate wife. The boys were tumbled together on their mattress like puppies, flushed with sleep, their dark curls still damp from their bath. Even asleep in their identical nightshirts with her identical embroidery on both collars, Graceanne could tell them apart. No one else in the household could. No one else in the household had made an effort to try in the three months they'd been back from the Peninsula. Mrs. Beckwith was too sickly, Pru was too self-absorbed, the servants were too overworked, and the vicar thought they were an abomination. Graceanne thought they were the most beautiful things she had ever seen. Sometimes just looking at them brought tears to her eyes and made her throat close, they were so perfect. If she never got to see a heavenly angel, she could rest content. If she never had another blessing in life, Willy and Leslie were enough. They were hers. Never, ever, would she say, "Yes, Papa," and let him take them away.

Graceanne'd had her one other moment of rebellion almost six years before, when she was seventeen, Pru's age, when she met Tony. She'd threatened to run off with him if her father did not give them his permission to marry. She always suspected the vicar relented more to gain the ducal connection than for fear of losing her. Then again, she'd come to suspect that she'd insisted so hard more to get out of the house and into the world than for love of Anthony Warrington. Oh, Tony was charming and so handsome in his new scarlet regimentals, so full of life and dreams for after he defeated Napoleon. How could any inexperienced, overprotected girl not fall in love? The fact that he was shipping out in six weeks only added to the high drama of the forbidden romance.

The banns were read, Reverend Beckwith performed the ceremony, and Mama cried. Pru was adorable as bridesmaid, and the nonesuch duke himself stood as his cousin's best man. The entire village turned out to witness little Miss Beckwith's grand match.

The rosy glow faded quickly when Tony's orders came before he'd had time to arrange Graceanne's passage to the Peninsula. She couldn't sail safely with the troop ships, couldn't travel properly by herself, and couldn't arrive officially at headquarters at all, in fact, until Tony got permission from his commanding officer, who was known to dislike officers' wives. They distracted his men, he believed. The younger and prettier, the more distraction.

So Tony left his new bride with his sickly mother in a small rented house outside Cheltenham, where the ailing woman could partake of the waters. Graceanne never lost the niggling doubt that Tony'd married her for just that reason, to provide company for his febrile mother so he could traipse off to war with a clear conscience. She spent a year in that dreary locale of antiquated invalids, the unpaid companion to a dying woman. Mrs. Warrington's worsening condition kept Graceanne even more isolated than she'd been in Warefield, where at least she had parish duties and her little sister. Tony's letters were sporadic, his homeward leaves always postponed. He did manage to return to England for the funeral. With no excuse to leave her behind, and no one to leave her with, Tony finally agreed to take Graceanne with him when he returned to the Peninsula.

This time he placed her in the care of the British ambassador's wife in Portugal, miles from his front-line position. Sometimes days or weeks away, Graceanne couldn't dampen his enthusiasm for battle with her fretting.

He did like to show her off to his fellow officers,

though, and he did visit her between engagements when he could. Graceanne provided hot baths, good food, had clean clothes whenever he arrived. After a day or two Tony would kiss her forehead and call her the best wife an officer could have, before he departed. He was undoubtedly fond of her, but Tony loved the war. He thrived on danger, laughed at the risks, reveled in the companionship of his fellow officers and his loyal troops. Graceanne hated everything about the war: the dirt, the heat, the wounded men passing through, the friends made and lost so quickly. She hated the confines of the headquarters, the rigid, narrow society of officers' wives. Mostly she hated the endless, encompassing fear for her reckless husband. She almost came to hate Tony for the chances he took.

Then she had the twins, and nothing else mattered so much. Her world was the nursery, not the battlefield. And Tony was even prouder of his young wife.

Then suddenly he was gone—they brought her his scarlet jacket and his sword for his sons—and she and the twins were bundled aboard the next ship and conveyed, willy-nilly, to the Warefield vicarage. No one asked her, no one gave her a choice. Now she was home in Warefield village, Warwick, back to being her father's obedient daughter, her mother's dutiful companion. But she was still Willy and Leslie's mother, and that would never change. She'd flee to America with the boys before she let some imperious nobleman put a decadent hand on either of their heads.

Of course she might have trouble booking passage with the few coins she'd managed to squirrel away from the pittance doled out by her father. She and her sons were living on his charity, the frugal vicar never ceased to point out, and Graceanne naturally believed that to be true. No one had ever discussed money with her, but she assumed her settlements to be negligible since her dowry was nonexistent. Tony used to pat her hand and tell her not to bother her pretty head about such dreary topics. The vicar told her what money she might be entitled to barely covered expenses, with a little bit put aside for the children's education.

So Graceanne never asked for money for herself. She made her own mourning clothes out of the sturdiest black material so they'd last longer, and she did without all the fripperies other females her age took for granted. The widow also tried to pay back in service what her father so reluctantly expended. She made fair copies of the vicar's sermons, writing half of them. She took over her mother's parish duties, the poor, the sick, the Sunday school classes, and the ladies' committees. Graceanne even made an effort at teaching Prudence prudence. She was also trying to manage the understaffed and underfinanced household.

Meanwhile, she was learning to manage her difficult father. There always seemed to be enough money for the vicar's own comfort and scholarly interests, so Graceanne practiced a subtle form of extortion.

She'd have more time to help him, Graceanne explained, if she could hire the twins a reliable nursemaid. Why, she might even be able to start cataloguing his precious collection of religious books. And just think, with more careful attention than Pru's wandering gaze, the boys might never get into his library again to practice their drawing on his latest sermon. As for the new pony cart Graceanne wanted, Heaven knew she could accomplish her errands among the parishioners and in the village so much more quickly than she could on foot. She could deliver six jars of soup to the shut-ins, stop at the butcher's, collect the mail, make sure the Rigg brothers knew about the change in choir practice, and still be home to help Cook prepare luncheon. And, the pièce de résistance, she could take the jabbering, mischievous little monkey children with her. She got the cart. And money for pencils and paper so the boys wouldn't use his, and pennies for treats so they wouldn't get underfoot in the kitchen so often, in Cook's way. Of course the boys had to be dressed warmly, coming from the hotter Peninsula climate. Their grandfather wouldn't want them catching infectious diseases, would he? Doctors were so expensive.

The only thing Graceanne hadn't been able to cajole out of the nipcheese cleric was money for Christmas. Unlike Pru, she knew better than to come between the vicar and his firmest beliefs. So she was knitting mittens and staying up late baking gingerbread men and taking the holly garlands off the pony cart before they reached the stable. They'd have Christmas one way or another. She'd manage, just like she was managing her father. And as for that dreadful duke, she'd manage his high and mighty lordship at Ware Hold, too!

Chapter Three

The Duke of Ware hated to play the fool. That was why he rarely overindulged. Spirits too often made a man forget his manners or his morals, loosened the connection between his brain and his tongue until Bacchus alone knew what drivel he might spew. Which was why, that morning after Almack's, when His Grace awoke with his head on the desktop in his library and the taste and feel of a desiccated hedgehog in his mouth, his first action was to reach for that addlepated letter he'd penned to Tony's widow the night before. Actually, his first action was to dismiss the footman who opened the drapes to let in the sunlight that pierced his aching head like an arrow dipped in particularly nasty poison, the kind of poison that made a fellow wish he'd die, and quickly.

His second action was to gulp at the hot coffee the obliging footman had brought, so Leland hired him back. The coffee restored too little of his equilibrium and too much of his memory—Almack's, Ellerby's warnings, Crow's cork-brained scheme to ask his cousin's widow for one of her twin sons, and how Fanshaw's idea didn't seem so caper-witted by three in the morning and three sheets to the wind. No one needed a matched set of boys, he'd reasoned. Carriage horses, yes. Dueling pistols, yes. Boys, no. By George, he'd actually written that fustian in his note, Ware recalled. *That* was when he reached for the blasted letter.

The problem with being a well-paying employer who was fair as well as demanding was that one's loyal staff tended to be efficient. They anticipated one's every need and desire. Hence the hot coffee. Thence the letter. Seeing a folded, sealed, sanded, and franked letter on His Grace's desk, one of the duke's devoted retainers immediately sent the missive on its way.

Ware had made a prime ass of himself this time.

He intended to apologize while he was at Ware Hold in Warwick, of course. It rankled, naturally, having to excuse his ungentlemanly conduct to a country nobody, but the female was his cousin's widow, after all. He intended to make amends by raising her allowance or some such. What he didn't intend was to be confronted with a raging harridan within hours of his arrival at the family seat.

Tony's widow stormed through the massive doors of the ancient castle like an avenging Fury, ugly black cloak gusting behind her in the gale of her fierce stride when she caught sight of her victim crossing the Great Hall. "You!" she shouted in a voice of doom that echoed in the high-ceilinged room, stunning the duke, his butler, three footmen, and a housemaid. One of the suits of armor rattled, Leland swore.

The Gorgon—or Graceanne, for he finally recognized his cousin's wife—advanced on Ware. A gentleman didn't run from danger, Leland had to remind himself, especially not in front of his servants. So he dismissed the servants. That was a tactical error, for it seemed Mrs. Warrington had been restraining herself until she had him alone. Valkyries had their standards, too. Now she lit into him, starting with unfeeling and inhumane, pausing only slightly for toplofty and despotic before the descent to rakehell and roué. She didn't quite accuse him of being a child molester, but he could see it dangling on the tip of her tongue. She'd already judged him guilty, and was most likely only biding her time before she grabbed up one of the medieval battle-axes from the wall to perform the execution.

While Mrs. Warrington was roundly cursing him in English, Spanish, Portuguese, and cockney navvy—the passage home must have been an interesting one, he figured—Leland took the time to observe Tony's bride. Bride, hah! He remembered a sweet young innocent, soft-spoken, dewy-eyed, as lovely and gentle as her name. He remembered thinking Tony was a lucky man. He still was; he didn't have to face this termagant anymore. Besides turning into a fishwife, Graceanne had grown thinner, darker-skinned from the Spanish sun, and even less fashionable. Her widow's weeds were a shapeless sack and her hair was scraped back in a straggly bun under a black mobcap his lowest scullery maid wouldn't be caught dead in. And her nose was red from the cold outside. A tiny drip of moisture hung from its end. She was magnificent.

Ware's mouth quirked up at the corners, which nearly sent Graceanne into apoplexy. "That's it, laugh. 'Tis all a great joke to you, that you might destroy whole families! 'I'd like to try my hand at child-raising,' " she quoted from that unfortunate letter. Leland winced, but before he could offer excuses, she was off again on her rant: "Why couldn't you stick to trying your hand at oil painting or poetry like the other idle, useless dilettantes of your class? To think that Tony died to preserve your way of life, when the French might have had the right idea after all!"

With her bosom heaving to keep pace with her tirade, Graceanne wasn't thin all over, Ware could tell. In fact, child-bearing had brought out more than rabid maternal instincts. With the proper dressing . . .

"You may win my father to your way of thinking," Graceanne was shouting, "and you may have your dissolute friend the Regent plead your case. You may spend every last groat of your wealth buying the law. For all I know, even God is on your side or He'd never put you here to torment me. But it does not matter! I swear by everything I hold sacred, you shall never take my sons away from me!"

Ware meant to offer his abject apologies then, truly he did. Instead, he heard himself make another kind of offer entirely. "Since you won't let me take the boy, my dear, perhaps you'd be willing to come with him? There's a vacant cottage at one of the tenant farms. You'd have every comfort those same groats can provide. I can be very generous."

"You can be damned!"

Lud, somehow he'd forgotten she was a vicar's daughter, not a town-bronzed worldly widow. Which just went to prove that a born fool could make an ass out of himself without alcoholic assistance.

Graceanne had gone absolutely rigid, her mouth opening and closing with no sound issuing forth.

Most likely she couldn't think of any words foul
enough for him. Before she did, Leland closed her
mouth in the most convenient—for him—way possible. He'd been wanting to taste those rosy lips for
an age. Now he had an excuse. Not a good excuse,
admittedly, but one that was just loud enough to
drown out his conscience.

He thought her lips would be warm from the fire
of her anger, but they were as cold as the wintry day
outside. And they were stiff, as unyielding as an ici-
cle. All in all, not a promising embrace. But she
smelled of lilacs, and enough of her hair had come
unpinned from that spinsterish bun for him to see
its honeyed gold color. He was satisfied.

Leland released her and stepped back, waiting for
the slap. He deserved it, had earned it, would suffer
it like a man. The slap never came. Instead, the thick
heel of one serviceable, no-nonsense, unfashionable
boot came down on his pump-clad toes with the ac-
companying command to "Go find a woman with
morals as low as yours, if you can."

And then, while the duke was hopping on one
foot, one serviceable, no-nonsense, and extremely unfashionable knee landed between his legs. "And go
get your own children, if you can."

Gads, he'd forgotten she was a soldier's wife, too.

Of all the imbecilic, hen-witted things to do,
Graceanne chided herself as she took up the reins of
the pony cart. Calling on a single gentleman alone in
his home—of course he thought she was a lightskirt!
Then kicking him. How could she have been such a
ninnyhammer?

There she'd been thinking how clever she was, to
bribe Jem, Ware Hold's gatekeeper, to send one of

his boys to her at the vicarage as soon as Ware arrived. She was going to get to the duke before her father could come to an arrangement with him, the way he did with her marriage settlements. She was going to give His Grace time to change from his travel clothes, refresh himself, perhaps have a bite to eat. Then she could approach him for a rational, mature conversation about his cockleheaded notion of stealing her son.

Instead, when she drove her cart through the formal gardens past the ornamental lake where the castle's moat used to be, and up to the front door, where the portcullis once protected against invaders, two grooms ran to hold her pony, as if poor Posy were a mettlesome destrier. A third groom came to hand her down, a procedure so unprecedented, Graceanne nearly tumbled them both to the ground. Then the massive front door opened long before she could reach for the knocker, and a bewigged butler bowed to her. Two footmen in liveried splendor silently posed at either side of the doorway, like bookends. Behind them the Great Hall was brighter than the December day outside, with more candles burning at two o'clock in the afternoon than the vicarage used in a winter month. Graceanne blinked. Two paces into the hall brought her dripping nose the aroma of mince pies cooking, even though the kitchen had to be miles away. One more step, and a welcoming warmth touched her frozen cheeks from roaring fires at both ends of the cavernous room, in hearths large enough to incinerate Sherwood Forest. And no one sat there. Both mantels held huge arrangements of holly and ivy and tinsel stars, while the imposing stairwell's carved banister and every wall in the place was decorated with swags of evergreens and red ribbons. And according to Jem's boy, only the duke, one man, had come to celebrate Christmas here.

There he was, walking across an Aubusson carpet so beautiful it could have hung on a wall. He was immaculate, elegant even in his informal wear that still bespoke the finest tailoring and a valet's fastidious attention. Tony would have called him top-drawer, bang up to the mark. Graceanne's mind called him greedy.

He had everything, His Grace of Ware. All she had was her sons.

So she kicked him.

To do violent bodily harm to another human being was outrageous, underbred, sinful. To kick a man who had such influence and control over one's life was worse. It was foolish beyond permission. Graceanne wished she could kick herself for being such a gudgeon. Instead, she drummed her feet on the pony cart's floorboard. Posy snorted in disgust. "Me, too," Graceanne agreed.

Why, the duke could see Papa removed from his living, frail Mrs. Beckwith thrown out into the cold, beautiful Prudence sold into white slavery, the entire family transported to Botany Bay. He could do anything, the all-powerful Duke of Ware, once he managed to stand up again.

He would hate her forever now.

How could she have been so indelicate? Such a want of conduct, Mama would be ashamed of her. Tony would be ashamed of her. No, Graceanne decided, clucking to Posy to pick up her speed from shuffle to amble, Tony would not be ashamed at all. He'd be proud of her ability to defend herself from unwelcome advances. He'd been the one to teach her, after all. Tony had worried about the rough soldiers, the Spanish peasants, the French Army. He should have worried about his own cousin.

Graceanne's indignation turned from her own idiocy to the duke's infamy. Obviously his reputation as a rake was well earned, the blackguard. Then again, she reflected honestly, it was easy to see how Ware would be very, very good at his chosen path to perdition. Susceptible women—not that she was one of them, of course; she was just being objective—would find his laughing hazel eyes and well-shaped mouth attractive. His dark curls just begged to be tousled, and the slightly hawkish nose only added character to an otherwise classically handsome face.

Ware wasn't as handsome as Tony, she thought loyally. But Tony's good looks were more boyish. Leland had the tiny lines and wrinkles of a mature man, plus an air of dignity and assurance quicksilver Tony never managed to attain. He was broader and taller than her husband, too, which was not necessarily a mark in Ware's favor, for his embrace made her feel overpowered, intimidated, and weak. She did have to admit that His Grace made a good figure, even compared to the young officers in prime physical condition she was used to. Yes, Graceanne could see where some gooseish women might succumb to the duke's appeal if they didn't mind being cast in the shade.

Even at their wedding Tony teased that the best man was more splendid than the groom. Heavens, the elegant duke was more splendid than the bride! All the village girls ogled him and the matrons sighed. There was just something imposing about Ware, commanding, confident . . . lordly. Except for the last time she'd seen him, whimpering on the floor.

Graceanne pulled her cloak more tightly about her. Never had she missed Tony more or felt so defenseless—not precisely defenseless, obviously— but vulnerable in her position as a woman. Not just physically, either. Women couldn't handle money or attend university; they couldn't hold decent positions or offices of power. If they visited a man alone, they were considered no better than they ought to be, and the one area that ought to be guaranteed safe, their nursery, wasn't.

No one would ever threaten to take a man's children away from him. No one would dare, even if he mistreated them. Why, her father often recommended from his pulpit beating the wickedness out of children, and the men in the congregation always nodded. He even threatened to practice his preachings on Willy and Les if they ever laid another grubby hand on his books. They'd only been looking for pictures.

This last thought reminded Graceanne that the Macgruder sisters had promised to order some picture books for her for Christmas. She ought to check, especially since having errands in the village was her excuse for going out this afternoon. Vicar Beckwith had been told that Cook needed some special herbs and spices, as if that would improve the woman's abominable culinary skills. At the low wages he offered, it was astounding Cook could boil water for tea. But Papa had optimistically agreed and had given Graceanne a few shillings to accomplish a miracle. Graceanne roused Posy into a half-trot so they might reach the village before nightfall.

The village was full of talk of the duke. Did Mrs. Warrington notice if the standards were flying yet over the Hold, signaling his arrival? Had she heard if he was bringing a party with him? The village could use the custom.

At the little lending library, the elder Miss Macgruder was positive he was bringing a bride home for Christmas. So romantic. The younger Miss Macgruder believed it was a band of like-thinking libertines he'd invited, for an orgy. The grocer's wife declared she heard Ware was looking for a wife; her husband said he was locking up their daughters. No one wanted to talk about choir practice or the Sunday school's Nativity play.

Even more depressed, Graceanne headed Posy back the way they had come. On the homeward trip she had to pass the hill from which Ware Hold commanded the surrounding countryside. It looked dark and forbidding, just like the old fortress it was, with its crenellated towers and arrow slots instead of windows. From this direction Graceanne couldn't see the lake or the gardens or the modern addition that had been built out of the torn-down curtain wall. All she saw was an impregnable stronghold that had been there forever. She'd be lucky not to land in the dungeons.

Graceanne entered the vicarage through the kitchen, after seeing to Posy. Cook was asleep in the corner, a half-empty bottle of cooking wine in her hand. Meg, the village girl who acted as nursery maid, was up to her eyebrows in flour.

"The master ordered me to help Cook this afternoon, ma'am. We're to make something special for tea. Vicar says as how His Grace is sure to visit and we're to be prepared."

If they were to be prepared, Graceanne thought, they'd bar the windows and doors and borrow

Squire's hunting rifles. Out loud she said, "I'm certain you're doing your best. Are the boys with my sister?"

"Oh, no, ma'am. Miss Prudence was that excited the duke was coming to call, she had to go ask her friend Lucy what she should wear. But don't fret yourself, I set the nippers to help make some Christmas decorations. Just for the nursery, you know, where the reverend can't mind. I taught the darlings to make paper chains." Meg wiped her nose on the back of her hand before going back to her kneading. "I found that colored paper and the glue you were using to make the costumes for the pageant. And some bits of feathers and that glittery paint you used on the angel's wings."

Graceanne clutched the side of the table. "You left three-year-old boys alone with that stuff?"

"Don't you go worrying, ma'am. I took the scissors away."

Chapter Four

*I*t took Graceanne two days to clean up the nursery, hallway, and servants' bedrooms from her darlings' handiwork.

It took Ware two days to recover from her. Since the constable, the magistrate, and the home guard didn't storm the little vicarage to arrest her, at least Graceanne knew she hadn't killed him. The *on-dit* in the village of Warefield was that His Grace was recovering from his latest London revels; that he was suffering from the French pox, and who could wonder why; that he'd been wounded by highwaymen on his journey north.

Graceanne offered no opinions on the gossip. She did snap at Prudence that all the idle chatter was a waste of time that could be better spent rehearsing the Christmas pageant or preparing the fancy tea-cakes their father suddenly insisted upon. The rebuke was enough to send Prudence fleeing the kitchen in a flood of tears, straight to Lucy's house to try out new hairstyles. Discounting Cook and Meg, this left Graceanne alone to assemble baskets of foodstuffs for

the poor, make Christmas treats for the children, and
bake for a guest who never arrived.

Meg's muffins were fed to the chickens—no one in
the parish was *that* poor—and the maid was sternly
admonished to keep a closer eye on the twins.
Graceanne wanted Meg to keep the boys presentable
at all times in case their regal relation came to
inspect.

"I'm nobbut a maid, Mrs. Warrington, ma'am, not
a magician."

"Try."

She went back to work, making sugarplums and
macaroons, honeyed ginger nuts and marzipan angels.
Graceanne also turned out small mince pies, which
were supposed to bring luck. Lots and lots of small
mince pies. With enough luck, or enough mince pies,
perhaps the duke would never come at all.

He came on the third day, looking far more elegant
than Graceanne recalled, and totally out of place in
the shabby parlor. He brought pineapples from the
Hold's forcing houses for her mother and a leather-
bound volume of sermons for her father. They invited him to tea, of course.

Of course he accepted. There was no hope he
wouldn't, the perverse man, not with Graceanne la-
boring in the kitchen, her hair damp with perspira-
tion, her fustiest gown spotted and stained. For spite,
before she went to change, she piled Cook's scones
on a plate with the tea service instead of her own
fresh raspberry tarts.

Upstairs in her shabby bedroom, glancing in the
small mirror, Graceanne decided a different dress
wasn't going to help matters. She also needed a bath,
a hairwash, and a nap to get rid of the dark shadows

under her eyes put there by worry over the dastard's machinations. More crucial than her vanity, however, was keeping the scoundrel away from her father. Besides, her other gowns might be cleaner, but they were all black, and not a one of them was any more attractive than the sacklike garment she wore. Graceanne hurriedly scrubbed her hands and face in the washbasin's lukewarm water, swiped at the telltale cooking debris on her skirts, and shoved her stringy hair under a voluminous black cap.

She raced down the stairs, then paused outside the parlor door to catch her breath. Heaven forfend the repulsive rake think she was hurrying to see him!

The duke was sitting at ease on the threadbare sofa, looking like he'd just stepped out of Bond Street. His snowy neckcloth was a marvel of starched perfection, his charcoal pantaloons hadn't the slightest hint of a crease, and his mirror-shined boots reflected every worn spot on the carpet. Ware looked to her jaundiced eyes like a tailor's dummy, someone who had never worked a day in his life.

Sitting next to the parasitic paragon was Prudence. The minx had no business taking tea with the company, much less sharing the narrow couch with an established libertine. Prudence was all pink muslin, lace ribbons, and blond ringlets—and rouged cheeks, unless Graceanne missed her guess. The little hoyden was sitting much too close to Ware, hanging on his every word, looking up at him through thicker, darker eyelashes than she'd possessed that very morning. No matter what commonplace the duke uttered, Pru's tinkling laugh chimed out and her dimples flashed. Graceanne looked for her mother's frowning reprimand at Pru's coming manners, but instead she saw a new lace cap on Mrs. Beckwith, rouged cheeks, and fluttering eyelashes. Goodness, no wonder he expected every female to fall at his feet! Thanking Heaven she was made of sterner stuff, Graceanne pursed her lips and stepped into the room.

There she was at last, hanging in the doorway like an untrained footman. Leland had been wondering how many more of the little sister's blatant lures he could shrug off before he uttered a crushing setdown. The baggage was an adorable bit of fluff, bachelor fare if he ever saw it, not that he was in the market for an unfledged bird of paradise. Even if Miss Prudence weren't a vicar's daughter, he'd always preferred his flirts to have some experience of the world. Virgins were the very devil. She'd make some man a cozy armful, though, if they didn't marry her off soon. Too bad Miss Prudence had been too young that summer Tony spent in Warwick; she'd be a great deal easier to turn up sweet than the prickly female Tony did marry.

Mrs. Warrington was already pokering up as she came into the room, and he hadn't even said hello. Leland sighed. He knew he owed the starchy woman an apology, perhaps two or three. He also knew she hated and distrusted him, perhaps with cause. The curst widow wasn't going to make this easy for him. He sighed again as he stood and made his bow, then accepted the hand she offered, but cautiously kept his distance.

"I never offered my proper condolences, Cousin," he said, trying not to wince at the sight of another awful gown and hideous cap. "I am sure you must miss Tony, especially at this holiday season. He was a fine man, a good soldier, a wonderful friend."

The vicar interrupted over her murmured expression of gratitude. "Yes, yes, but as you say, this is the season of joy, no time to mourn." Leland couldn't spot a single token of the season, much less of joy, in the dreary room, but he returned to his seat after the widow quietly excused herself to go help Cook with tea.

Prudence immediately took up the conversation: "And it is a special season of celebration for Warefield, with Your Grace in residence after so long. Shall you be making a lengthy stay? If so, perhaps you'd consider holding a ball at the castle. My friend Lucy says her sister remembers when there were parties all the time at Ware Hold."

"That is enough, Prudence. His Grace did not come to be importuned with your girlish nonsense," the vicar scolded. Then, "Have you had a chance to look over my report about the church steps, Duke? I'm sure you'll see I was correct about the dry rot."

Leland let the small talk flow around him with an occasional nod or a noncommittal comment. He could make social chitchat in his sleep. Meanwhile, whilst the object of his call made herself scarce, he looked around again. No, there were no ornaments, not even a sprig of holly. The furnishings were sparse and worn, the drapery faded, the wallpaper peeling. There were no servants to speak of, and he was the only one to come to Mrs. Warrington's assistance when she returned with the heavy tray. There was meager fare for refreshment, scones that were as hard as rocks and tasted as appetizing, and poor quality tea. Leland noticed how Mrs. Beckwith was quick to turn a cup so the chipped handle didn't show. Her clothes and Prudence's were more fashionable than

the widow's, but decidedly village-made and of inferior materials.

Ware knew to a shilling what the vicar earned.
Despite his reputation as a man-about-town, the
duke was cognizant of every detail of his country
holdings, too. His domain was decidedly not popu-
lated with impoverished preachers. Reverend Beckwith was not spending his generous stipend on his
family, that was clear. Perhaps the man gambled or
had another secret vice. But why the devil was
Tony's widow pretending poverty? There she sat,
like the colorless little mouse he knew she wasn't,
humbly knitting in the corner. He couldn't imagine
what kind of game they all were playing, unless it
was a scheme to get more money out of him. They'd
catch cold at that!

"I'll send my head carpenter to inspect the church
steps," he offered while taking a bank draft out of
his pocket. "Meantime I did bring my annual dona-
tion to the poor box. 'Tis the season to give, after all.
You must be a charitable man yourself, Reverend."
That was a fairly broad hint to find out where all the
money went, and wide of the mark at that.

"To a point, Your Grace," Beckwith answered.
"My daughter makes gloves and mittens for the
needy, as you can see. And no one goes hungry. We
send baskets around at Christmas and Easter."

"From the poor box money, Papa," Graceanne said
from her corner. "His Grace should know where his
offering goes." And where Beckwith's didn't. So the
mouse still had teeth after all, and she wasn't protecting Beckwith's cheese. Curious.

"To be sure, to be sure. After that, I believe God
helps those who help themselves." This pronounce-

ment must have sounded harsh for a man of the cloth even to Beckwith, for he changed the subject instantly. "But come, Duke, perhaps you'd like to see my collection."

"I'm sure His Lordship has more important things to do, Papa. We mustn't delay him." Graceanne was determined to keep the two men apart. Her father was just as bent on having a private talk with the nobleman.

"This will take but a moment. A man of His Grace's discernment will surely be interested in the historical significance."

Ware looked around the room. Mrs. Beckwith was smiling vaguely, Prudence was pouting, and Mrs. Warrington was mangling her wools into a regular mare's nest. Why in blazes was she frowning at him again? He didn't want to appear toplofty as she'd accused, so said he could spare some time, to the vicar's satisfaction.

Beckwith led him down the hall and through a locked door, the first locked door Ware had ever seen in a parsonage, even in London's stews when he made his charity calls. If a minister doesn't have faith in humankind, he wondered, who will?

Catching his guest's bemusement over the keys, Beckwith explained, "The imps of Satan are everywhere."

Lud, Leland thought, the fellow was always a religious fanatic, but now a page or two of Beckwith's prayerbook was missing.

But the man did know his Bibles. Beckwith's collection of religious texts was extensive. Some volumes were ancient, most were valuable. The duke wouldn't want to read many of them, but he could recognize their worth. There was even an illuminated manuscript, in another locked cabinet, that he'd be proud to have in his own library of rare editions. No wonder the household was on short rations if Beckwith was as compulsive a collector as the accumulation of books indicated. If that was how the cleric chose to spend his money, Ware had no complaints as long as the man got the locals baptized and buried. And as long as Tony's children weren't on bread and water to support the man's hobby. He cut short the vicar's lecture.

"Perhaps I can see the children now?" he asked after they'd returned to the parlor. He might have announced he had smallpox, the way Mrs. Warrington lost what little color she had and everyone else found something better to do. Mrs. Beckwith announced the knickknacks needed washing before the holidays, so she filled her lap with china shepherdesses before being wheeled out of the room. The reverend recalled his Christmas sermon needed polishing. Oddly, he took with him a pewter mug, a bowl of nuts, and a carved wood tobacco humidor. He also took two framed miniatures from a piecrust table. "My parents" was all he said.

Even Prudence was willing to peel herself from Ware's side. "If you are going to entertain the little beasts in the parlor, I'll go memorize my lines for the Nativity. You are coming, aren't you, Your Grace? I am Mary again this year." She tossed her curls for effect. "Of course I am too old for the children's play, but Papa insists that if we are going to have the pageant in church on Christmas Eve, it must be dignified. He wants no little girls who giggle and get tongue-tied, so I volunteered."

"And I'm sure you'll be everything saintly and demure." Actually, Leland was sure the little tart would be thrilled to be treading the boards, even in church.

Before she left, Prudence put her magazines and her mother's workbasket on the mantel, and the lid down on the pianoforte. She took two needlepoint pillows with her, saying, "I'll ask Meg to bring them down now."

Leland thought they were all as queer as Dick's hatband, especially when Mrs. Warrington, whom he thought was the only sane one of the bunch, moved the fireplace screen. Then she started putting out the few candles and lifting an oil lamp to the already crowded mantelpiece. She moved the screen again, wedging it in the hearth. At least she finally had some color in her cheeks, he noted admiringly, even if it was from blushing at the peculiarities of this household. Or exertion, as she moved the blasted screen again. At least the rosy tinge wasn't from the rouge pot.

All of Graceanne's unproved color fled her face, though, when Prudence returned a moment later. The younger girl curtsied uncertainly to Ware, then whispered in her sister's ear. He could hear Mrs. Warrington gasp, then whisper back, "But when I told them I wanted everything neat for the company, I didn't mean the nursery fireplace!"

Chapter Five

*D*ash it, Ware thought. Before this no woman had ever been afraid to be alone with him. The way the widow was clenching her fists, he wouldn't be surprised if she picked up the poker the next time she dithered at the fireplace. She was even more attics-to-let than the rest of her family if she thought he'd make improper advances after her previous response. He cleared his throat. "Mrs. Warrington, I owe you an—"

My stars, Graceanne fretted, Ware was going to think they were all lunatics! Heaven knew what Papa had said, but the duke was angry after he'd gone to see the collection. She could tell by the way his lips thinned. Graceanne also noticed how he unobtrusively observed the lack of amenities in the house—and now the lack of courtesy! And, oh, dear, she still hadn't had the opportunity to beg his pardon for her own shocking behavior. With his thick brows already lowered in a frown, he was most likely wondering how soon the court papers could be drawn up giving him custody of Willy. "Your Grace, please forgive—Oh, excuse me."

"Pardon. No, ladies first."

Graceanne licked her lips before starting again. "Your Grace, I cannot tell you how ashamed I am of my dreadful words and actions when I called at your home. I am so sorry to have—"

Before she could say precisely what she was sorry to have done, Ware held up his hand. He knew what *he* was sorry she'd done. "Please, say no more. I also owe you an abject apology."

"In your—"

"You were provoked. I have no excuse for my own less than noble conduct."

"But I—"

"Shall we call it quits? Do you think we have eaten equal amounts of humble pie?"

Graceanne stopped wringing her hands. "Not very palatable, is it, Your Grace?"

He muttered, "Even worse than the scones at tea," which finally brought a smile to her face, which so enhanced her appearance that Leland was reminded why he'd made his dishonorable proposal in the first place. He smiled back. "Do you think we might start over?"

Graceanne had to remind *herself* that one could "smile and smile, and still be a villain." She nodded anyway, and Ware was just speculating that he could win her over after all, when a disheveled serving girl came in without knocking. Her grayish uniform was wet and rumpled, and she had a wriggling, blanket-wrapped bundle in her arms.

"Here's the first 'un, ma'am. I figure he wouldn't stay clean long enough for me to dress t'other without someone watching." She dumped a child in Mrs. Warrington's lap and tramped out.

"Hello, my cherub," Graceanne said, peeling away the blanket and kissing damp curls. "I'd like you to make your bow to His Grace, the way we practiced."

The little fellow did, looking up at Leland with hazel eyes that matched his own. "If you're His Grace," he chirped, "whose grace is Mama?"

Graceanne blushed. They obviously hadn't practiced enough. "My Grace is part of my name, sweetheart. The duke's grace is his address, part of his title."

The boy lowered his brow in concentration, a habit that somehow looked familiar to Leland. Perhaps Tony . . .

"My papa was a major," the sprout solemnly announced.

Leland squatted down to the child's level, and just as seriously agreed, "That's a very proud title."

Tony's son patted the duke's arm. "Don't worry. Maybe someday you'll be a major, too. I'm going to be a major in this many years." He held up two chubby hands and spread his fingers out twice.

"Are you?" Ware asked, sitting back down in his chair, having found squatting to be deuced uncomfortable. "Wouldn't you rather be a duke and live in a big house and—"

"That's enough," Graceanne said, scooping the boy into her lap. He climbed down immediately and began inspecting the tassels on Ware's boots. Graceanne watched him with a worried look, but continued: "Stop filling his head with such flummery. He will never be a duke."

"He might be. You cannot know for sure. What if I fell off my horse tomorrow? Granted, it would be a first, but I could be struck by lightning. One never knows. Besides being a true Warrington, the boy has all the makings of a duke. He is confident, intelligent—"

"And he's not your heir. This is your namesake, Leslie, the second-born twin by ten minutes. Wellesley, Sir Arthur's godson, is the elder. Willy is the quiet one."

Embarrassed, the duke looked down, to find one tassel unraveled and the other missing altogether. "The deuces! Uh, pardon, dexterous, isn't he?"

With his eyes on his brand-new boots, Leland missed Graceanne's grab for Leslie, who disappeared under the sofa. She gathered up the gold cord instead, to see if she could reconstruct the shredded tassel. Silly affectations anyway, she thought, wondering how much they would cost to replace. But she mustn't let a petty expense distract her from the point she had to make: "Even Willy is only so temporarily in line for the succession that I cannot understand why you insist on calling him your heir. Surely at your age you intend to remarry and have any number of sons. Therefore— Oh, dear, I shouldn't give him my watch to play with."

Leslie had climbed over the back of the sofa and was standing next to the duke, examining his diamond stickpin. To distract the boy so he could continue his conversation with the mother, Leland unhooked the watch from its fob chain. He tried to defend his ignorance. "I thought children liked watches."

"That's infants, Your Grace. They like the ticking. Older children tend to be . . . Oh, my." She'd have to sell her wedding ring to repay the duke for this day's work if he didn't leave soon.

Ware put the pieces of his grandfather's ticker back

in his pocket and watched the child, who was *not* his heir, thank goodness, try to climb the window curtains. Amazed at the widow's apparent nonchalance as she plucked her son from certain disaster, he tried to explain. His Grace of Ware was not used to justifying his behavior to anyone, least of all to a scheming widow in a harum-scarum household. He did feel he owed some excuse for that bacon-brained letter he'd sent, though. "I was married twice, Mrs. Warrington, with no issue either time."

"But your wives died early, Tony told me. That's just bad luck. Your next wife might have twins. I've heard such things run in families."

Leland got up to fetch Leslie, who was now trying to stand on his head atop the pianoforte stool. With his back to the widow, he said, "I never fathered progeny outside the marriage bed, either."

"You mean you can't? With your reputation as one of London's greatest rakes?" Graceanne clapped her hand over her mouth when she realized how very improper this conversation was becoming. "I'm sorry, Your Grace."

What? She was sorry he was impotent or sorry she'd been so indelicate? He'd show her impotent! "I didn't say I was incapable of the act," he snarled, "just that the outcome has not been productive. Perhaps you'd like me to demonstrate?"

Graceanne was saved by Meg from having to make some kind of reply. "Here's the other 'un. Do you want me to clean the ashes or mop the floor before the bathwater seeps through the ceiling?"

Ware missed Mrs. Warrington's answer, watching how Leslie took his brother's hand and led him to the guest. Leland was prepared for twins, but this was uncanny. They were the same boy!

He looked up at the widow, who clucked her tongue, used to this reaction. "They are just twins, my lord, not two-headed pigs in a freak show."

Leslie was making the introductions: "He's Papa's cousin, Willy, and Mama says we're to call him His Grace."

The duke could see now that they were not the same people at all. Willy made his bow, but with his eyes cast down; then he went right back to his mother's skirts.

His brother told him, "Don't worry, Willy. He's only a duke."

"Why don't you call me Cousin Leland? Or Lee, if you prefer. That goes for you, too, ma'am, if I might be permitted to call you Cousin Graceanne."

She nodded. "Cousin Leland."

"Cou-lee!" Willy pronounced, still from the safety of his mother's side.

"No, that's a dog," Leland told him. "A collie. A sheepherder. You know, woof-woof." Willy clapped his hands, dropped to all fours, and started barking and woofing around the room, Leslie hard on his heels.

Willy was the quiet one?

Graceanne called them to order. "Boys! We have company."

Leslie wanted to know if that meant they could have the good cakes, not Cook's scones. Graceanne saw the duke's raised eyebrows and looked away. Willy, meanwhile, had changed his chant to a sing-song "collie cake" at the top of his lungs.

"Can we, Mama, can we? Meg didn't give us anything to eat all day!"

"Collie cake, collie cake, collie cake."

Graceanne turned helplessly to the duke. "May I

leave them with you for a moment? There is no one else to send to the kitchen."

The duke hadn't managed to eat half of one of Cook's stone scones. "Of course. I'd like to see the 'good' cake myself."

Graceanne chewed her lip uncertainly, but she left to prepare a respectable tea this time.

When she returned with a well-filled tray, Cousin Leland's neckcloth was limp, his superfine coat was awry and missing a button, and his carefully combed curls looked like a sparrow had made a nest there. He had a slightly dazed look. "They have a bit of energy, what?"

"It's the cold weather," she explained as she put the tray down atop the pianoforte, well out of her darlings' reach. "They do not get enough exercise." She spread a ragged tablecloth on the floor and began to lay out heavy crockery dishes and sturdy mugs of milk. "Here, sweethearts, your favorite raspberry tarts. And I brought you each a gingerbread man, if you'll promise to be very good while Cousin Leland and I have our tea."

The duke was relieved to see she was setting only two places on the floor. He was also relieved to see she was placing another raspberry tart on a pretty porcelain plate. They were his favorites, too. He got up to assist her, and tried to straighten his cravat while her back was turned. "They seem to do fine in here."

"Yes, but today is special. Usually they have to play upstairs so they don't disturb Papa's studies or Mama's rest. There's not nearly as much room to run and jump." Graceanne realized she was giving him more ammunition to find the vicarage inadequate, so she hurried on: "But we do get outdoors most days.

Just now there is less time, what with the preparations for Christmas and all."

Leland could not help looking about him. Christmas might be months away rather than less than a week, judging from the dearth of decorations. "Your preparations must be behind times indeed."

Graceanne's hand shook slightly as she poured the tea. "Yes, well, ah, I meant teaching the village children their parts for the Nativity pageant and rehearsing the choir. One lump or two, Your Grace?"

"One. And I thought it was to be 'cousin.'"

"Cousin." She handed over his cup and plate, then took her own seat after righting one spilled mug of milk.

Leland sat again, too, taking a bite of a truly excellent raspberry tart. "Delicious," he announced. "Your cook must be as temperamental as my French chef. Some days ambrosia, the next day offal. The only reason I put up with him is his way with pastry."

Inordinately pleased, Graceanne confessed that she was responsible for the better fare. "I learned in Portugal, when there was not much else to do. Unfortunately my baking for the holidays has also taken time away from the boys. Mince pies, sugarplums . . ."

"I remember helping to stir the Christmas pudding as a boy, making my wish. Have you and the children done that yet?"

Graceanne stirred her tea. "I'm afraid Papa would not permit such a thing," she said in a voice filled with frustration. "I see you have noticed Papa is very strict in his notions of celebration." She frowned at the bare walls, the cheerless arrangement of faded silk flowers. "He is very devout, you must know, and resents the incursion of pagan superstitions into the religious observation. Since many of the Christmas traditions are holdovers from the Druids' winter solstice rites, Papa has tried to avoid all those trappings."

"And all the lovely aspects that make Christmas such a pleasure, especially for a child," he said under his breath, but Graceanne heard. She privately agreed, but loyalty demanded she defend her father.

"But we do have a Nativity pageant and the choir will sing carols."

"Reverend Beckwith must know he'd have no audience at all to listen to his sermons if he forbade those."

"The congregation members respect my father's piety in church," she said. And then they went home to uphold all the old traditions, but she didn't tell him that. The Christmas pudding for wishes, the Yule log for luck in the new year, the holly and ivy to ward off evil, the mistletoe for fertility. Good heavens, did he know . . . ? She hurried on: "And you mustn't think the boys are missing out on all the anticipation and celebration. We've been decorating the nursery"—may he never learn how—"and both twins have small parts in the play." Mostly because she could not leave them home when she held rehearsals; His Grace needn't know that either, just that her sons were not being deprived. "And of course they will have special treats and a few little gifts." She nodded toward her knitting basket and the mittens sticking out the top.

The boys were getting mittens for Christmas? His tenants' children did better! Yet the twins did not look downtrodden or underprivileged. They were certainly healthy and spirited little tykes, obviously doted upon by their mother. They were handsome to boot, if he had to say so himself who shouldn't, seeing how the lads were the spit and image of himself at their age. Of course he and Tony were often mistaken for brothers instead of cousins, so alike were they in appearance. Nothing could be more alike than these two peas in a pod, he marveled again, watching Leslie and Willy playing at soldiers or whatever with their gingerbread men cookie figures.

He couldn't understand a word of their game, no matter how he listened, although the gibberish seemed to make sense to them.

As if reading his thoughts, Graceanne told him they'd jabbered like this long before they learned to speak the King's English. "In fact, I despaired they'd ever communicate with anyone else. And yes, they understand each other perfectly."

"And they seem to share so equally." He wrinkled his aristocratic nose when the twins traded half-eaten cookies. "I thought little boys were more possessive than badgers."

Graceanne laughed. "They don't always get along this well, but if one falls, the other cries. They've always been like that. Willy lets Leslie take his toys, but Leslie gives Willy the bigger piece of cake."

She studied the leaves left in her teacup, wishing she could read the future there. Her future was now. With a deep breath Graceanne said, "It would be cruel to separate them, Your Grace. Cousin."

He sighed. "And you. I can see that. Please do forgive my thoughtlessness, that letter, even the suggestion of taking Willy away. Please understand I was feeling desperate. I truly do want sons of my own."

"Then you won't . . . ?"

Hope was shining in the widow's blue eyes. Leland hated to dim that light, but he had to tell her. "Willy—Wellesley—is still my heir, no matter what your wishes, or his, or mine. He'll need to know about the lands and people, to learn the responsibilities facing him, the same way I did."

Graceanne looked at Willy, his face smeared with raspberry jam. "If you can teach him to use a napkin, that should be enough for now."

The duke didn't smile. "For now."

Graceanne understood the door was still open, the threat was still left hanging, but she'd won some time today. "Come, boys, we must let His Grace go about his business."

"G'bye, Collie," they giggled in unison, tumbling out of the room after giving him a quick, unexpected double hug.

The duke brushed crumbs off his pantaloons. Graceanne dabbed ineffectively with her napkin at the raspberry smears on his once-pristine shirtfront. Her cheeks grew pinker than the stains when she realized what she was doing. "H-habit, Your Grace."

"They like me," was all he said, in wonder. Then he asked if he could call another time.

Graceanne couldn't have heard right. "Excuse me, Cousin?"

"I asked if I might come by again, to spend time with the boys."

Graceanne let her napkin flutter to the floor. Goodness, not even Tony had ever wanted to spend time with the boys.

Chapter Six

*H*is heirs were slap up to the mark. The duke's valet was packing to return to London, but the boys were marvelous. They might be a trifle overexuberant, but high spirits were not to be despised. Ware had always hated those miniature wax dummies his friends trotted out for inspection to be dutifully admired—the ladies always cooed—then placed back on their shelves. What was there to admire in a child with no conversation, no imagination, no sparkle? Neatness? Neatness mattered in a valet—who might be persuaded to stay on with a raise in salary; the fellow did have a way with boots—not in a little boy. Besides, high spirits were natural in Tony's sons. Eton and Oxford could tame any unruliness, Ware complacently decided, ignoring the fact that no amount of rigid school discipline had checked Tony's wilder starts. Warrington had been his mother's despair until he married and became some other female's worry. Aunt Claire had been ecstatic when Tony chose a quiet girl from a strict upbringing. Tony's marriage hadn't given his hey-go-mad cousin any better sense of responsibility, but it had given the duke his heir and a spare! Leland raised a brandy nightcap to the fallen hero. "You were a credit to the Warrington name," he toasted. "Your sons are all a man could ask for to succeed him." And his wife wasn't half bad either, but Ware didn't say that aloud, just in case Tony could hear him. The old castle had ghosts enough.

Graceanne was a puzzle the duke pondered long after snuffing out his bedside candle. In the dark he could visualize her eyes, her face, her form, and be stirred by the images his mind conjured up. Hell, a ghost would be stirred by *those* images. Then he pictured those horrific black sacks that covered the widow from head to toe. They were enough to dampen any man's ardor, even one who hadn't had a woman since leaving London and wouldn't have one while he was resident in the family pile. No true gentleman fouled his own nest, and the Duke of Ware had never been one to tup serving wenches at the local tavern. He required a little more refinement in his convenients. Which brought him back to the vicar's daughter.

There was something deuced havey-cavey about the female. Her fortune wasn't on her back, that was for certain, nor, to judge from the state of the vicarage, was it going to lighten her family's burdens. Even the children she obviously adored were being shortchanged with mittens for Christmas. And she was doing her own baking. So what the devil was she doing with the money?

The duke fell asleep determined to uncover the widow's secrets. And her hair, her shoulders, her ankles . . .

To that end, and others the duke chose not to examine more closely, he arose the next morning, paid his valet's extortion demands, and drove to the manse.

Miss Prudence almost threw herself into his arms when she saw the rig he was driving. "Oh, Your Grace, I've never ridden in a sporting vehicle! Why, Lucy will be green with envy. Her beau only drives a gig."

She almost threw herself on the ground when he said he'd come to take her sister out instead. "I've promised the boys, you see, and cannot disappoint them, no matter how I might wish it otherwise."

When Pru flounced out of the room, Graceanne put down her account books and turned on him. "What is this Banbury tale of promising the twins a ride? You did no such thing, thank goodness, or they'd have slept in their overcoats to be ready."

Ware's smile was so charming she couldn't be angry, especially not when he shrugged his broad shoulders and confessed, "I came to offer you and the boys a ride, and I didn't want to have to tool some silly chit around the countryside instead. A promise to them was the only polite excuse I could think of. Will you come? You did say the children needed more exercise."

They did, and the account books never balanced anyway. Besides, she was secretly delighted that Ware wasn't falling all over Prudence like every other male in the neighborhood. It was a long-overdue boost to her sorely tried vanity that this exquisite in fawn breeches and caped riding coat preferred her, Graceanne's, company to that of her beautiful younger sister. Of course Ware needed to have her if he was to have the boys, but so what? A mother's pride was gratified, too. With her father's strictures ringing in her ears, she accepted. When she'd told the vicar there was to be no more talk of the duke taking Willy to raise, he'd been disappointed. When she mentioned Ware's request to call again, he'd grown angry.

"You're to have nothing to do with the man, do you hear me? He's a rake. Why does he want to visit children? Mark me, daughter, if he doesn't want Wellesley, it's you he's after. And I won't have any Jezebel living under my roof."

All in all, Graceanne thought she was being very daring—until she saw the curricle outside. "It's too high. It cannot be safe. The horses are too highly strung and they'll go too fast and the boys will fall out. I'm sorry, but . . ."

Ware's eyes crinkled at the corners. "I wouldn't have expected Tony's wife to be so lily-livered. But come, ma'am, you're insulting both my driving skills and the manners of Castor and Pollux. Perfect gentlemen, I assure you."

The twins were already being introduced to the matched bays by His Grace's tiger. She did have to admit the horses seemed remarkably even-mannered for high-bred cattle. Any animals that stood still to have their noses patted first by Leslie in the groom's arms, while Willy hopped up and down, calling "Horsie, horsie," were not likely to spook under the duke's capable hands.

"But the seat is so far from the ground!"

"That's what makes the ride so exciting! But I assure you neither lad will come to grief. I have it all planned out. You'll hang on tight to one on your lap, and the other will sit wedged between us. John Groom will keep his hand on the boy's shoulder from his perch behind."

Graceanne was not convinced. Willy and Leslie were still shouting and jumping about, dangerously close to the horses' hooves, she thought, but the groom did seem to have his eyes on them, and a calming hand on the horses. "I fear the children will not sit still well enough."

"Of course they will. You're not babies, are you?" Ware called over to the boys. "Babies wriggle and scream too much and upset the horses, so they cannot go for curricle rides. That's the rule."

Willy held up three fingers to prove he was far beyond infancy; Les tried to tell the duke he was old enough to shave.

"There, are you satisfied now?"

She'd have to be. She'd need a crowbar to separate the twins from those horses, else. She nodded, which earned her a warm smile from Ware.

"Good. They're boys, not hothouse orchids. You'll have to let them grow up someday, you know."

"Surely not until they can dress themselves!" she pleaded.

The boys had been having one of their private conversations, and now Leslie approached the duke and tugged on his sleeve. "Collie, Willy wants to ride the horsie."

"Oh, only Willy?" Leland teased. He stooped down to their level. "I'm sorry, lads, but Castor and Pollux are carriage horses. They're not used to being ridden."

Leslie and Willy were not used to being denied. They went to their mother. Les stuck out his lower lip and Willy stamped his foot. "Want to ride the horsies!"

"But Cousin Leland has explained, darlings, it

wouldn't be safe. You know that Posy doesn't like you on her back."

"But these horsies are twins! John said so!" Both children started to cry.

Graceanne was wishing the wretched duke, his carriage, and horses to perdition. The duke, however, commanded, "Stop that nonsense," in a voice that had Meg in the upstairs window stop mooning over John below. The bawling ceased. "I thought you told me you weren't babies? It's too bad I can make promises only to real gentlemen, not infants, for I would have promised to bring a riding horse next time if you behaved today."

Noses were wiped, eyes dried, and the boys clambered over the wheels and into the curricle.

"And you were worried they would fall?" the duke asked as he helped Graceanne onto the bench. "They're as agile as squirrels!"

The argument over which twin got to sit alone was instantly quelled by Leland's masterful decision that Willy would have first choice because he was the elder, and then Leslie would get the center seat on the way back.

As he walked around the carriage to the other side, Leland told John Groom that he felt like Solomon. His bubble of pride burst when the tiger grinned and wondered, if he was so wise, how come Master Wellesley was sitting on Mrs. Warrington's lap?

"How the deuce can you tell that's Willy?" the duke asked, confounded. He hadn't seen a mark different, and he'd been looking.

" 'E's the quiet one. Sticks by 'is ma more."

"Then what in blazes was all that argle-bargle about?"

" 'E had to prove 'e weren't a baby, now, didn't 'e?''

The widow just smiled. Leland didn't find that smile quite as appealing as some of the others he'd fought harder to win.

Graceanne finally relaxed under the carriage robe when she saw how competently the duke tooled the ribbons. He was careful of ruts, watchful for small animals near the hedgerows, and kept the pair to an even, moderate pace. Assured that John Groom was keeping one strong hand on Leslie's shoulder, she soon eased her death grip on Willy and the railing. The boys were too enthralled to be troublesome. They looked so happy, she couldn't hold back a sigh.

"Are you cold?" Leland asked, looking over briefly.

"No, I just couldn't help wishing . . ."

"Wishing . . . ?" he prompted her. " 'Tis the season for that, after all."

"No, I was just being gooseish, wishing I could give the boys ponies of their own when they are old enough."

She could give them a stable of their own if she wanted, he knew. And Warrington boys belonged on horses as soon as they could walk. Then again, what did a female know about such things? She was like to make a mull of it. Astounding himself with such fiercely protective emotions, he offered, "I'll see to it when the time is right." Which would be as soon as he and John could find the perfect mounts, but no need to worry a fussbudget mother yet. Then, gads, he mused to himself, if she beamed like that for a couple of ponies, imagine what she'd do for a pair of diamond earbobs.

There was something about his smile, and Greeks bearing gifts, that made Graceanne distrust his offer. She became downright panicky when the curricle turned off the road to the village and headed toward Ware Hold on its hill.

"I thought we were going to the village, Your Grace. That is, perhaps we should turn back now. Willy, are you chilled?"

Ware turned and grinned, feathering the corner between the Hold's gates. "What, did you want to show off for your friends in town like Prudence? I thought to take the boys back to the Hold to see the decorations."

"No, no, that wouldn't be at all the thing." She couldn't quite come out and say she feared for her virtue, but some of that worry must have shown on her face.

"You're not a green girl, Cousin, who's never let out alone."

"But I still have to mind my reputation." His reputation was what she minded most. "Small-town gossip is not a comfortable thing. And the vicar's daughters . . ."

"But my aunt Eudora is up from London. There cannot be the tiniest tidbit for the scandalbroth. She wants to meet Tony's boys. Will you come?"

Graceanne felt that she'd been outflanked again, but she nodded.

Going through the enormous doors of the castle, past the bewigged and bowing butler, the boys were dumbstruck for once. Graceanne kept tight hold on two little hands as two heads swiveled from the rigid footmen to the armored knights to the weapon-filled walls. Graceanne's head swiveled, too, from the irreplaceable Dynasty bowls to the framed miniatures to the collection of carved jade horses. "I don't think this is a good idea, Your Grace."

"Nonsense." Leland turned to the right-hand liver-ied sentry and assigned him to escort the children to the kitchens. "This is Master Wellesley, and Master Leslie, or vice versa. They would appreciate some hot chocolate and one of Henri's pastries, I'm sure."

The footman gulped. "Me, Your Grace?"

"Unless you wish to imitate an andiron for the rest of your life."

Graceanne reluctantly transferred the boys' hands to the servant's immaculate gloves. "Be good, dar-lings, and don't touch anything."

"Not even the pretty horsies?"

"On second thought," Ware decided, turning to the other footman, "you go along, too. After they've eaten, I'm sure there is a ball or something in the old nursery."

Before the children were halfway across the vast cavern of the hall, a small, gray-haired woman dressed in the latest style approached, tapping her cane. "So there you are, Ware. I've been waiting an age. Had my tea without you."

Leland made the introductions to his aunt, Lady Eudora Warrington.

"Remember the gel from the wedding. Your father still such a starched-up prig?" Before Graceanne could think of an answer to such a question, the old lady fired off another: "D'you gamble, missy?"

"Why, no, ma'am. My father—"

"Just what I thought, he is. I cannot abide niminy-piminy females, Ware, even if they are good breed-ers. Told you so. Now I'll have to go trounce my maid again. Already owes me two years' salary."

Scarlet-faced, Graceanne still had to ask, "But I thought you wanted to see Tony's children?"

Aunt Eudora pointed her cane to where the footmen were leading the boys away. "See 'em, don't I? Got the Warrington look, at least. Now you can go put 'em in the icehouse or whatever. Take 'em out when they're eighteen or so and fit for society." With that, she tapped her way across the carpet and disappeared through an arched doorway.

Her head still spinning, Graceanne permitted herself to be led down a hall and into a library five times the size of the Misses Macgruders' bookshop. The duke seated her on a leather armchair near the blazing fire and said, "Tea will be along shortly."

"But no chaperone." It was a statement, not a question. Oh, Papa was right, she never should have come. The duke was resting one arm on the mantel, looking so confident and at ease and attractive that she was tempted to throw one of his priceless Sevres vases at him. And there she'd been worried about the boys!

Leland laughed and gestured toward the door. "See? It's open, all very proper. You're safe, I promise."

"But you've lied to me before. Twice now, I believe. Once about promising the boys a curricle ride and once about your aunt."

"No, she did want to get a look at the twins, I swear. But please, Mrs. Warr—Cousin Graceanne, I did want to speak to you, away from the parsonage."

She folded her hands in her lap as grimly as a schoolmistress. "Yes, Your Grace?"

"I . . . that is, what have . . . um, are you sure you don't gamble?"

"Of course not, Your Grace. My father would never have permitted such behavior. While I was with the army, the wives led very circumspect lives. There were no polite gaming parlors, if that's what you are thinking. Naturally the officers indulged. If you are afraid I'll chouse your aunt Eudora out of her pin money, you are far off the mark."

"No, no." But he sounded relieved nevertheless, adding to Graceanne's confusion. He ran his hand through his hair. "Confound it all, there is no delicate way of putting this."

Graceanne was certain now that another slip on the shoulder was in the offing. First he wanted to make sure she wasn't expensive to keep. She jumped to her feet. "No, there is no polite way to ask a lady if she will—"

Just then a mighty crash came from somewhere down the hall, followed by minor noises, slamming doors.

"Oh, dear, I knew we shouldn't have—"

The butler entered with the tea tray and two footmen to help serve. Leland merely raised an eyebrow. The butler bowed and said, "I believe Monsieur Henri has just tendered his resignation, Your Grace. Will that be all?"

Graceanne couldn't make a scene, not with two footmen standing at attention in case the sugar bowl was emptied. She couldn't leap up and run away from this makebate philanderer or toss his extravagant, ostentatious repast in his lap. So she sat and drank her tea and ate his pastries and made small talk about their favorite Christmas carols. And she seethed.

Then came the unmistakable sound of glass shattering. Graceanne's teacup fell from her hand. Thank goodness it was empty, and the carpet so thick the delicate Wedgwood only bounced. Besides, the footman almost caught it before it hit the floor.

The butler returned. And bowed. "Not one of the stained glass panels, Your Grace. Will that be all?"

Chapter Seven

Graceanne was on her feet. "Please, Your Grace, I must leave."

"No, no. Milsom will handle everything. He always does." The duke blocked her way to the door before she could bolt like a nervous filly. "I haven't yet had a chance to ask you—"

"Please, it will only embarrass us both."

"Then you *do* know what I'm talking about."

"Yes, to my eternal shame."

"Aha, so I was right! You *have* done something underhanded with the money!"

"The money?" If he'd said he wanted her opinion on the Corn Laws, Graceanne couldn't have been more surprised. She sat back down. "What money?"

"It's a little late to play the innocent, Mrs. Warrington." He took up his position in front of the mantel, then started pacing. "Or did you think I was such a here-and-thereian, I'd never ask where the money was going?" He didn't wait for Graceanne's answer, which was just as well, for she didn't have one. "I've been racking my brain to think what it could be.

Clothes? Jewelry?" He gave her one disdainful look in passing. "Not likely. I've seen your Posy, so it's not fast horses. You say you don't gamble, and I believe you."

"Am I supposed to be thankful for that?" Graceanne murmured into his tirade, her head rotating from side to side with his long strides.

"So I asked myself, what could it be? Is she paying off some terrible debt? Buying Consols for her old age? Keeping a lover?"

"Your Grace!"

He came to a halt in front of her, glowering down. "So tell me, what in the blazes are you doing with Tony's money?"

"Oh, *that* money!" Graceanne sighed in relief. "You must know I didn't have any dowry to speak of, just a pittance from Mama's family. The settlements, therefore, were negligible. Papa says my widow's jointure barely covers the cost of what the twins break—that is, what they breakfast on."

"Cut line, ma'am, I know to the shilling what your portion is. I ought to—my man of business helped draw up the marriage papers. What I am talking about, if you wish to play the game to its conclusion, is Tony's money. The money I hold as trustee and whose interest I deposit at your bank monthly, having started the account with a substantial sum. The money that is supposed to ensure Tony's children a happy, healthy childhood and his widow security. The money, in short, that is withdrawn and never spent!"

"I . . . I never knew Tony had any money. He never spoke to me about it. We never wanted for anything, but neither did we live grandly. I thought his army pay . . ."

"The army pays chicken feed. Of course Tony had money of his own; his grandfather was a duke. There was no property, since they lived at Ware House in London, but a tidy competence. How do you think Tony bought his commission?"

Graceanne stared at her fingers. "I thought you must have purchased it for him." She shook her head. "And his mother lived in a rented house."

Now it was Leland's turn to study the Turkey carpet he had almost worn out. "Aunt Eudora moved into Ware House," was all he said. It was enough.

Graceanne was so silent for a moment, obviously thinking, that Leland could hear a clock ticking, and feet pounding down a hall somewhere. Many feet. He let her think. Then he handed over his handkerchief. Damn and blast, he never meant to make her cry. It wasn't as though he was going to have her clapped in irons, either, especially if what he now suspected was true. He started pacing again.

Graceanne dabbed at the tears that trickled down her cheeks and snuffled into the fine linen. "Thank you," she said automatically, staring at a private hell so intensely that she didn't hear the shouts in the hall. Many shouts.

At last she spoke: "That's why he didn't want me to spend time in your company. He didn't care about my good reputation, or your bad one. He just didn't want us to converse. It's his collection, of course. I've heard that some men get like that over gambling, where they will lie and cheat their own families to support their wagering. He told me there wasn't enough money to bother about, that he would handle everything for me the way he always did, that women had no head for business anyway. My own father. The temptation must have been too great."

"That's not much of an excuse. If temptation is too great for a man of the cloth, how are we poor mortals expected to manage? Right now I am tempted to go wring your father's scrawny neck! To think of you acting the servant in his home so he can purchase moldy old books makes my blood boil. I've half a mind to have him hauled before the magistrate." His pacing grew more rapid.

"You mustn't, please. My mother is of a nervous disposition. That would kill her."

"Then what would you have me do? I cannot just plant him a facer, a man his age, and I certainly cannot issue a challenge to a cleric. Of course, I have it in my power to see he's not a clergyman in my district anymore."

"Please, the church is his life. He really is a devout man." Graceanne sniffled again, which did not ease the duke's anger one whit.

"Except for greed, deceit, and dishonor, to say nothing of being the starched-up prig Aunt Eudora called him. You cannot intend to let him get away with this."

"Exactly how much . . . ? That is, how tempted was he?" Graceanne wanted to know.

Leland paused long enough in his pacing to listen to the dying commotion in the hall, which she seemed not to hear, thank goodness. Then he named a sum that had the widow gasping. Graceanne knew the value of things from doing the household accounts; this was far beyond any computations she'd handled.

"Why, that's a king's ransom!"

"Not quite," he said dryly. "It wouldn't even pay Prinny's debts for a month. But that's the capital, of course, which should stay intact so the children have a legacy when they reach their majority. Unless Willy is duke by then, in which case only Leslie inherits. Meanwhile, the interest and earnings on investments should be enough for living expenses and incidentals. That's decent living, mind you, befitting a gentleman's sons, no more scrimping and cheese-paring. I had always intended to pay the boys' schooling"— he hadn't thought of it till then, but he should have— "so you needn't count that in your figuring. Nor the ponies."

"Oh, my." She'd never been fonder of Tony than at that moment, nor of His Grace! With a radiant smile, she said, "What a marvelous Christmas present! I don't know how I can ever thank you."

He kicked the edge of the fireplace. "Thank me? You should be wishing me to perdition. I should have seen you settled back in England myself, but it was easier to assume you were more comfortable with your parents. And then I should have looked into the matter sooner rather than suspect you of any hugger-mugger."

"But you couldn't have known. And I think you are taking on too much responsibility. I should have asked to see Tony's papers."

Leland was about to explain that looking after those dependent on him *was* his responsibility as duke, when the butler cleared his throat in the doorway. "Your Grace?"

"Yes, Milsom, what is it?"

"I thought Your Grace might be wondering about the slight disturbance. The fire is out now." He bowed and backed out of the room.

Leland resumed his pacing. "So what about the reverend? What shall you do?"

"I shall cast up my accounts if you don't stop moving to and fro," she said in exasperation, rubbing her temples.

Leland smiled. "See the power of money? A bit of a windfall and no more meek little sparrow. The humble widow is already giving orders to dukes. Not that you were ever quite humble," he amended, taking a seat across from her. "But seriously, you don't have to stay in your father's house any longer."

Graceanne pondered her choices. "My suddenly taking a cottage in the village would be degrading to my mother. And it would leave her and my sister no better off. They'd still be at Papa's mercy."

"You could move in here," he suggested. "The boys being my heirs, no one would think anything of it."

No one would think anything good of it, he should have said. Graceanne could just hear the gossip now. "I think not." Rather than discussing his reputation, she said, "It wouldn't be healthy for the boys to live so far above our station. Think of the comedown when you marry and have heirs of your own, as I am sure you'll eventually do."

"What? Do you think I'll toss Tony's family out into the snow?"

"Of course not, Your Grace." But his wife might.

"I thought you had agreed to stop 'Your Gracing' me, Graceanne. Please, Leland is adequate. *Cousin* if you insist on the formality."

She did. "Cousin. Besides, I am not sure Ware Hold can survive the twins."

He laughed. "You're right. It's withstood siege for only two or three hundred years. Well, if you won't move into the castle, perhaps you'd consider Ware House in London?"

"With Lady Eudora? No, thank you! I think that

would merely be substituting one form of tyranny for another. Maybe I should move away altogether, be truly independent for the first time in my life. Bath, perhaps, or Brighton, where the boys can play on the beach in the summer."

Leland got up and walked toward the desk, where a decanter and glasses stood. "Madeira, Cousin?"

"No, thank you, my father thinks imbibing is— why, yes, Cousin, I do believe I would enjoy a sip of sherry."

While Leland poured, he spoke. "I shouldn't like you to move where I cannot see the boys."

Leland really meant he'd miss seeing the sprouts grow up, miss the riding lessons he was already planning and the hunting, fishing, and swimming expeditions his own father never took him on. Grace thought his words must imply a threat. His Grace was being agreeable now, but cousin or not, he was still the imperious duke. And he held the power and the purse strings. She mustn't forget that for a moment. "I suppose I'd hate to move where I knew no one."

Out of relief that she wasn't emigrating to Canada or something impossible, he handed her a glass and said, "Well, you know me. My offer of a cottage in the woods still stands, or a little house in Kensington . . ."

She did know him. And she must never, ever forget that he was a rake of the first water. She slammed the wineglass down on a table beside her, hard enough to rattle the collection of ivory figurines there. A drop of wine sloshed out onto the carved cherrywood. Graceanne hurriedly used her handkerchief, the duke's actually, from when she was weeping, to dab at the spill. "That is not and never will be, an option, Your Grace."

"Back to 'Your Grace' again, eh? I suppose I owe you another apology, ma'am. Just as you cannot help mopping at spills, I cannot help flirting with a pretty girl." Which wasn't true at all, Leland admitted to himself. There was something about this woman . . . "At any rate, you won't want to decide anything till after Christmas, when I'll have a chance to visit the bank. Do you want all the bills and such sent to me to handle?"

Graceanne was taking deep breaths to try to regain her composure. Then she decided to take a sip of wine instead. The tingle on her tongue worked better. "I am not a nodcock, Cousin, who has never seen an account book. I am sure I can manage my own finances."

"It's not the way things are usually done, a woman in charge." With misgiving he eyed the fragile wineglass, the delicate ivories, and the spark in her blue eyes. "But I suppose we can try that arrangement for now. I'll make provision for the funds to be at your sole disposal at the first of every month, with no one else to have access without my approval. That should put a crimp on the reverend's sticky fingers."

Graceanne nodded her satisfaction. "Then on the first of January I shall be free to make my own decisions for once. A new life for the new year." She savored the freedom, and the wine. One of the unfamiliar experiences gave her the courage to ask, "Do you think . . . that is, I hate to bother you. It's vulgar to speak of money and such, but might I have an advance or whatever?"

"What, outrunning the bailiff already?" he teased.

"And here you just assured me you could manage to live within your means." But he stood up and went to the desk, where he opened a drawer and then a cash box. "How much blunt do you need, my dear?"

Her cheeks were warm; that must be the wine, not the familiarity. "Oh, just enough for Christmas. I'd like to send something to Tony's batman in Dorset. He was injured trying to save poor Tony, only to lose him to a fever, and he returned on the ship with us, seeing to our comfort the whole way."

"Confound it, I should have seen to him." He added a few more bills to the pile in his hand.

"And I'd like to buy some gifts, even if there's not much time to shop. Do you think there will be sleds for the boys here in Warefield? Cook says it will snow for Christmas, and they could have so much fun. And a new set of dishes for Mother, a dress length or two for Prudence. Velvet, I think. A new uniform for Meg. No, a new uniform and another nursery maid!"

Leland kept adding to the stack, smiling. She hadn't mentioned anything for herself, so he did. "And a new bonnet, I hope, for me and the boys."

"A bonnet? Whatever could you and the children want with a bonnet?"

"So we don't have to look at that monstrosity you've been wearing. Save it for the snowman we'll build if Cook is right. And get yourself some prettier gowns, too. Tony wouldn't like you looking the dowd."

She looked down. "No, he wouldn't. Perhaps one or two if I find the time to sew."

He laughed. "And you said you were a downy one. You don't need time, sweetheart. You have money! The village seamstress will stay up Christmas Eve to see you outfitted properly, for enough of the ready."

"A new gown for Christmas would be lovely, even if it must be black."

"Make that two or three. I'd like you to be here with me and Aunt Eudora on Boxing Day to help give out the gifts, so Willy can meet the tenants. My relatives should certainly be dressed as well as the farmers." He shrugged and emptied the rest of the cash box into a leather purse which he handed to her. "My Christmas present." Before Graceanne could argue about the money coming from her account, he asked, "But what about your father? Should I speak to him?"

Graceanne clutched the purse and raised her chin. "No. If I am to stand on my own, I shall do it. And I intend to ask him for the return of the money he spent."

"*Brava!* Stand firm, my Grace. Kick him where it hurts most"—she inhaled sharply—"in his pocketbook. Ah, and here are the boys, just in time."

Milsom carried the exhausted twins, one under each arm.

"Did you have a good time, darlings? Thank Cousin Leland for the visit."

One look at his butler's face and the duke said, "I think we should thank Mr. Milsom, too." And double his Christmas gift.

The boys made their proper bows and thank-yous, then: "I peed in a water closet, Mama! You pull a chain and the water goes whoosh and ends up where the moat used to be."

Graceanne clapped her hand over Leslie's mouth. She didn't get to Willy in time.

"And I peed behind some bushes."

Trying not to laugh, Leland asked, "What? Did you go outside, then?"

Milsom stared over their heads. "I believe that was the conservatory, Your Grace. The orange trees."

Chapter Eight

"God gave Adam sovereignty over all the creatures of the earth," Reverend Beckwith preached. "Including Eve. It isn't right for a woman to have that kind of authority."

Unfortunately for Graceanne, she was the sole recipient of this day's sermon. She'd come back from Ware Hold and handed the twins over to Meg for a nap—they did not resist, for once—then confronted her father in his study.

"I have spoken to His Grace, Papa," she began to say.

"And I suppose he filled your head with all manner of nonsense."

"If you call a handsome competence nonsense, yes." Then she went on to explain that while Reverend Beckwith might have used the money for reasons he deemed worthy, Tony would not have agreed. She did not agree, and the Duke of Ware did not agree. It was only the invocation of Leland's name, and his threats to hold the vicar to account, that had Beckwith cease his diatribe about preserving the past, the revered texts. "I doubt the sacred writings would crumble to dust without my children's patrimony. Some other cork-brained collector would be happy to keep them for posterity's sake. I am not."

The vicar grumbled, "And I suppose you'd rather let Ware gamble the whole thing away, or spend it on his ladybirds."

"I'm not saying the duke is a saint, but I cannot imagine him misusing the funds left in his trust. Nor could he possibly need more wealth. Besides, he truly wants what's best for the boys. He likes them."

Beckwith snorted, ruffling the hairs in his nose. "Hah! You always were as green as a goose. It's called petting the calf, you moonling. So you'll move in with him and he'll have his heirs, his fortune, and a ready-made mistress. Well, don't come crawling to me when my lord rakehell gets tired of you and those hell-born babes, missy."

Graceanne tried to keep her tongue in check. This is your father, she kept repeating to herself. Aloud she said, "It's not like that at all. I am not going to move into Ware House."

"What? He didn't offer you carte blanche? It must be because he doesn't want the brats underfoot."

If Beckwith weren't so busy caressing the pages of his latest, and most likely last, acquisition, he'd have seen his daughter's flaming cheeks. "He did—that is, he likes the children. He did invite us to live at the castle, but I know how small minds work." She ought to, from living at the vicarage. "So I refused his offer. I thought I might stay on here for a while, for Mother's sake." When she saw how his eyes lit up, she added, "I'll pay my fair share of expenses, but no more. And I'll go over the household accounts with you so we are both satisfied."

The vicar was thinking of how he could put some of that corrupt, worldly money to holy use. "And the bills will go to Ware's man of business?"

"No, His Grace agreed that I can be trusted to look after my sons' welfare. I shall see every bill that comes across this desk, and I shall pay only those I authorize."

That's when the good vicar began quoting Genesis. "Furthermore," he added in a burst of last-ditch effort, "God made woman's brain smaller. He wouldn't have done that if He'd wanted them to understand finances."

Graceanne knew better than to argue Scriptures. "That's absurd. Mother handled the account books for years."

"And squandered half our income on the poor," Beckwith griped, but still making his point. "And look what happened because she overtaxed her mind. Now she's in a wheeled chair most of the time."

"Papa, she's in a wheeled chair all winter because this house is too cold for her arthritis. You won't permit enough fires to be burned to keep the place warm. That's going to change, too."

"Now, wait a minute, girl. You can fritter away your inheritance on furbelows and folderols for those limbs of Satan, but no woman is going to dictate how I spend my money."

"I wouldn't think of it, Papa. My brain is too small. When I put such bills in your pile, I'll just consider that you're repaying what you borrowed from Tony's estate."

Prudence was not happy with Graceanne's new circumstances either at first. "It's just not fair! You got to marry a handsome soldier and go to a foreign country and be a duke's relation and now this! You always get everything! Why, Papa won't even let me go to Squire Maxton's Christmas ball! And Liam asked me for the first dance!"

"Liam Hallorahan had no business asking you anything, when he knows Papa does not approve. And you'll have plenty of chances to find a handsome beau next year, when you are eighteen. I'll make sure of that."

Prudence began to see the advantages of having an older sister with deep pockets, especially when she accompanied Graceanne on her first-ever shopping spree. Of course Pru pouted and stamped her foot when Graceanne insisted an orange silk gown was too old for her, but she allowed as how the peach sarcenet was as pretty as anything Lucy had, after Graceanne threw in a Kashmir shawl, new slippers, and a painted fan. Honestly, Graceanne thought, dealing with the twins' tantrums was easier. They were less costly to bribe back to smiles, too.

Other than that temporary setback, the shopping trip was a great success. Henry Moon and his son were willing to make the sleds. They couldn't be varnished in time for Christmas, but they'd be sturdy enough, the blacksmith promised, even for her little demons, ah, darlings.

Mr. Anstruther at the local emporium had toys for the twins and trinkets Prudence couldn't live without, although she'd managed to for seventeen years. He didn't have any "quality" dishes, however. There was no need, he explained, since Ware got its china ordered special from London or direct from the manufacturers, and even Squire's wife went to town once a year for her fancy household furnishings. No one else thereabouts had any call for porcelain dishes. Mrs. Anstruther, however, did uncover some color plates of china patterns they could order up Birmingham way. She'd send a boy straight off if Mrs. Warrington was certain that's what she wanted, expensive plates that wouldn't last a day with those hellions—no, honeys—in the house. They'd be there by Christmas morning if it didn't snow.

Graceanne next visited some of the less fortunate of her father's parishioners and hired the women to finish her mittens and scarves, and their husbands and sons to whittle tops and wooden animals for all the Sunday-school children.

The milliner's was the last stop. Prudence snatched up a chip straw bonnet with jonquil ribbons, just the thing for her new gown. Graceanne knew she'd get no peace unless that, too, joined the pile of parcels filling the pony cart. Pru was a selfish, spoiled chit, but she was Graceanne's sister. And really, she deserved some joyful spots in her life, too. Graceanne was happy being able to provide them. She was even happier finding a black satin bonnet with lavender lining and ribbon rosettes that was far and away the prettiest hat she had owned since her wedding. No matter that it was black, it would match her new lace-trimmed black gown of finest merino and the velvet one with satin ribbons. Her cheeks seemed rosier next to it, her blue eyes brighter. Or perhaps that came from thinking if His Grace would like it.

Foolish beyond permission, she told herself. She had no business thinking such things, not with her husband dead less than six months. And certainly not about a confirmed rake like Ware. He was far beyond her touch, Graceanne reminded herself, and further, beyond her experience. Whatever else, she must not let the recent amity between them blind her to his autocratic nature. Just as she'd considered a velvet toque, then chose the black satin, His Grace could change his mind about Willy. The same way she decided what she wanted, then purchased it, Ware could have anything he wanted, including her son. The power that came from funds in hand was new to Graceanne, a blessing; she must never forget that Ware considered such power his birthright. Still, it did feel good to look presentable. And maybe next month she'd buy the toque.

The last days before Christmas were too few by half, with all the new things Graceanne wanted to do: shopping, fittings, hiring extra staff for the vicarage, and some new furnishings, too, so the place would look respectable if not festive. Her father grumbled, but he did find the funds for his share someplace, likely the same place he kept deference to his noble patron.

Ware did ride over the next day on a huge roan stallion, and he did give each of the boys a turn up in front of him while Graceanne stood wringing her hands in front of the door of the vicarage. The children were ecstatic, of course, and begged, "Faster, Collie, faster." Any faster and Graceanne would have palpitations. Ware's grin was as wide as the boys'.

He was still grinning later, after a session with the vicar in Beckwith's study. Graceanne couldn't hear what was being said, not over Willy and Les's whoops as they rode the broomstick ponies Ware had brought, but her dealings with the vicar were easier after that. Not more pleasant, just easier.

Another lightening of Graceanne's burdens came when Prudence surprisingly offered to take over choir practice. Since this was the first and only unselfish act Graceanne could recall her sister performing, she distrusted it immediately. Liam Hallorahan's fine tenor voice just might have something to do with Pru's commitment to the choir, Graceanne suspected. His handsome looks and green-eyed admiration for the chit might have even more to do with it.

With no Catholic church in miles, Liam had taken to attending Warefield's chapel. "For certain and it's the same God, no matter the name on the door," Liam declared, and "B'gorra, aren't we all God's children anyway?" Not even Vicar Beckwith could bar the church to someone who wanted to worship, especially when he attended in company with the second most influential family in the neighborhood. Squire Maxton was a reliable parish donor, his wife one of the leading do-gooders for the community. Unfortunately, Mrs. Maxton loved music. Her warbly soprano insisted the choir needed Hallorahan.

What the choir didn't need was Pru making eyes at the good-looking young Irishman behind the vicar's back, but that's what it got every Sunday until Graceanne took over as director and insisted on a little more decorum. She supposed she ought to be keeping an eye on her hoydenish sister now, to save her from heartbreak later, but Liam would be leaving in a month or so anyway. Pru would get over her infatuation soon enough. Besides, Liam and Pru weren't her problem just then; replacing the old but newly shredded wallpaper in the hall was, where the broomstick ponies had lunged out of control.

"Not a shilling of mine will go to that, daughter!"

"If the paper weren't so old and shabby, it wouldn't have ripped."

"If those urchins had an ounce of discipline, it

wouldn't have ripped. Why, I've a mind to use those broomsticks where they'll do the most good.''

So Graceanne bundled the twins into the pony cart and went about her errands. Despite all of her new tasks, she couldn't let the usual parish duties fall behind. The sick still needed visiting, for instance. It was amazing what an improvement a visit by Graceanne and her boys made. Why, May Turner got right out of her bed and shooed them out the door.

"I'm feeling so much better, Mrs. Warrington, after these few minutes, I think I'll go visit my brother. I'll have to hurry now. Looks like it's coming on to snow.''

Little Letty Brown with her broken leg took one look at the twins and started hopping around the room, gathering her toys. "There, I told you she'd be walking soon," Graceanne told Mrs. Brown.

And the baker's wife, who was almost near to term, was so encouraged by seeing two such happy, healthy, energetic little boys, she decided to stop fretting and go help her man downstairs immediately. "And you know how important it is to humor women who are breeding, I'm sure. Otherwise they might have twi-twitches.''

Only Old Man Hatchett seemed to have a relapse. "Oh, no," he called through the closed door. "Don't come in, ma'am. I'm suddenly feeling that poorly, I'm afeared it might be something contagious. I'd never forgive myself an' your precious bairns come down sick.''

Somehow her duty calls always seemed shorter when she took the boys along. Graceanne's other visits to the village, without the twins, seemed to take longer than ever these busy days. Everyone wanted to stop her and congratulate her on the good news they'd heard as soon as the vicarage placed its first robust order for groceries.

There wasn't a man, woman, or child in Warefield who wasn't happy for that nice Mrs. Warrington. No one deserved it more, losing her husband so young and having to live with that nip-farthing Beckwith. Troubles seemed to come in pairs for the sweet young thing. Now maybe she'd be able to hire a proper nanny for those terrors, or send them off to school. Or the navy.

If the villagers wanted to take time to rejoice with Graceanne over her good fortune, callers at the vicarage wanted to know its precise amount. The squire's wife came for tea as soon as she heard they'd hired a decent cook. Her questions bordered on the discourteous, but she had a nephew bordering on River Tick. In an attempt to deflect the inquisition, Graceanne had the inspired notion of having the twins down to take tea with the adults. No, Mrs. Maxton wasn't ready to share Leslie's macaroon or Willy's watercress sandwich, without the watercress, naturally. And no, she didn't think she'd invite that nephew down for Christmas after all.

Graceanne was irritated at all the time the entertaining took, especially when the ladies insisted a good coze was impossible with little ears present. Her mother, though, was delighted with the influx of new company, especially since Mrs. Beckwith didn't have to be so ashamed of her parlor. For her mother's sake, Graceanne poured out the tea and passed the plates, and smiled at the nosy old biddies when she would rather have been wrapping gifts or finishing the pageant costumes or any of the thousand other things on her list.

Graceanne was so busy, she didn't miss His

Grace's presence for the two days he was gone to visit friends in Oxford. The duke had stopped to see if Graceanne had any commissions for him before he left, but she didn't, not with the sleds and the dishes already ordered. She wished him Godspeed and watched him drive off in his elegant curricle, caped greatcoat over his wide shoulders. Then she went back to consulting with the sexton over decorations for the church.

No, she didn't even notice the duke's absence, except when the vicar forbade her to put the evergreen garlands in his church, and made sure their cost was added to her side of the ledger. And she didn't wish Ware would come back soon, except for the children's incessant questions: "When is Collie coming home?" and "Do you think he'll bring us something?"

No, she didn't miss him at all.

Chapter Nine

Christmas came, as it usually did, whether anyone was ready for it or not. Had there been more time, in fact, Graceanne would have found more to do. Now that it was the afternoon of Christmas Eve, all she had to accomplish was a dress rehearsal of the Nativity play in the empty church, minor repairs on the twins' costumes, and a nap. The boys couldn't be expected to stay up later than their usual bedtime without a longer than usual nap; nor could they be expected to understand that concept, especially as agitated as they were. Leland's return hadn't done much to dim their excitement, not when he mentioned a surprise or two for good little boys—tomorrow.

Every other minute a dark head would pop up from the pillows to ask if it was tomorrow yet.

Finally Graceanne took them down to her own room, where the three of them could share her bed. She cuddled their little bodies next to her, pulled a quilt over them all, and started to tell stories and sing carols.

When she awoke, Willy smelled of her rosewater and Les was wearing her new slippers on his hands. They must have slept some, for her slippers didn't smell of rosewater yet and the rest of the room was more or less intact. At least Graceanne was refreshed. And at least it was now time to get the boys bathed and dressed, with Meg's help.

Then it was Graceanne's turn, with no help. She tried to ask Prudence which gown she should wear that night, which to save for Christmas Day, the velvet or the merino. Pru was too busy complaining that Mary had to wear a shawl on her head, and how was she supposed to go out caroling with the choir later if she looked like a scarecrow?

Graceanne chose the velvet, with its satin ribbons. She put on the pearls Tony had given her in honor of the twins' birth and went down to supper, to her father's lecture about the pitfalls of vanity, avarice, and trying to catch Lord Ware's eye. Prudence came in for her share of strictures on modesty and filial obedience. Even Mrs. Beckwith was censured for getting above herself, entertaining gentry, and serving three courses at supper. Of course, Graceanne noted, her father didn't turn down any of the new cook's offerings. They all said, "Yes, Papa," and "No, Mr. Beckwith," and went on eating the best food to grace this table in anyone's memory. The silence was broken only when Beckwith remembered another fault, another sin.

Graceanne couldn't help contrasting this meal, with its varied selections, to the plain fare at the nursery dinner, where the children laughed and sang and chattered about everything. Perhaps she should take her meals there from now on, she considered. What were a few spills or stains?

Then it was time to put on their warmest cloaks and walk across the path to the church. Even Mrs. Beckwith was going, all wrapped up and leaning on the arm of the new maid. Sick or well, servant or master, young or old, everyone in the little village of Warefield would be attending church that night. The twins skipped ahead of Meg, darting off into the darkness, then giggling at the nursemaid's frantic calls. Graceanne didn't want to call them to heel yet; better they expend those high spirits outside the church doors.

The party from the manse separated once they were inside the stone church, where the sexton already had the candles lighted, reflected in the stained glass windows. The vicar took up his robe and stood by the pulpit, meditating. Mrs. Beckwith settled onto the bench reserved for the minister's family, along the wall nearest the lectern, while the servants filed into back pews. Prudence took her seat in the small choir section behind the vicar, where the chairs had been pushed to one side to leave room for a few bales of hay, a makeshift manger, and a ladder draped in dark fabric.

Graceanne and the boys stayed in the tiny vestry, gathering the other Sunday-school students who were to be actors for this night. While the congregation assembled in the church, she adjusted headpieces and located props and soothed anxious nerves. Just before her father started the service, she handed out the children's Christmas gifts, their mittens, little tops, and clothespin dolls, to keep them quiet. One of the mothers was to stay with the cast while Graceanne joined the choir for the first hymn.

From where she was sitting she could look past her father's rigid back to her mother's uncertain smile.

Graceanne nodded in reassurance. Past them, nearly every row of the small church was filled, both sides of the aisle, with some parishioners standing by the door in the rear. That was more to make an easy exit when the vicar got going, she knew, than from lack of seats. The unfortunates in the first few rows had no such option, sitting almost immediately under the vicar's watchful eye. They couldn't even choose to sit farther back in the darker recesses, where one might have a catnap during Beckwith's orations, since these parishioners had their names on the pews, like Squire's family. Graceanne saw that Lucy Maxton had brought her betrothed along, but she couldn't see what had Prudence in such a swivet about him. The young man had no chin. And Mrs. Maxton must have purposely forgotten to air her furs until that afternoon again, for she was swathed in beady-eyed boas, and Squire was already sneezing and wiping his eyes. Graceanne knew from her childhood that the wheezing was bound to get worse halfway through the vicar's sermon. She used to make mental wagers over which would give out sooner, her father's voice or Squire's patience.

The very first row, of course, was reserved for the Warringtons. If His Grace got up and walked out, it wouldn't be his mortal soul in danger but the vicar's job, so for tonight, at least, they were assured a shorter than usual harangue. Thank goodness, she thought, for the children's sakes. And then she thought, Goodness, doesn't His Grace look fine tonight!

He wore cream-colored pantaloons and a brown velvet coat that almost matched the color of his hair. His shirtpoints weren't as high as Lucy's intended's, nor his gleaming neckcloth so intricate, but Leland was the one who seemed better dressed and more confident in his attire. Besides, he had a strong, firm chin, with just the hint of indentation. He was definitely a man to the fiancé's youth.

As much as Graceanne had been studying His Grace during the invocations, he had been watching her watching him, and now he smiled. Mortified, Graceanne quickly lowered her eyes to the prayer book in her lap. But she knew it by heart, and soon enough her mind started to wander again, right in his direction. It must be the diamond in his neckcloth that drew her eye, or the heavy gold ring on his finger that flashed when he turned the pages, or the tiny sprig of holly in his buttonhole. Or the light in his eye when he caught her staring again. This time he winked.

Graceanne forced her concentration back to the matter at hand. This was church, and Christmas! She had no business staring at one of the worshippers, no matter how attractive. Besides, it was time for the next hymn.

At least the choir was paying attention, Pru's and Liam's voices melding gracefully around the others'. So they had practiced, contrary to her fears. The only jarring notes to the ancient hymn came from the congregation: Mrs. Maxton's warbly soprano and Ware's aunt Eudora's off-key squawk trying to drown her out. Graceanne looked up—she just couldn't help herself— to see that Ware was mouthing the words, with no sound coming out that she could hear. Tony had been tone deaf; most likely the duke was, too. Somehow that made Graceanne feel better, that he wasn't entirely perfect. She also felt better when she noticed the black armband he wore in respect for his cousin. Good, she thought. If he respected Tony's memory, he would respect Tony's widow. There would be no more of his shockingly indecent proposals.

Papa had begun his sermon while Graceanne daydreamed of what being such a man's mistress could mean.

"I see faces I haven't seen in this church since last Easter. What? Does God celebrate only holidays? I hear voices I know have taken the Lord's name in vain. Are you not ashamed now to sing His praises? I know there are those of you who have lusted and coveted and lied and cheated. Repent of your sins, I say, lest you burn in the hellfires of eternity."

A less self-righteous man might have figured out by then why he saw some of his parishioners so infrequently. Not Papa. But how could even Papa be talking of sin on this of all days, when he was supposed to rejoice with his flock in the birth of hope? Then again, she'd been thinking of sin, so she was just as guilty. Squire started coughing again.

"I know there are those among you"—the vicar's eyes were fixed on the first pew, and Graceanne didn't think he meant Aunt Eudora—"who have gambled and fornicated. On Sundays!"

Squire harrumphed, and Pru giggled from beside Graceanne. Gracious, whatever the duke said to Papa that day in the study must have been dire indeed, to call down such retribution. His Grace was looking thunderclouds back.

"And I know there are those among you who would profane the sanctity of Christ's birth with merrymaking and overindulgence, with pagan rituals and self-serving avarice."

Now a great deal of the congregation began squirming. Maybe they'd been sitting too long; maybe they'd been thinking of the lamb's wool back home, the goose dinners, and the presents.

Just when the vicar was winding himself up for the grand finale of calling damnation down on all their heads if they didn't repent, a small voice from the back of the church called out: "Mama, is it time to go home yet? We're going to miss Christmas!"

Graceanne mightn't know which child it was wandering down the center aisle, but she definitely knew whose child. With her face as red as the new mittens her son wore, Graceanne watched Meg dive for the child and miss. Two footmen in the duke's livery managed to corner the boy between them and lead him back to the vestry while the rest of the parishioners laughed.

So furious he could hardly speak, the vicar pounded on the lectern, but it was too late. No one was listening; no one was going to take him seriously when his own family didn't. Glaring at his elder daughter, he signaled for the final hymn.

With the closing refrains, the choir began to walk down the aisle toward the back of the church, and the sexton dimmed some of the candles, enough that the congregation could pretend not to see the frantic scurrying as the chairs were moved back and the hay bales were moved forward.

Then Squire's youngest son took his place at the lectern and began to read: "And it came to pass . . ."

When he reached the lines where the shepherds were out minding their sheep, the blacksmith's boy, with white robes and crook, herded his small flock down the center aisle. The matching lambs, woolly headpieces, red mittens, and all, gamboled in front of him making sure their furry tails wagged.

"And, lo! A star arose."

From the top of the shrouded ladder a silver star appeared. One of the lambs breathed, "Ooh!" but the shepherd managed to get in his lines about being amazed.

"And an angel spoke to them."

The Anstruther girl was atop the ladder now, her brother holding on to her ankles. One wing was lower than the other and her halo kept falling into her eyes, but she told the shepherd to follow the star, so Toby Moon did, herding his little lambs around the perimeter of the church and back to the vestry. One lamb baaed the whole way, one woofed.

Then it was Mary and Joseph's turn. Pru's pillow stuffing was realistic, and she drooped convincingly over Joseph's arm as they wearily limped toward the altar, where the Anstruther boy came out from behind the ladder to point toward the hay bales. There was no room at the inn. But there was a cow. Timmy and George Bindle could still be heard arguing over who should be the front end, forgetting to moo. Annie Carruthers was the horse. Her father's prize Percheron had a shorter tail now. There were two feathered creatures who alternately quacked and honked, and one pig in a dyed-pink pillowslip who was so embarrassed, he refused to oink.

Mary was masterful, though, kicking the pillows aside and retrieving the blanket-wrapped "infant" from behind the bales of hay while all eyes were on the animals and their antics. As she placed the baby in the rough manger, the star rose again and the angel's sweet young voice rose in a song of joyful adoration. Mary gazed adoringly—at the redheaded Irish Joseph, who still had his arm around her. They sang a duet of rejoicing.

The shepherd and his lambs followed the star

again, then the three kings, bearing gifts and retrieving fallen crowns, wandered toward the altar and made their speeches. By this time one of the lambs remembered the spinning top in his pocket, and the other remembered he hadn't relieved himself after dinner. As the rest of the choir filed back in for a reprise of the angel's hallelujah, this time carrying lighted candles, Graceanne grabbed Willy and his top. Then she looked around helplessly, wondering what to do with him while she took Leslie outside. She couldn't hand him to her father, that was for sure, unless she wanted poor Willy served up as mutton, and Meg was all the way in the rear of the church.

"Rejoice, rejoice, a King is born," sang the choir, the kings, the congregants.

"Mama, I've got to—"

The duke stood and took Willy from her, and sat back down with the child in his lap as casually as if he'd taken a pinch of snuff, one-handed. He winked again as she fled outside with her other son through the nearby side door.

Graceanne reentered the church just in time for the closing benediction. The duke must have been watching for her, since he nodded and patted the empty space next to him. Lady Eudora was still cackling on his other side. Gathering up the remains of the duke's quizzing glass first, Graceanne put Leslie down in that spot next to Ware and started to move farther into the pew. The duke merely lifted Les onto his other knee and gave her an innocent smile. The vicar cleared his throat. Graceanne sat.

For the very first time, Tony's widow and sons took their places in the Warrington pew with the duke's family while her father blessed them all. Not a one of them believed he meant it.

Chapter Ten

"Sorry I cannot shake your hand, Vicar," Leland said as he left the church, "but as you can see, my arms are full." He could have handed one of the sleeping boys back to their mother, but Graceanne was busy gathering hats, mufflers, and sheepskin costumes. She was also accepting laughing congratulations from all the villagers on the success of her pageant.

"Never seen it done better," beamed Mr. Anstruther, his own arms around an angel and an innkeeper.

Everyone was smiling, wishing each other the joys of the season, patting backs, sharing hugs, shaking hands. The vicar's "Rejoice in the Lord" struck a somber note, but only until his flock reached the outside and Squire's wife started "God Rest Ye Merry, Gentlemen," and everyone joined in on their way to the carriages or as they began the walk toward the village in the silent, starry night.

Aunt Eudora was already in the duke's crested carriage, rapping her cane impatiently on the floor. She had even less Christmas cheer than the vicar, Leland thought, looking around for Graceanne.

She hurried to his side. "Goodness, I didn't mean to leave you there like that. Here, give me the boys so you can see Lady Eudora home before she catches a chill."

"That woman is so coldhearted, she could give an iceberg lessons," he joked, handing over one of the twins. "Aunt Eudora will find the flask I left in the coach soon enough. Then she'll be content for a minute while I help you home. The boys are too much for you to carry together. You take Willy and I'll follow you to the vicarage."

"This is Leslie," she said with a smile at his muttered frustration. "It takes time. Thank you, and for your help during the service. The boys can be a trifle, ah, rambunctious at times."

"Just a trifle?" he teased. "But they were the highlight of the pageant. Why, they even stole the show from that precious angel on her ladder. You did a superb job of directing, Mrs. Warrington."

Graceanne opened the vicarage's side door and proceeded down the hall. She tiptoed past her father's study, where light shone under the closed door. Beckwith must have already retreated there to pray over the wickedness of mankind, and the servants would be celebrating with their own families or in the kitchen. "Gammon," Graceanne whispered. "Drury Lane has nothing to fear. Did you see the three kings almost come to blows at the end? And Prudence's shocking display—why, I thought Papa would suffer a brain storm right there."

If he hadn't before, he would now, seeing Pru and Liam alone in the vicarage parlor, where the carolers would assemble later. The way they jumped apart didn't look like choir practice to Leland.

Graceanne pursed her lips. "Prudence, I think you should go help Cook fix the hot cider. The others will be here soon, and you'll want to serve them and be on your way. Liam, perhaps you could start checking for the lanterns. They might be in the barn."

And they might be right in the front hall closet, where Graceanne had made sure days before that they'd be handy for those going wassailing.

"Masterful, my dear," Leland congratulated her, after Prudence stomped off and Liam nervously bowed and hurried in the opposite direction. "But surely your mother—"

"Would have found her bed by now. Her delicate nerves, you know."

He knew that Graceanne had too much in her dish if the Beckwiths expected her to play duenna for that harum-scarum miss. He frowned as he followed her up the narrow stairs, and up again to the children's rooms under the eaves. His brows lowered even more when he saw the humble accommodations.

"Oh, I haven't finished decorating," she hurried to explain, misunderstanding his scowls. "I wanted to leave something for a surprise in the morning. I'll work on it later. This should be a Christmas they'll remember forever."

It would be if he had anything to say about it.

She led him through the nursery room and into the boys' tiny bedchamber. "Watch your head," she cautioned too late, for he was already rubbing it.

Tarnation, the newest tweenie at Ware Hold had better quarters. "Lud, you'd better stop feeding them."

Graceanne didn't even smile at that. She'd been worried herself that the boys would bash their skulls on the low eaves. Even when—and if—her father deemed them civilized enough to take up residence on the family floor below, there was hardly enough room. Perhaps when Prudence married. She had put Leslie down on the bed and was reaching to take Willy from the duke.

He, meanwhile, was looking around for another bed. "Is there another room, then?"

"What, for two tiny children? This isn't the castle, Your Grace." She didn't mean to be so belligerent, she was just embarrassed for the conditions. "Most of your own tenants make do with less."

"But these are not tenant children. These are my cousins." He held up a hand when he saw how she started to get that pinched look, then he patted Willy's back and put him on the bed next to Leslie. "No, I don't mean to pull caps with you on such a night. Even I would find that sacrilegious, brangling over babies on the night of the Christ child's birth. But pulling caps reminds me that I haven't had a chance to compliment you on your new bonnet. It's lovely, Cousin."

"Thank you, Your—Cousin." Graceanne busied herself with unbuttoning Leslie's shoes so he couldn't see her blush. Leaning over the bed, she told him, "Even if there were another room, they'd never sleep apart. As infants they were fretful without each other's company in the same cradle. Later, when they were ready for cots instead of their crib, I had two made. Every night I'd put them each to sleep in his own little bed. Every morning I'd find them tangled together in one bed or the other. Now I just give them a wider mattress." She looked up quickly. "I do expect them to outgrow it, like other children stop sucking their thumbs or carrying favorite blankets around."

"Hopefully that will happen before they go to university." He bent over the bed, too, working on the other twin's boots, and his hand brushed her arm.

Even through the layer of fabric she felt uncomfortable with his touch. The tiny room, the sleeping children, the feeling of being a family—but they were not a family, and she must not forget. "I can do that, Cousin. Thank you."

"Surely you have help?"

"What? To undress two little boys? It's only dukes who forget how to put on their own clothes! Remember, your aunt is waiting in the cold carriage."

"She'll keep. She's eager to get home only to the hand of piquet I promised her, to give her poor abigail an evening off. Aunt Eudora is likely in the coach now, marking a new deck."

"She cheats?"

"That's why she's always so desperate to get up a game. None of her cronies will play with her anymore." He removed Willy's shoe and stocking and stared at the little foot he held. "It's so small."

His very reluctance to leave bothered Graceanne. She wanted him to like the boys. Why shouldn't he? Everyone else did, except Papa, but she didn't want him to like them too much. She wasn't jealous, she told herself, that the boys already adored their cousin Collie. This was different. This was fear of a man who was used to getting what he wanted. She quickly tossed a blanket over both children and made sure Willy's foot was tucked out of sight. "They'll do better like this until I see you out. And I can warm their nightshirts by the fire downstairs

while I make sure the carolers get off on their way."
She stepped back toward the door so he would have
to follow. "Don't worry. They won't wake up."

Leland stood up, and bumped his head. "Blast!
Pardon." He stared at her as he rubbed at the same
sore spot. He'd been just as aware as Graceanne of
their proximity, the intimacy of the setting. He could
still smell her rose perfume. (Or was that Willy? By
Jupiter, the lads needed a man's influence!) And he
was just as conscious of that accidental touch. Except,
of course, that it wasn't accidental at all. The nearness
of that midnight velvet had proven irresistible.
Frowning at his own lack of scruples, he asked, "You
still don't trust me, do you?"

"I . . ." She couldn't lie. He must have known the
answer anyway. "No."

Guiltily, he told her, "You shouldn't."

He meant she shouldn't trust him not to try his
damnedest to seduce her. She thought he meant she
shouldn't trust him not to kidnap her children. She
almost pushed him out the door.

"But I'll try to restrain myself, I promise."

He'd try to restrain himself from stealing her babies? What kind of promise was that? Graceanne
vowed to return to her cheese-paring ways, saving
every shilling—wasn't she her father's daughter?—in
case she had to flee.

The duke laughed now. "Don't look so horrified.
I am still a gentleman. I'd never do anything without your permission. Like asking for a good-night
kiss."

Now she was truly appalled, and he laughed the
harder. "The boys, I meant."

He leaned over and kissed each boy's cheek, without waiting for her permission, Graceanne noted. So

much for that vow. Still, she was a little relieved. Enough that she didn't smile too brightly when Leland stood up—and gave his head another resounding thump on the pitched ceiling.

She had to stop being such a clinging mother, Graceanne told herself after she had the boys in their warm nightshirts and tucked under the covers again. They were safe, they'd have a happy Christmas, Leland would be a conscientious guardian to their inheritance. So why couldn't she leave them and go about her other chores? Instead, she wanted to hug them and squeeze them until they were almost part of her again.

They were growing too fast. Graceanne remembered when the boys were infants sharing one cradle in her bedroom, in their tiny suite. Tony would carry the cradle into the parlor when he came on his rare visits. They'd laugh about keeping their privacy, but she'd always move the cradle back as soon as he left. Now she was worried her sons would get too big to stand in this little room without bumping their heads!

Giving herself a shake, Graceanne went to fetch the rest of the ornaments to be hung. That garland of evergreens Papa wouldn't permit in his church went in the nursery room, but the foil stars, red bows, and paper icicles got hung on strings from the curtain rod to the doorframe, so Willy and Les would spot them as soon as they awoke. Too bad she couldn't see their faces then, but she'd be there when they found the sleds and other toys in her bedroom later. That would have to be enough.

Even after the last bow was hung, Graceanne lingered in the room. She pushed aside a hanging star and opened the curtains enough to look out. She could just see the candles and lanterns of the carolers making their rounds through the village, although she couldn't hear the songs. Humming one of her favorites, she stood and watched the lights bob through the night. They reminded her of the native celebrations in Spain, when the people of that poor, war-ravaged country all gathered with candles and prayers and songs of joy to celebrate *Feliz Navidad,* Merry Christmas. They filed through the streets and hillsides in a seemingly endless line of smiling faces. They were dirty, tattered, sometimes hungry, but they had their faith and each other, their candles in the dark.

And she was alone.

No, she would not get melancholy about Tony, not on this night. She hadn't seen him for months before he'd been killed, so it wasn't as if she had any fresh memories of him. She hardly remembered more about him than his smile and his good-byes, anyway. Instead, thinking about Spain reminded her of the trinkets he'd brought her whenever he made one of his infrequent and short visits. Combs, fans, lace mantillas—they were all packed in boxes in the attic because Papa took one look at them and declared them heathen trumpery, frivolous to boot.

Graceanne picked up a candle and hurried across the hall to the attics. A moment's search found her trunks, and the box with the mementos of Tony's careless affection. Yes, there was a black veil she could be wearing, and the combs weren't trumpery at all, but exquisite works of art. She'd wear a pair for Christmas, another present from her husband, along with her gowns and bonnet and the new independence his money gave her. "Thank you, Tony," she whispered. "Especially for our sons."

Under the laces, as she remembered, was a little hand-carved Nativity. Tony had given it to her last Christmas, sheepishly, because he'd forgotten to buy her a real gift and that was all he could find at the last minute. It would be perfect for the boys' mantel, especially since they couldn't reach it. Let them remember their father, too, despite the new affection for their cousin Leland.

Thinking of the duke made her look out the little window on this side of the parsonage, where she could see Ware Hold guarding its hillside. All those lighted windows for Leland and his aunt. She wondered if he ever got lonely in that enormous pile, if he ever missed his deceased wives.

Graceanne had seen his first duchess once, when she was still in the schoolroom. She wasn't introduced, of course, but then, almost no one was. The duchess kept to herself and her houseguests. Ware's second wife was too sickly to get out, Graceanne remembered hearing. The second duchess had her own chaplain attend her at the castle, so she never attended church in the village. But did she love her husband? Or was theirs an arranged marriage, a convenient economic merger? More important, did he love her? Graceanne guessed not, if he could treat other women so casually, like commodities.

No, she didn't trust him a bit.

She went back to the boys' room and arranged the Nativity set over the fireplace just as the sexton rang the bells for midnight, Christmas midnight. Peace on Earth, goodwill to all men. Well, she'd try.

Parting the curtains again, Graceanne looked for

the carolers' lights. They'd be returning soon to deliver the poor box donations, and she had to be on hand to serve the hot cider that was all the vicar would permit. She made sure there would be coffee and tea, too, for those who had tasted enough wassail on their waits. Just as she was about to close the drapes, a snowflake drifted past, then another. Her boys would have snow for their new sleds after all. Thank you, Lord. Happy birthday.

Finally she pushed aside stars and bows and icicles to kiss her sons good night. And bumped her head when she stood up.

His Grace was also listening to the midnight church bells, watching the first snowflakes, and thinking of Tony Warrington's twins.

After the carolers left, young Prudence hanging on her Irishman's arm, and castaway, too, if he didn't miss his guess, Milsom had brought up a new bowl of wassail. Then the servants gathered in the Great Hall for the lighting of the Yule log. At the first tolling of the bells, His Grace had lit the enormous ash log in one of the huge fireplaces, using a bit of last year's wood. He hadn't the slightest idea if it was last year's wood or yesterday's, actually. Hell, he'd been at some dull house party or other last year, and the year before that, but Milsom would have carried on. He always did.

The butler had handed over the burning ash splinter, then toasted the House of Ware when the new fire caught. The servants lifted their glasses of wassail and said, "Hear, hear." If the log burned till Twelfth Night, tradition went, Ware's house would prosper.

How the bloody hell could it prosper if the butler had to light the fire and the servants make the toasts?

There was supposed to be family and friends assembled, not paid retainers and one crotchety old cardsharp who needed two footmen to hold her up after an evening at the punch bowl. And he, Leland Warrington, the Duke of Ware, was supposed to pass that burning ember to his son, blast it! Damn his past wives!

Chapter Eleven

The stars, the sleds, the storybooks—nothing compared to the snow! In all of her thinking what fun the children could have with their new sleds, Graceanne had forgotten that the boys had never seen snow. There was nothing to do but to push the presents to the side, bundle the twins in their warmest clothes, and let them loose outside.

Oh, the wonder of it! Oh, the wetness of it! Thank goodness for the new mittens and caps and mufflers, for Les and Willy needed three sets of dry clothing, once before breakfast, once after, then again before church. Graceanne didn't mind, hearing their laughter.

They danced in the snow, rolled in it, tasted it, tossed it. Heaven and the stained-glass windows be praised, the boys were too young for hard and heavy snowballs, but they did manage a lopsided snowman with Graceanne to lift the head on. She did not dress the snowman in her old black hat, as Cousin Leland had suggested, not when every Christmas-morning worshipper could look out the church windows and recognize it. And not when she needed it for mornings like this, rather than ruin her new satin bonnet with such child's play. Instead, she fashioned a merry wreath of holly and ivy for a crown, and cut up some of the foil stars for eyes and a nose. With a big red bow around his neck, the snowman looked as happy as she felt, even in her old black gown.

Breakfast in the nursery was a hurried affair because she'd promised to teach the boys how to make snow angels as soon as they were fed and dry again, and because their noisy excitement couldn't be restrained in the still-sleeping house.

Outside again, Graceanne found there was no way she could explain the concept without lying down in the snow, waving her arms and legs up and down, then hopping up to show the boys the impression in the snow. *Now* the old black bonnet was ready for the dust bin. Willy and Les filled the parsonage yard with angels, then swore they weren't too wet or tired to try their new sleds.

The hill behind the church wasn't much of an incline, at least so Graceanne thought before she helped drag those sleds up it a hundred times, or so it felt. Leslie screamed the first time he went down, and every time after that. Willy just grinned. She finally convinced them they'd wear the sleds out if they didn't stop soon. Besides, there were gifts for the rest of the family. Didn't they want to see?

The Beckwiths were still at the breakfast table—Papa had thought a longer than usual grace was called for that morning—when Graceanne in her new black merino and the boys in their new nankeen suits entered the dining room.

"What's this, daughter? You know I don't permit those—"

"It's Christmas, Grandpa! Look what we helped wrap!"

Willy handed the vicar a wad of tissue paper that Graceanne had to peel apart, the vicar refusing to touch it, to reveal a new pipe. Leslie held out a piece of paper, a ribbon, and a warm muffler.

"Very nice, very nice, I am sure, but you know I don't approve of—"

"Here, Aunt Pru, all these boxes are yours. Mama didn't let us help wrap."

"Mama, how come Aunt Pru got more presents than Grandpa? Wasn't he as good this year?"

"Hush, darlings. Let your aunt open her gifts."

Prudence dutifully pretended to be surprised by each new delight she uncovered, the peach sarcenet, the hat and gloves and fan, just as if she hadn't whined and wheedled over every item. She permitted each boy to kiss her cheek, then wiped it.

When it was Mrs. Beckwith's turn, Graceanne left the room.

"It was too heavy, Grandma," Willy explained.

"And too fra-fra— Mama said don't touch."

"That's 'fragile,' darling," Graceanne said, wheeling in the tea cart. Both shelves of the cart were filled with the new dishes—cups, saucers, bowls, serving platters, teapot—all in a dainty pattern of violets and vines.

Mrs. Beckwith held up one teacup to see the light shine through the delicate porcelain, and started weeping.

Willy frowned at his mother. "I told you plates weren't a happy present." But Leslie put his arms around his grandmother, who clutched the teacup to her breast, and said, "Don't cry, Grandma. You can play with our toys."

* * *

The boys were so good—and so tired from their morning in the snow—that Graceanne felt comfortable leaving them beside her mother in the family pew during the church service. She was so happy today, in fact, that she didn't even resent that no one in her family had thought to buy the boys any gifts. That her father should have done so was out of the question, and her mother hardly left the house, but Pru? That she might have spent a ha'penny of her pin money on her own nephews never occurred to her. Graceanne shrugged and joined the choir behind the pulpit determined that nothing was going to spoil the rest of this perfect day.

The joyous uplifting of voices in song that she expected was not quite so joyous, not nearly perfect. There were some stuffed noses and scratchy throats among those who had spent the chilly night out caroling, and there were some bleary eyes and unsteady hands among them, too. One seat was empty altogether. When a particularly sour note sounded next to her, Graceanne shuddered and turned to her sister. Yes, Pru was definitely off key today, and off her looks, too. In fact, Graceanne noted, the chit had a decided greenish cast to her complexion. The one piece of dry toast on her plate at breakfast must not have meant Pru was waiting for the noonday feast after all.

Good, Graceanne thought, and not just because Pru hadn't bought the children Christmas presents or complimented her on her new gown and hairstyle. Maybe Prudence would learn from experience if her head ached enough, Graceanne thought, for surely neither Papa's sternness nor Mama's vagueness were teaching the girl moderation.

When Graceanne turned back to check on the twins, her mother was sitting alone on the bench. Before she could panic overmuch, Graceanne saw the boys ensconced on the seats next to Leland, in the Warrington pew. Lady Eudora was asleep, snoring slightly, and the duke was his usual handsome, elegantly attired self, smiling at her when he noticed her attention. He, at least, seemed to admire her new look.

She'd gathered her hair into its usual bun that morning, but then raised the knot of hair higher on the top of her head, held with two tortoiseshell combs. Then she'd draped the black lace mantilla over the whole. It wasn't quite a match for the lace on her soft woolen gown, of course, but with Tony's pearls, she felt quite the thing. Leland's warm regard seemed to agree with her assessment. It brought a flush to her cheeks, too.

The boys were playing with the duke's quizzing glass, a different one from last night's, necessarily so. Gracious, he must have a drawerful of the things, that he let three-year-olds play with them. After he collected all the pieces, he offered the boys peppermint balls from a little sack in his pocket. He must have come prepared, Graceanne thought, unless the highest peers in the realm usually carried sweets with them to church. She doubted it, and felt warmer toward Ware because of that, warmer than she wanted herself to feel.

After the service, Graceanne had to endure the comments of all her longtime neighbors about how nice it was of His Grace to take such an interest in the boys. She smiled and nodded, yes, it was. And she was looking a real treat, too, Squire remarked in his tally-ho voice. "One thing doesn't have aught to do with t'other, does it, missy?" he asked with a wink and a grin before his wife pinched him and dragged him to their carriage.

Of course the duke was next to greet her. Where else would he be when she was wishing the ground to open up, but right there to see her embarrassment? His hazel eyes were twinkling, but Leland merely bowed over Graceanne's hand and asked if he might call after taking his aunt home, for he had a few trinkets for the boys he'd like to deliver.

"For the boys? You didn't need to buy gifts for them. I told you I was going to. All that money you gave me . . ."

"I didn't have to. I wanted to. Isn't that the spirit of Christmas?"

The spirit of Christmas was hopping up and down and running to the window every other minute to watch for their beloved Collie's arrival.

"But it is snowing again, darlings. His horses might have trouble getting through the drifts." Two identical lower lips started to tremble. "But I'm sure he'll try. Come, let's look at the new picture book until he gets here. If he doesn't come, we'll go play in the snow again." Where His Grace and his curricle had better be, ditched, for disappointing little children on Christmas Day.

But no, they soon heard carriage wheels crunching in the snow. The boys scampered down the stairs, which they were never supposed to do, squealing, which they were certainly not permitted to do in this part of the house. They were trying to open the door—another taboo or Graceanne would never know where they were—but luckily they were still too short to reach the latch.

Graceanne shooed them aside, straightened her skirts, and said, "Now, remember to bow, and do not ask if he brought you anything." Then she opened the door.

His Grace was framed in the doorway, his curls all windblown and the shoulders of his greatcoat powdered with snow. He was wearing a grin as wide as the one she'd put on the snowman, and his booted foot was raised to kick at the door for entry, since his arms were heaped with mounds of packages.

"A few trinkets for the boys, you said. Why, you look like Father Christmas himself!"

"They are not all for the children," the duke told her as she led him into the parlor. Where else was she to entertain a visiting nobleman? Upstairs in the nursery again? Her family prepared to depart when Leland added, "I was having such a fine time shopping that I bought gifts for everyone."

Prudence, who had been drooping over a fashion magazine, perked up like a half-dead seedling that's just been watered. She wasn't getting to attend the party at Squire's tonight, despite having a new gown, but Lucy Maxton never got a gift from a real live duke. Pru hurried to help relieve Ware of the gifts, so he could shrug out of his greatcoat.

Of course it was left to Graceanne to take the damp coat to hang in the hallway and go to the kitchen to order tea. When he raised an eyebrow as if to ask why she was still acting the menial, Graceanne laughed and said, "It's the maid's day off. Oh, how I have wanted to say that like some grande dame come down in the world. But it truly is the new maid's holiday, and I really don't mind, if you'll promise not to let the children act like pigs at the trough of your gifts while I am gone."

It was Pru, however, who was in a snit when Graceanne returned. The duke had let the brats each open a present, sets of wooden jackstraws, but he made the rest of them wait for Graceanne's return. "What took so long, Gracie? You should not keep Cousin Leland waiting."

"Cousin Leland? His Grace is no cousin of yours, Pru."

"He is too, by marriage."

Graceanne looked toward her mother to remonstrate with Prudence over her coming ways, but Mrs. Beckwith was anxiously trying to explain jackstraws to Willy, and why it wasn't a good idea to stick them in his ear. Leslie was playing with his set on the floor between the duke's legs while Leland conversed with the vicar. Leslie's chubby little fingers wouldn't manage that game for a few years, but he seemed to be having no trouble whatsoever shoving the narrow pieces down His Grace's high-top boots.

"Leslie, Wellesley, come get our present for Cousin Leland. No, Your Grace, do not—"

There was a crunch, a snap, a "Blister it! What the deuce?" and another crackle.

"—stand up. Yes, well, I apologize for taking so long, but we seemed to have misplaced the gift the boys and I made for you."

The package the boys proudly handed to him seemed to have been misplaced in the dustbin. There were crumbs and smears and a few rips in the paper. "You shouldn't have," he said, and sincerely meant it.

"Open it, Collie, open it!"

So the duke stepped back, gingerly, and sat down again. He untied the string. Actually, he had to cut the knots with his pocketknife, which he hastily tucked back in an inside pocket. The paper fell off by itself to reveal a dirty sheepskin square protecting—what?

"It's a pen wipe, Collie! We made it out of the lamb hats from the pageant. See, we colored it here, and Mama showed us how to put your initials here. See?"

"I see it's the finest pen wipe I have ever owned," the duke nobly swore while Prudence snickered and the vicar snorted, "At least I got a pipe."

Leslie was looking uncertainly from one adult to the other. Willy was frowning.

"But I do not smoke," the duke whispered to the boys, "so this is a much better present."

Then he started handing out gifts, with only an occasional cracking sound as he moved around the room. To the vicar he gave a leather-bound volume, *A Dissertation on the Proof of the Existence of Angels,* by a well-known Oxford don. "I visited my old religion professor and had him sign it for you. It's not ancient, but it might be a worthy addition to your collection."

"You mean you know Robert Jordan? I believe him to be one of the foremost theologians of our day. Why, he—"

The reverend would have gone on, but Ware had turned to Mrs. Beckwith with a soft, flat bundle. Inside was a tablecloth runner and napkins, the finest damask embroidered with clusters of violets. "However did you manage that?" Graceanne asked when her mother seemed struck speechless.

He grinned. "I cheated and bribed Anstruther to lend me the illustration of the dishes you ordered. While I was in Oxford I had a clerk at one of the linen-drapers search out anything that matched."

"All that trouble," Mrs. Beckwith cried. She was weeping again, and one of the boys, dashed if Leland knew which, told him not to worry. "Grandma didn't like her dishes either."

"Lud, I never thought of that. I can exchange them—" So he had to be reassured that Mrs. Beckwith adored her new dishes, and her new linen.

The duke next handed Graceanne a small box that looked ominously like jewelry. "I cannot accept . . . that is, it wouldn't be proper for me to . . ." What she meant was that she'd die of mortification if Leland handed her the diamond bracelet or whatever expensive frippery gentlemen gave their mistresses.

"Nothing improper at all, Cousin. Open it."

He was right. There was nothing to take exception about in a plain gold locket, except that it was empty. "I meant it for locks of the twins' hair," he explained. Of course there was nothing to do then but for Graceanne to find her embroidery scissors and cut a curl from each boy. Prudence gnashed her teeth. The children were showing more forbearance.

Pru's gift, when Ware finally got around to her, was too big for a jewelry box. She wasn't quite successful in hiding her disappointment, no matter how inappropriate such a present might have been. Graceanne was relieved when the chit managed to show proper enthusiasm for the charming ceramic dresser mirror with its painted figures on the back, though she wished her sister could have refrained from throwing her arms around the duke in appreciation. He stepped back hastily enough, she noted, saying something about a pretty bauble for a pretty reflection, calculated to feed the young girl's vanity. Which was just what Prudence didn't need, Graceanne thought.

"Mama says pretty is as pretty does. What does that mean, Collie?"

"Uh, it means it's time to open another of your presents, bantling. Here, these two, I think. They are to share." One was a small tin trumpet, the other a little drum.

Prudence left off admiring her blond ringlets in the mirror to groan, but a frosty glare from Graceanne kept her in her seat. The next package contained a pair of child-sized wooden swords.

"So you can play at pirates and soldiers, all kinds of games, even St. George and the dragon."

Graceanne half expected him to produce the dragon next, but it was Mrs. Beckwith who groaned this time, thinking of the vases they could knock over, the furniture those swords could gouge. "I think I'll just take my lovely gift to the dining room before the table gets set."

Prudence and the vicar both offered to wheel her, but Pru won, so Beckwith decided he could get a bit of reading in before luncheon.

"Will you join us, Your Grace?" Mrs. Beckwith asked from the doorway. For once she was not at all embarrassed to make the invitation, not with a fine goose cooking, Graceanne's minced meat pies heating up, and her new china. Why, her table would be fine enough for the Prince Regent himself.

"I am sorry," the duke said, "but I am expected home for nuncheon with my aunt. Another time, perhaps. But I would like to invite you all for tea this afternoon. The kitchens have been busy, although there are just two of us. And the castle is looking quite festive."

The vicar declined at the word *festive.* He intended to spend the afternoon of this holy day in church, praying. Mrs. Beckwith, torn between the pleading look on Prudence's face and the disapproval on her husband's, was decided by Willy's "Us, too, Collie?"

And Ware's "Of course you, too, halfling."

"I think I've had too much excitement for one day, Your Grace, but thank you. Yes, Prudence, you may go without me, if Graceanne accepts."

The boys were tugging on her skirts and Pru was looking like she'd cosh her with the mirror if Graceanne said no. Outmaneuvered again, if her plan was to avoid the licentious lord, she nodded. Pru made her best curtsy and sighed, "Until later, Cousin Leland." Good, he'd be busy fending off her little sister.

When all the Beckwiths were gone, Ware let the boys loose on the rest of the packages. Under the maelstrom of wrappings and ribbons, Graceanne saw puzzles and picture books and tin soldiers, but also some vastly inappropriate gifts, like cricket bats and dart sets.

After everything was unwrapped and the children were playing with the boxes, Leland asked, "Will you excuse me? I have to—"

"It's out back," Leslie told him.

"Empty my shoe."

He must have been like a child in the toy shop, Graceanne reflected while Leland was gone, buying everything that appealed to him, without regard for age or ability. Cricket bats and swords and darts, my goodness. He might as well hand the boys a cannon and be done with it. And that drum and trumpet were enough to give a mother a headache just looking at them.

Leland came back with yet another gift, another horror for Graceanne. This one wiggled and barked, and had a red bow around its neck. "Oh, dear, Papa will never let them keep a dog."

Leland was on the floor with the children and the pup. "Then the little fellow can stay at the castle, and the boys can come visit."

"You tell them that," she answered with a touch of bitterness. The twins were delirious. A dog of their own was even better than snow. And it wasn't just any dog, Ware declared, it was a real, honest-to-goodness, purebred collie. So the twins instantly and simultaneously named the dog Duke, since their own duke was Collie.

"Makes sense to me," Leland agreed. "Duke it is."

Graceanne felt she was drowning. "But are you sure it's a boy?"

"Yes, Mama. See, here's his—"

"I think Duke needs to go outside. Run get your coats and mittens." Graceanne started to gather some of the toys, the catastrophes waiting to happen. Then she turned to the duke, still sitting on the floor with the puppy, looking up at her like a naughty boy. "I can't help but see a pattern here, Your Grace." She held up the dart set and waved it at him. "This is the stuff of a parent's nightmare. Cricket bats for three-year-olds? And a dog? Come, you had to have known better."

He just grinned, the same grin Willy and Les wore when they escaped Meg and picked Mrs. Beckwith's last flowers, "For you, Mama."

"I didn't think you'd find me out so soon." Leland stood and looked down at her, seeming not at all like a little boy anymore. She took one step backward and would have toppled over the toy drum if he hadn't put his arms out to steady her. Leland re-moved his hands from her shoulder, but not instantly. He gave her one more smile, then bent to pick up the drum.

"I bought everything the vicar would hate the most, the noisiest, most destructive toys I could find." He grinned again. "That way, he'll throw you out and you'll have no choice but to move to the castle."

Chapter Twelve

$\mathcal{D}$angerous. The man was positively dangerous. And endearing, which of course made him more dangerous. He returned after luncheon to fetch them in a sleigh, for the twins' sake, he said, but his own face was glowing with excitement. Graceanne couldn't have thought of a better treat for a snowy Christmas afternoon. Prudence could. Her hair would be mussed, her complexion wind-damaged. She went anyway, rather than sit home bored when all her friends were getting ready for the party at Squire's. Besides, none of the other local belles had been invited to her cousin the duke's, so she went, but not graciously.

The twins, on the other hand, were in alt, even though Duke got left behind in the barn "to keep Posy company." It was a big sled, with two large, shaggy farm horses to pull it and bells ringing everywhere. They tried to keep their wet boots from Prudence's skirts—they really did.

Not even Prudence could keep to her crotchets when she entered Ware Hold's Great Hall. Graceanne and the boys had already seen the immense room decorated, of course, but not like this.

"I wanted it to be a surprise," said Leland, standing proudly to one side, right where the liveried footmen would have been if they both hadn't succumbed to the grippe right about the time they heard who was coming to tea. Leland's surprise was a magnificent fir tree, eighteen feet high at least, decked top to bottom with glowing candles in holders. When his guests had looked their wide-eyed fill, Prudence even clapping her hands, he explained, "It's a Christmas tree. Actually it's a German tradition, called a *tannenbaum*. Princess Caroline had one, and the idea took hold in London. I found them so charming, I wanted one for the castle."

Pru giggled then. "Papa would have conniptions! Not just heathen, but Hanoverian to boot. Why, I thought he'd go off in a swoon when you mentioned Father Christmas this morning."

Graceanne smiled, too. "That's a lovely tradition and this one is . . . is wondrous! It's magnificent, Cousin Leland, but are you sure it's safe?" She kept a steely grip on each boy's wrist.

"Of course it is. Milsom here wouldn't let anything untoward happen to his castle. Look over in the corner, where there are buckets of water. And a footman is on duty whenever the candles are lit, although dashed if I know where he's gone. Milsom will see someone in his place, I'm sure."

"Stop being such a spoilsport, Gracie."

The duke laughed and swung one of the boys up in his arms. "Willy?"

"No, silly, I'm Leslie!"

He shrugged and turned to the boys' mother. "Yes,

Grace, don't be a marplot. It's Christmas, time for magic, not worrying! But come. Aunt Eudora is waiting in the Adams parlor, with the wassail bowl."

"Oh, good," chirruped Prudence, not soothing Graceanne's nerves a whit.

The Adams parlor was to the rear of the castle, in the modern wing. It wasn't quite as large as the Great Hall, just large enough to fit the entire congregation of the Warefield church. Instead, it held one old lady and another Christmas tree. This one was only ten or twelve feet high, and it was decorated with red bows instead of candles.

"See, nothing to worry about."

Nothing except the Axminster carpet, the Queen Anne chairs, the Chippendale tables, the Dutch Masters paintings, and the old lady.

"Don't expect *me* to play nursemaid while you get up a flirtation with some mealymouthed vicar's daughter, nevvy."

Thinking she was the object of the supposed flirtation, and delighted that it be so, Pru replied for the duke: "Oh, I'm not at all mealymouthed, Lady Eudora. And you don't have to worry about the children. Gracie hardly trusts me to watch them, so she wouldn't let an old tartar—that is, she wouldn't expect anyone else to babysit the brats."

Graceanne didn't know where to look, except at Leland, who was covering his laughter with a cough. Lady Eudora banged her cane on the floor a few times, then declared, "At least this one's got some spirit. Do you play, girl?"

"Play? The pianoforte? Only indifferently, my lady. Gracie usually plays while I sing." She fluttered her eyelashes in the duke's direction. "I've been told

I have a pretty voice." She'd been told she sang like an angel and looked divine by the candlelight atop an instrument. "Would you like me to perform?"

"Faugh," Aunt Eudora answered. "Every prunes-and-prisms chit in London trills her notes and thumps away at the pianoforte. I meant, do you play cards?"

Pru's face fell. She'd really wanted to impress the duke.

"Our father would not permit gaming," Graceanne reminded the old lady, who started to hobble away in disgust, back to the wassail bowl.

"But I've always wanted to learn!" Pru almost shouted, lest Ware think her some country gapeseed, which she was, of course.

Eudora turned around. "That's more like it. You'll do, gel. What did you say your name was?" And she started to lead Prudence away, toward a card table set up at the opposite end of the room.

Pru looked back helplessly. "But I thought His Grace . . ."

"M'nevvy's feeling patriarchal. It's enough to make a person bilious. Come. And bring two cups of that lamb's wool."

"Not for money, Aunt Eudora," Leland called after them as Graceanne murmured, "Oh, dear, and you said she cheated."

"What? Are you afraid I'll be having your sister raiding the poor box like that skinflint father of yours?" Lady Eudora turned back to Prudence. "Don't worry, gel. I'll lay out your stake. Pennies only—makes the game more interesting, don't you know."

"And I can keep whatever I win?"

"Oh, dear," Graceanne said again, louder.

Leland chuckled and took her arm. "I think Miss Prudence can handle herself." He led her toward an inlaid table where the wassail bowl sat. The boys had already found the tray of sugarplums next to it. Graceanne had no way of knowing how many the platter used to contain, but she suspected the Ware staff would not send up a half-empty plate. Well, it was Christmas.

"A toast," Leland was saying, holding out a cup of the warmed brew. When she took it he poured another and raised his. "To Christmas. To good cheer and goodwill."

"To peace," Graceanne added, taking a cautious sip. It was delicious, this mixture of ale and spices. She sipped again. The duke, meanwhile, was offering a taste to each of the boys from his own cup. "I don't think they should—"

"A tiny bit won't hurt, just to toast the holiday. Besides, they need to experience more of the world, more than they ever will in the vicarage."

Oh, well, she thought, it was Christmas.

Leland was leading the boys across the room toward the decorated tree. "Do you know, I think Father Christmas made a mistake this year."

"Grandpa says there's no such thing, Collie."

"Ah, then perhaps that's why he got confused. You see, Father Christmas cannot deliver presents where no one believes in him, that's the rule. So he had to leave some gifts here instead of at the vicarage."

"Do you believe in Father Christmas, Collie?"

"Well, I'd like to," Leland said, rummaging under the low branches to the rear of the tree. "But I particularly wished for a pair of matched grays for my new phaeton, and look what he delivered instead." He pulled out from underneath the tree two identical wooden rocking horses, with real manes and tails, leather harness, and glass eyes. The boys jumped aboard and neighed and whoaed and rocked until Graceanne nervously started chewing on her lip.

"That is a most wonderful surprise, Cousin. But are you quite sure . . . ?"

"That they can't pull my phaeton? Definitely." He brushed pine needles off his shoulder, then led her to a nearby sofa, where she could watch the boys' antics. "Come, you must learn to relax more. They'll be fine, I promise. You cannot keep them wrapped in cotton wool, you know, and expect them to grow up to be decent men."

Graceanne hadn't been thinking of the twins so much as the carpet.

"I couldn't bring the rocking horses with me in the curricle this morning, of course, so I'll have someone haul them over to the vicarage in a wagon as soon as the weather clears. My man will make sure they get up to the nursery, out of the vicar's way."

Good, then she'd only have to worry about them wearing holes in the wood flooring and falling through into Papa's bedroom. She had another sip of the wassail. Leland was right, there was no use worrying today. She stared over at him as he watched Willy dismount and ask Les if he wanted to ride the other horse awhile. The fond affection she saw in the duke's smile made her say, "You'd make a wonderful father."

He sat up straighter and, she swore, puffed his chest out. She might have complimented his prowess with the ribbons or at culping wafers. "I would, wouldn't I?"

"Well, yes, if you ever managed to tell your children apart."

"Unfair, Gracie, you've had three years to work with your peapod brood! Furthermore, I have the perfect solution right here." He took a small box out of his pocket and called the boys to him when they seemed to be tiring of the wooden horses. "Here, my lads, is one last present on this most special of days."

Les climbed into his lap and Willy leaned against his leg for a closer look. "That's girl stuff, Collie," he said when the box was open.

"Not at all. See, I have a ring on, and a stickpin. I thought of getting you signet rings, but your fingers are growing too fast, so I settled on these. Look, these are your initials, *L* for Leslie, *W* for Willy. They are stickpins for your neckcloths, just like mine."

"Silly, we don't wear neckcloths. We're just boys!"

"Yes, but you have lapels on your coats, and collars on your shirts. Boutonnieres are au courant."

"What's a 'boot on ears'?"

"What's 'awker aunt'?"

"It means all the fashionable gentlemen are wearing pins in their buttonholes."

"Especially those who don't know their name," their mother teased with a giggle. "Perhaps you'll even start a new fashion for gentlemen who tend to get castaway, little pins with their addresses engraved on them so the Watch can send them home in a hackney." She giggled again.

The duke eyed her narrowly, then moved the wassail cup away from her reach. "Enough of that, my girl, or you'll be the one needing help finding your way home. Here, Les, Willy, not only will you be all the crack, but no one can mix you up again."

"But we don't get mixed."

"And Mama doesn't get mixed."

"But poor, old, silly Cousin Leland does, so won't

you help him out?" At their nods, he took the *W* and
reached for the boy on his lap. Graceanne coughed
delicately. He switched to the boy by his leg. When
he had both pins affixed on their collars, Leland sat
back with a satisfied smile. "There. Now, why don't
you go ride the horses a few more minutes before
Milsom comes to get you for tea?"

"They really should have a nap," Graceanne worried.

"On Christmas? Gammon, they can sleep the rest
of the year."

While the grown-ups were debating, the level of
Graceanne's wassail cup was descending. By the time
Milsom arrived, both boys were sound asleep under
the Christmas tree. Ware sent him off to fetch tea for
the adults, except Aunt Eudora, who was also sleeping, her head on the card table. Pru wandered
around admiring the furnishings and the decorations,
then joined Graceanne and the duke when two footmen and the butler brought in the tea things.

As soon as everything was laid out to Milsom's
satisfaction, he snapped his fingers to the footmen
and nodded at the sleeping children. Small boys
sprawled on His Grace's carpet did not fit Milsom's
dignity. The twins were removed from the parlor like
so many dirty dishes.

After an elegant tea, the three adults moved to the
pianoforte in the corner, the finest instrument
Graceanne had ever played. Prudence had recovered
from the morning's indisposition and sang beautifully, directing her voice and soulful gaze at the
duke. Graceanne joined in for some of the old carols
and Ware hummed along. He truly had abominable
pitch, but, begging their pardons, enjoyed himself
nevertheless. Then Pru sang some Gaelic carols by

herself. Graceanne didn't want to know where or
how she learned them, not today.

They stopped singing when the boys ran into the
room, energies back to full gallop. Milsom bowed.

Leland told Graceanne, "See, no loud noises, no
alarums."

"I do see. Thank you, Mr. Milsom."

Milsom bowed. "My pleasure, madam. And the
steward says the door to the wine cellar can be re-
paired tomorrow, Your Grace."

His precious wine cellar? With the bottles laid
down in his father's time?

Her babies put to sleep in the damp, dark caverns
beneath this place?

Prudence was tired of being ignored. "Do you
know, Cousin Leland, you've done such a lovely job
of decorating for the holidays, I don't understand
how you forgot the mistletoe?" Milsom sniffed and
bowed himself out as Pru struck a pose next to the
fireplace. "I helped Lucy Maxton make the kissing
bough for the manor, and I think it's quite one of
the nicest Christmas traditions, don't you?"

"Oh, quite!" He gathered up both boys, one under
each arm, and carried them toward Prudence, who
was, of course, standing under a beribboned bunch
of the berries. "Les, Willy, here's a lesson a gentleman should learn early in life: Snatch kisses whenever you can!" And he held them up to kiss the
cheek Prudence begrudgingly presented. He lightly
bussed her forehead, almost as an afterthought, before bending down to the twins' level. "Now, why
don't you try getting your mother over here, Willy,
ah, Leslie?" He looked in vain for an initial. "The
deuce! Did you lose the pins already?"

"We put them on the horsies, Collie."

"So they don't get mixed in the wagon!"

He sighed. "Bright lads. Now, why don't you be even more clever and drag your mother under the mistletoe?"

They giggled, Prudence bristled, and Graceanne said, "Come, boys, it's time we went home."

Then the butler was at the door, handing out the wraps. "Blast, Milsom, this is not the time to be so dashed efficient!"

"Yes, Your Grace. Your mittens, Master Wellesley."

Leland waited, but no one corrected the butler. "Lucky guess. Fifty-fifty odds, anyway." Milsom sniffed.

Graceanne almost purred with pleasure on the sleigh ride home. "I think this was the nicest Christmas I've ever known, surely the best the boys have had. The pageant, their first snow, Christmas trees and sleigh rides, rocking horses and a puppy."

"And a pen wipe."

She laughed. "It's the stuff dreams are made of, a memory they'll cherish all their lives. I know I will. Thank you for making it so very magical."

Her warm regard almost made up for that missed kiss under the mistletoe, Leland told himself. Almost. That and how she'd said this was her favorite Christmas, not one from her childhood, not one with Tony. It had been one of his finest Christmases, too. His youth wasn't spent in a strict religious household like hers, but his parents were cool and distant, his tutors and servants merely polite. He never remembered such joy as a child, and never the pleasure of creating such happiness for others. Recently there'd been only stuffy house parties, inane flirtations, the repetitive rounds of London celebrations.

But today, with his family near him, or the closest he had to one, his house brimming with children's laughter, yes, today was magical. Almost enough to make him wish that—no, it could never be. For now he'd be content with a nearly perfect day. After all, only one boy puked on the ride home. On Prudence.

Chapter Thirteen

The glow of Christmas continued. On Boxing Day, when all the tenants and servitors came to toast their lord's health and receive his blessing, and his largess, in return, Leland wanted his cousins at Ware. It was important for the boys to meet those dependent on the Warringtons, the duke felt. Graceanne felt this was foolish, when the boys weren't remotely likely to inherit, but, as the duke pointed out, this was part of their heritage, too, prospective noblemen or not. Every man from titled gentleman to yeoman farmer should know the source of his income, respect it, and care for it. That's what this day was about.

Respecting the source of *her* income, Graceanne accepted, although she was nervous about the reception she was likely to get from the duke's tenants—and their wives. So she dressed with extra care and took her place near the duke and his aunt in the Great Hall, shivering despite the warmth from the two huge fireplaces. Milsom handed her a glass of sherry.

Once the visits began, she realized she had nothing

to fear. She'd known most of these people all her life. They weren't suddenly going to think ill of her for appearing at the duke's side; most thought it about time she and the boys took their rightful place. She didn't receive one slighting remark from the women, not one suggestive leer from the men, except from His Grace, after he'd raised his glass one time too many. After the tenth or twelfth farmer's toast, Graceanne and Milsom made sure Leland's cup was filled with the children's punch, not the potent lamb's wool.

The boys had a wonderful time, helping hand out presents, playing in the snow with the tenant children, being introduced and admired by everyone. The old-timers told Graceanne the twins were the spitting image of His Grace as a lad, and a rare hellion he was, too. They told Ware that it was good to see children in the old fortress, good to see a new generation of Warringtons running up and down the ancient halls. Continuance, that's what one old gaffer called it, so they toasted continuance, and Ware was well satisfied. The water closet wasn't working properly and Willy's ball was missing, he'd have the devil's own headache on the morrow, but his line had continuance. And the physician reported that Aunt Eudora would make a full recovery.

The week after Boxing Day, Leland called at the vicarage often, going sledding with the twins once before the snow melted, making sure the rocking horses were delivered, consulting about Duke the dog's training. He brought a collar and leash his stableman had crafted, fruit from Ware's succession houses, a box of toys from his own nursery days. When Graceanne protested that he should save such treasures for his own son, he replied that since that son was not even a twinkle in anyone's eye, the twins may as well enjoy the stuff rather than let it molder in an empty nursery. Besides, she could send the box back when he got around to having a son; Willy and Les would have long outgrown such childish pursuits as tin soldiers. Judging from how His Grace spent hours on the floor with the twins configuring miniature battles, Graceanne doubted a boy ever outgrew the pastime.

He was everything thoughtful, and she was careful not to be alone with him.

She refused the invitation for another party at Squire's house on New Year's Eve because of her mourning period, and couldn't help feeling that Leland decided to visit friends in Oxford for the holiday on that count. Prudence reported he'd already accepted, then canceled, throwing Mrs. Maxton into a swivet. Pru was in the sulks again because she wasn't to go either, the vicar's excuse being that she was still too young, her mother was too weak to chaperon her, and there might be bad influences among the unknown guests. Pru hardly came out of her room the entire week, claiming an indisposition, which was almost as much a relief to Graceanne as Leland's departure. Pru's petulance was aggravating; Leland's kindness and consideration were all too tempting. Speak of bad influences!

Graceanne always hated New Year's Eve. She disliked that false, spirits-generated joy of noisy fetes at the embassy in Portugal, and she used to dread the prayerful, contemplative New Year's Eves the vicar celebrated. She'd always felt stranded in the parsonage with nothing but her life speeding by, reminding her of what she was missing. New Year's Eve made her feel alone. This year was looking rosier. She no longer had to worry about her sons' futures; now she could dream for them, with hope.

Les could be a soldier like his father. The cavalry, of course. He'd be brave and dashing, ready for anything. She'd start praying now for an end to war. And Willy might take up the law. He had more patience than Les for books and quiet pursuits. The clergy likely wasn't an option: This household was enough to make anyone a nonbeliever. Perhaps both boys would go into trade, sail off to new lands to find fortunes. No, she couldn't bear that. Leland would say she was tying her apron strings too tightly, but she was having enough problems facing pony lessons in the spring; she couldn't contemplate her sons' leaving. That was the problem with New Year's Eve, and being alone.

Then it was Twelfth Night, when three castaway kings from the village made the rounds, handing pennies to the children. And the decorations had to come down lest they bring bad luck in addition to the vicar's wrath. So Christmas was over, the magic and the melancholy.

The duke was leaving. Of course. He had his glittering London life to lead, parties, not piquet with his aunt. He had the theater, not the blacksmith, the butcher, and the innkeeper's brother done up as Wise Men. Lobster patties instead of flavored snow; highbred horses instead of highly polished ones; bucks and bloods and blades for friends, not babies. And ladies of his own class.

Graceanne told herself it was good that he was leaving. The boys were getting too used to him and his extravagant lifestyle. He spoiled them. With their own competence they could enjoy a comfortable life, but they were not nabobs' children. And it was better he left now, before they were too dependent on him.

Graceanne knew she was in as much danger of relying too heavily on Leland for companionship, for intelligent conversation, and shared joy in the children. She had an allowance. For the first time in her life she could be independent, make choices about her life and her sons' lives—after he left. It was too easy to let him decide the boys were old enough for ponies, not old enough for a tutor, that skating was too dangerous, but rolling down hills *sans* sleds wasn't. Those should have been her choices, but he'd smiled and teased and made her loosen the leading strings.

She would miss him, too much already. She feared that the longer he stayed, the more she'd miss him when he left. And he would leave. 'Twas better he went now, before he took part of her heart with him.

"What? The widow sent you haring back to London in the dead of winter with a flea in your ear about claiming one of her children? Told you it was a bacon-brained idea."

"No, Crow, you told me it was an excellent idea, that she'd be more than happy to part with one of the nuisances." The two men were in White's, which was less than a quarter filled. Crosby Fanshaw was in his peacock plumage, Leland was in much more somber garb. His mood matched. She hadn't quite sent him off with a flea in his ear, not at all. It was more like a tickle, a tingle, a whispered siren's call. He'd had to leave Warwick if he was to stay a gentleman. But he wasn't happy about it.

Fanshaw polished his quizzing glass. "Well, can't

figure women at the best of times. There was m'sister, trying to foist her brats off on the mater constantly. So I suggested she send the worst of 'em, the middle boy, off to join the navy. Midshipman, don't you know. They take 'em small. Make a man out of the little savage. Caught the brat using my four best neckcloths to tie his sister to a chair. He said they were playing Joan of Arc. My four best, I say! Anyway, m'sister starts shrieking, babies start wailing, m'brother reads me a lecture about family feeling, and I start packing." He shrugged his padded shoulders. "Bachelor quarters is better'n that, even if town is thin of company. Tailors ain't so busy, besides." He raised a glass. "Glad to see you back, though."

The duke stared into his glass of cognac, swirling the amber liquid around. Ware House wasn't exactly bachelor quarters, but it was certainly quiet and empty and dreary after the Hold. No decorations, no neighbors calling, no children's laughter, no—

No, it was just after-holiday megrims, he told himself, that had him blue-deviled. He'd get over it as soon as he found a new diversion.

"So what was she like, Tony's widow? A drab? A dasher?" Crosby wanted to know.

Leland studied his drink some more. "No, not a drab, once she had some decent clothes. Not a stunner, either—that was the sister. A regular Diamond, that one."

Crow perked up. "Aha, a bit of dalliance there?"

"What, my wards' aunt? Besides, the chit is seventeen, a mere babe."

"You're the one who said it was experience that counted, not years."

"Yes, but this one is a gorgeous bit of fluff and

knows it all too well. That's about all she knows. Graceanne, ah, Mrs. Warrington, has it all over her for intelligence."

"So the widow wasn't an antidote after all?" Crosby refused to believe his friend had spent nearly a month in the countryside without getting up a flirtation with some fancy piece or other.

Leland smiled, but at his memories, not at his friend. When he saw Graceanne Christmas morning, with that veil over her blond hair, singing in the choir, then on Boxing Day, when she held the children to wave to the departing tenants, he'd thought her more beautiful than any Madonna ever painted. Even sledding, her hair coming undone, her nose red, and her cheeks rosy, she'd been so enchanting that he would have tumbled her right there in the snow if it weren't for the children, and a still-healthy respect for her self-defense methods. No London Incomparable had that vibrancy, the brilliant warmth he saw in Grace that made her so very exquisite. Despite their beauty, the town belles were as sterile as a framed portrait in comparison.

"No, Mrs. Warrington was not an antidote," he finally answered. "Very attractive woman, actually. You said yourself Tony had good taste. The usual nice blond hair, pretty blue eyes." Like summer sunshine was nice, like azure tropical seas were pretty.

Crow nodded, careful not to disturb his neckcloth. "New arrangement, don't you know? Devised it m'self. Call it the Fanshaw Fall."

Leland studied the intricate arrangement, happy enough to change the subject. Two or three pieces of linen had to be used to give that thickness, that height, that stranglehold. "Looks deuced uncomfort-

able to me. You'd do better to name it the Crow
Killer."

"Your taste in women was always better than your
taste in clothes," the baronet retorted, not a bit concerned over his friend's less than enthusiastic response to his sartorial ingenuity. He was also not a bit
deterred from pursuing details of Ware's latest *affaire*.
"So the pretty widow was warm and willing, eh?"

Now Leland laughed, but without a great deal of
humor. "Not at all. She is a vicar's daughter to the
core. You know, good works, good thoughts. I do
believe she is that rarest of *aves*, an honest woman."

"Good grief, that's the worst kind." Crow shuddered delicately. "Good thing you fled, old man—
you might have found yourself leg-shackled."

"Don't be absurd. You should see the family she
comes from. The father's a moralizing old jackstraw
who'd rob his parishioners blind if he thought I'd let
him get away with it. The mother's a cripple, in spirit
more than body, I think. And that sister is bound to
land them all in the scandal broth. I don't know what
Tony was thinking of, to ally himself with such a
sorry bunch. At least the children turned out all
right."

"So your heir passed muster, did he?"

"My heir is the best—no, one of the two best children there could be. You should just see them, so
bright and sweet and trusting. Learning their letters
already, they are."

Crow wrinkled his nose. "Now you're sounding
like m'sister-in-law cooing over her latest rug rat. At
any rate, you've got your heir and can stop worrying
about sticking your spoon in the wall and the Crown
getting all of Ware."

The duke's fingers drummed on the table next to him. "But I don't have the rearing of him—them—dash it. She'll spoil them, smother them. That vicar will try to bleed the spirit out of them. I can take a hand if things get bad enough, but they aren't mine. I have to step back and let Graceanne do her job." As much as it rankled him, she was the boys' mother. "And your mention of sticking my spoon in the wall reminds me I have a job I'd like to ask of you."

"Not a very useful sort of chap, you know, but anything I can do."

"I'd like you to stand guardian to my wards if anything should happen to me."

"Me? Children?" The quizzing glass dropped to the end of its ribbon. "Haven't you been listening, Lee? I'll send 'em off to the navy! How old are the brats, anyway? They must be old enough for school!"

"They're practically babies, you clunch, and I'm not asking you to be nursemaid. Graceanne is a good mother, just a trifle overprotective. But if something happens to me, Willy will be rich beyond Vicar Beckwith's wildest expectations. You'd have to protect the boys and their mother from him."

"Unless she's remarried by then."

Graceanne remarried? Leland hadn't thought of that at all. And he didn't like the notion above half. What, some other man raising Ware's heirs, most likely living in Ware Hold, holding his widow? No, Tony's widow, confound it! "Damn and blast! She cannot remarry!"

"Can't stop her, in the blood it is. Widows remarry. Especially ones with looks and full purses, which she already has. You cock your toes up, some lucky chap gets himself a real plum, calling a duke his son."

"Deuce take it, there'd be fortune-hunters and basket-scramblers sniffing 'round her skirts before I was in the ground."

Crow nodded. "If not sooner, on expectations."

The two friends were silent for a moment, contemplating. At last Leland pounded the leather armrest of his chair. "Blister it, none of that would happen if I had a wife and babes of my own!"

Crow shook his head sadly. "And here I thought seeing the infants would cure you of that rumgumption. Looks like the opposite. Lady Sefton's holding a rout next month. May as well start looking there."

He may as well. He couldn't worry about some other man raising Tony's children, and he couldn't live the rest of his own life in Graceanne's pocket, either. Besides, now that he was in London he had other interests to take care of, not just heirs and the Hold. There were other investments, other properties that needed tending. There were definitely more willing women.

Before Lady Sefton held her rout, and the newest crop of debutantes made their curtsies, Leland received a note from the Foreign Office. There was some trouble with the Prussian allies—power, money, the usual things—that called for his skills at diplomacy and his sober head at the stalled peace talks in Vienna. No Duke of Ware had ever refused the Crown. He'd have to go.

Before he left, Leland wrote to Graceanne in Warwick, assuring her that her finances were secure, as they'd discussed. His man of business, Eric Olmstead, would keep an eye on her accounts, and Milsom, who was now at Ware House, Grosvenor

Square, London, could always get a message to him through the Foreign Office in case of emergency.

A ha'penny's worth of good that was going to do her, Graceanne thought as she read his letter. By the time Ware got any of her correspondence, Pru would be long gone.

Chapter Fourteen

Days were easier than nights. Dreary January gave way to a brighter February, and Graceanne settled into her new, more comfortable life. Even the vicar reluctantly agreed their situation was improved. There were enough candles for him to read as late as he wanted, enough food that his stomach didn't rumble embarrassingly during his sermons, and enough servants and nurserymaids that his pesky grandsons were not underfoot as much. Through his new correspondence with Professor Jordan, he was able to purchase some modern, modest texts, but still worthy additions to his collection.

Mrs. Beckwith recovered some of her health and some of her animation under the new regimen. She even began to make social calls now that she was not ashamed to reciprocate, and parish visits, since bringing bread to the needy did not mean taking it off her own table. Graceanne or one of the servants—they now had a cook, a man-of-all-work, and three girls who came from the village every day to clean and serve and help Meg in the nursery—would drive her in the pony cart.

At first Prudence was also reaping the benefits of Graceanne's windfall. Not that she ever did much, but even fewer chores fell on Pru's shoulders now. Therefore she could spend most of her days with her bosom bow, Lucy, at the manor, to everyone's relief, from Graceanne to the children to the servants, who were all targets of Pru's derisive and demanding nature. Prudence was helping Lucy plan her trousseau, she claimed, and Graceanne hoped it was so, and not helping Liam Hallorahan supervise Squire's new racing stable. Pru was filling out under the new cook's plain but decent cooking, growing more womanly by the day, and Graceanne worried the young Irishman might find her sister even more appealing.

Somehow Graceanne's days were as filled as ever, even if she didn't have to do all the baking and shopping and parish work. She still taught Sunday school and still helped her father make clean copies of his sermons, mostly to keep the peace with him. She still saw to the running of the household to conserve her mother's strength, and she still kept the household accounts. In addition she spent hours over her own bank statements, making budgets, figuring interest, trying to plan for emergencies so she would not have to call on the duke. That extra money each month meant her security, so she stayed careful with her pence and pounds and did not turn into a spendthrift overnight.

Whatever excess of time Graceanne might have found was devoted to the boys. She took them on long tramps on nice days, to exercise the dog and the children. The sheepdog seemed to know his job by instinct, having adopted the twins as his own small flock. Duke always kept Willy and Les in sight, and tried his best to keep them together and out of danger. Unfortunately, he perceived the sexton as a sheep-stealer and the village dogs as wolves, but Graceanne was working on that. She was also working on teaching the boys their letters and numbers, after swearing to Leland that they were too young for formal schooling. The only fault he'd be able to find with their education was the lack of schoolbooks: Indoors they read from picture books, outdoors from tombstones in the church graveyard next door.

Her days were busy, but Graceanne no longer fell exhausted into her bed right after dinner. Now she had time to sit with her reading, mending, or letters, and think of all the time she had yet to fill. Endless hours, countless nights.

Then Liam Hallorahan came to ask Vicar Beckwith for Prudence's hand.

The vicar said no, to no one's surprise, not even Liam's, Graceanne suspected. She was only surprised Mr. Hallorahan managed to leave with all his skin.

After that there wasn't a restful night's sleep to be had, what with Prudence alternating between shrieking and sobbing and slamming doors. The first night the twins woke up crying; the second night Mr. Beckwith moved a cot into the church; the third night a trembling Mrs. Beckwith pleaded with Graceanne to talk to her sister.

"You're what?" Graceanne sank down on the one chair in Pru's room. Prudence was stretched out on the mattress, a blanket over her head. Maybe she heard wrong. "You're not really . . . ?"

The blanket nodded, yes.

"Dear Lord, how did that happen? No, I know how it happens. That wicked Irishman had his way with you, didn't he? Why, that dastard should be shot. If I were a man, I'd call him out, I would."

There was a mumble from under the bedcovers.

"What do you mean, it wasn't his fault? There was somebody else, too?"

Now Prudence sat up, indignation writ on her tear-puffed face. "Of course not, you gudgeon. I meant it wasn't Liam's fault. It wasn't even his idea. I thought Papa would let us marry if I wasn't a . . . you know."

"But now you're breeding!"

"Well, I didn't *know* that would happen, did I? No one told me!"

No one thought she needed to know. Graceanne wanted to tear someone's hair out—her own or Pru's, she couldn't decide. "You should have found out, for heaven's sake! And you should have known better in the first place. What were you thinking?" she wailed, well aware the nodcocks hadn't been thinking at all.

"I was thinking that I had to get out of here, that's what. That if I stayed another year I'd grow old and ugly without ever going to parties and having fun. That I'd never meet any young men and I'd be on the shelf and living with my parents forever. Or end up marrying a farmer and having his grubby brats."

"Now you'll have Liam's grubby—er, children." Graceanne couldn't quite see how a horse breeder was much above a wheat-and-barley farmer or a hog grower, but she didn't have a chance to clarify that.

"Well, I never wanted a baby. I just wanted to go places. Liam goes to Tattersall's twice a year to the auctions. That's in London, you know. And he goes to horse fairs all the time. He said I could go along."

Graceanne doubted any of those venues were proper places for a lady, and certainly not one with an infant. "When is the baby due?"

Pru rolled over, tired of the conversation. "Oh, I don't know."

"What do you mean, you don't know? Haven't you been counting? Pru, you have to know, to make plans!"

"Stop shouting at me! Everyone's always shouting at me! And I made my plans: I am going to marry Liam and get out of here. I didn't want any baby, I told you. And no one ever told me I had to count. What, did you think Mama was going to tell me about breeding?"

No, Graceanne couldn't picture their anxious mother explaining the marriage bed to her seventeen-year-old daughter. Mrs. Beckwith never told Graceanne a thing, not even on her wedding day. Tony only laughed and said he'd show her.

"I thought I could get rid of it somehow if I didn't want it."

Some of the army wives had hinted about such things, but Graceanne certainly didn't know of any.

"But Liam said that would be a sin."

And lying with an innocent girl wasn't? No matter, what was done was done, and if it couldn't be undone, or redone differently, had to be fixed. "Papa said no?"

"He said he'd see me burn in Hell before he let me wed a Papist. I think they are one and the same to him. And no one else will marry us, since I am underage."

"But did he know about the baby? Surely that must make a difference, even to Papa."

"Liam was supposed to tell him when he asked

permission for us to marry." She sat up in the bed. "*You* can go talk to him, Gracie. He listens to you."

If the Almighty himself was whispering in Beckwith's ear, the vicar wouldn't have listened. No daughter of his was going to marry out of the only true church, and that was that.

"But what do you expect Prudence to do, Papa? This isn't just a flirtation she'll grow out of if you forbid her to see the young man. This is a baby!"

The vicar slammed shut the Bible he'd been studying as though he could slam shut this conversation. "Then she can have it at the workhouse for all I care. Or let her go live in sin with her stableboy. She has already sinned. What difference can it make to her immortal soul?"

"But what about the child, Papa? Will you permit your own grandchild to be branded a bastard? Its life would be ruined forever, through no fault of the baby's."

"That is no grandchild of mine. Prudence is no longer my daughter." He opened the Bible again, to the front, and pointed to the family listings. *Prudence Lynne Beckwith* was drawn through with a heavy black line. Several. If Graceanne hadn't known the name, she couldn't have made it out.

She shook her head. "You foolish old man. Did you think crossing her out of the family Bible was going to make the problem go away? Your daughter, your daughter Prudence, sir, is upstairs in her bedroom here, growing bigger with child even as you contemplate her life in the hereafter. What are you going to do about that, sir?"

"I'm going to write next Sunday's sermon, girl,

that's what. About serpents' tongues and disrespectful children and silver-tongued devils. You think something should be done about your sister's condition, you do it. Get that . . . that Jezebel out of my house. You're the one with the money and the influential friends, so go make your wicked arrangements. I blame you for the whole evil mess anyway." He opened the Bible and began to read, his lips moving.

Graceanne wasn't being shut out. "I? I am to blame, Papa? How can you say such a thing? I never encouraged her to meet with Liam. I never left them alone. I think she's been planning this since before I came home from the Peninsula."

Without looking up, without hearing her logic, the vicar growled: "Yes, you. You challenged my authority, you and your twice-damned duke. You're the one who put ideas in her head, ideas above her station, made her want what she couldn't have."

"That's unfair, Papa. Just seeing what Lucy Maxton had was enough to make Pru jealous when she had so little. Why, if you'd just let her laugh and dance like the other girls, she may have paid more attention to your lectures. You lavished everything on your precious books." She waved her arms toward the glass-fronted cases. "And ignored the needs of your own family. You didn't even give her your affection, Papa, how could you expect her not to look elsewhere?"

"Bah. To an Irishman? He cannot even vote."

"Neither can women, but what's that to the point?"

"The point is you encouraged her to think she could make decisions for herself, contrary to mine, counter to the natural order of things. Now she has to pay the price. Or you do, since you think money is more important than religion. Get out of my sight, girl, you are keeping me from God's work."

If there was one thing Graceanne was sure of, it was that not even God could want Pru's baby to be born out of wedlock. Mary and Joseph were married, weren't they? If He wasn't going to take care of the situation, and the vicar wasn't going to take care of the situation, Graceanne was damned well going to have to take matters into her own two hands.

Thinking this was very much a case of slamming the barn door after the cow ran out, Graceanne went to see Liam Hallorahan at Squire's. She didn't stop at the manor or pay her respects to Mrs. Maxton; she didn't stop to think what gossip would arise. She just drove Posy around back to the new paddocks and stable complex. She pulled up alongside the cleared racing oval and handed Posy's reins to one of the grooms who was standing around watching the training runs. Liam's red hair stood out in the knot of men observing at the rails, and Graceanne marched purposely toward him, giving Squire a brief nod.

"A moment of your time, Mr. Hallorahan?"

"Sure and I wouldn't deny a pretty lady, ma'am. Excuse me, Squire. Carry on, lads."

Graceanne was fractionally aware, in one tiny corner of her mind, that Squire's mouth was hanging open and some of the stablehands were sniggling and elbowing each other. "Choir business," she firmly declared. In a way it was, although Liam and Pru had been making a lot more than music.

With her arm resting lightly on his, Liam drew her away from the others. When they were in full sight, but out of hearing, he grabbed her hand and asked,

"Pru? She's all right, Mrs. Warrington? Nothing's wrong?"

The desperation in his voice reassured Graceanne. The handsome Irishman hadn't just been leading her sister down the primrose path; he seemed to care. She bit back her first answer, that no, Prudence was not all right, she was *enceinte*. He already knew that. "Yes, she is fine," she said instead. "Or as fine as can be expected while expecting. I, ah, came to ask your intentions." Good grief, Graceanne thought, that sounded like a cheap melodrama. Her lines should have been declaimed by a maiden's father or brother or someone who at least stood higher than the villain's shoulder. Not that Liam Hallorahan was a true villain. He didn't even look the part. He was tall and broad, but his sun-weathered face had laugh wrinkles and freckles, and he was running hard, callused hands through his hair in a distracted manner.

"I'm sorry," she began again. "I know you asked my father in an honorable fashion for permission to marry Prudence. I meant, how shall you accomplish that, in light of his refusal?"

"And how soon, you'll be after wanting to know, I'm sure. B'gad, and it's all I've been worrying over meself."

Graceanne noted that his brogue returned under duress. She patted his arm the way she would have comforted one of the twins, except Liam had muscles of iron under his corduroy jacket. She nodded. "And I came to offer my help. I have some money put by, if you need it to purchase a special license. I don't know how expensive they are. Do you?"

Liam smiled at her, showing dimples—he really was a most attractive man, not that hard muscles and dimples were any excuse for Pru's fall from grace—

and gently touched her cheek. " 'Tis a fine lady you are indeed, Mrs. Warrington, but things are nary so simple. Aye, a special license would do the trick, but archbishops don't hand dispensations to poor Irish Catholics. Your highborn English lords could get a license to marry their stepsisters, likely, given enow money and influence. I misdoubt they'd let me in the door unless I had that pot o' gold I've been seeking me whole life."

Graceanne suspected he might be right and cursed the duke again for being out of the country. "Then it will have to be Gretna Green."

"Aye, they're no so fussy over the Scottish border. But that spaleen vicar—pardon, your da—said he'd have me arrested for kidnapping should I take Miss Prudence away. I'd pay the old blighter no never mind, but happens there's another problem. I've promised Squire here I'd take three of his best mares back to Ireland and me father's stud this month to be bred. He's already made all the arrangements and bookings. And me da needs the income."

"And Ireland is in the opposite direction from Scotland," she finished for him.

He nodded. "And there's some't else. I never thought to take a man's daughter without his blessing. That's laying bad cess on a marriage. I'm thinking we'd better go to Ireland with the horses and get me own da's blessing."

How nice, Graceanne thought. Then the three mares and Pru could all be breeding at the same time.

Chapter Fifteen

Graceanne made all the arrangements.

First she had to meet with Liam again, since Prudence wouldn't come out of her room. He didn't come to choir practice or church, not with the vicar around, so she met him outside the lending library in the village and set tongues to wagging again. That was as good a camouflage as any, Graceanne thought, for keeping Prudence's secret.

Liam was so relieved to have any kind of solution offered to him and was so appreciative of her help that he kissed her hand. Then he kissed both her cheeks.

"Mr. Hallorahan!" she exclaimed, blushing furiously under the Misses Macgruders' gasped shock.

" 'Tis a brother's affection I'm showing, lass," he whispered in her ear, "merely a brother's." But he was flashing those dimples. The town was getting a diversionary smoke screen indeed, and Prudence was getting more than she deserved.

But not in Pru's estimation. "But I always wanted a pretty wedding like yours. And if I can't tell Lucy, what good is it? Some skimble-skamble wedding over the anvil is not at all what I had in mind, Gracie. Besides, by the time I get to Gretna Green, I'll be so fat even their filthy blacksmiths will laugh."

As patiently as she explained to the children that while birds could fly, little boys must not jump off the barn roof, she told Pru there was no choice. Somewhat less patiently did she listen to her sister's new complaints.

"I don't see why I cannot just drive off with Liam when he takes the mares next week. At least that would be romantic."

"What? And advertise your disgrace in front of the whole village? Perhaps I should have the Sunday-school children strew orange blossoms in your path."

Pru screwed her face into a pout. "It's not as if we aren't going to be married as soon as we find someone who'll do the thing. Besides, I don't care if I never see this place again. Good riddance, I say. So why should I care what these cabbageheads think, anyway?"

"So Mama can hold her head up in Warefield, that's why." And so the Duke of Ware doesn't learn that his wards' aunt is no better than she ought to be, Graceanne hoped, but she didn't say to Pru. She just plotted her intrigues a little deeper.

She made sure that they both went to bid Liam a polite farewell at Squire's, and she made sure Pru went to church—with her cloak kept on against both the chill and prying eyes. Let everyone see the chit wasn't grieving; let no one see she was swelling like a dead cow on a hot day. Then Graceanne drove Prudence to visit Lucy briefly, to announce her carefully rehearsed good fortune: a friend of Gracie's, another army officer's widow, was going traveling, possibly to Austria for the peace talks, and she wanted a companion. What luck!

One week after Liam left, Graceanne drove Pru out of town in a hired carriage to meet her friend in Worcester, she told Mr. Blanchard at the local hostelry as he helped load all the bags and boxes. Pru had insisted that it would look odd if she didn't have new, fashionable clothes for her journeying. Her old clothes didn't fit, anyway. Graceanne's purse did.

Liam was supposed to be waiting in Worcester, resting the mares. The hired driver and post boy mustn't know this, of course, so Graceanne dismissed them to return to Warefield without her, saying she was going to visit with her friend a day or two before returning home. Graceanne and Pru took a room at a respectable inn, at Graceanne's expense, to await the friend's arrival. Pru wanted only to see the shops; Graceanne wanted only to see her gone before someone recognized them.

Liam finally appeared, with a cumbersome traveling coach he'd managed to hire. It wasn't as fancy as the one Graceanne had chosen for the ride, nor as well sprung. According to Pru, it was also odorous, drafty, and the squabs were bound to hurt her back. Furthermore, Liam was going to drive it himself to save expenses and to keep an eye on the mares tied behind.

"We're going to take forever just getting to Cardigan, I know it. And I'll have no one to talk to the whole time, Gracie."

"Of course you will. You can ride outside with Liam."

"What? In the cold and the wind? Besides, you were the one who worried what people would think."

"Yes, but they are now supposed to think that you

are already man and wife, so there is nothing odd in your traveling together."

"But I don't have a ring," Pru slyly noted. "Innkeepers' wives are sure to notice such things."

So they had to go buy her a ring, at Graceanne's expense. Liam needed his money for their traveling costs.

Pru was still not resigned to that old coach. "I don't understand why you can't accompany me, Gracie, at least till the Welsh border."

"This is my first night ever away from the boys, Pru, and I am as anxious as a broody hen. I couldn't bear to be away a moment longer than I have to."

"For pity's sake, Gracie, the brats don't need you. You left four nursemaids to watch them."

Graceanne smiled. "Wait until you are a mother, Pru. Then tell me how you feel about leaving your baby behind."

"I won't feel like that, I know. If you think I am dragging a puling brat around with me when we go to London, you are even more harebrained than I thought." She tugged her new fur-lined mantle closer about her. "Truly, Gracie, the slow pace is sure to make me queasy with nothing to do and no one to talk to. Couldn't you at least hire me a maid?"

"You can sleep or read those books you insisted I purchase for you or start sewing baby clothes. You've never had a maid a day in your life, Prudence Beckwith, and you're not going to start now on my sons' income. If I thought my budget could spare it, I'd hire a girl for myself so I don't have to spend tonight alone at an inn. At least you'll have Liam."

"Smelling of horses," Pru muttered angrily, but she gave up and got into the coach without so much as thanking Graceanne for her efforts. It was Liam who hugged Graceanne good-bye and swore to take care of her precious sister. Graceanne walked back to the inn, shaking her head. That poor man.

Despite her widow's blacks, the veil, and air of distraction, Graceanne still got looks from the men in the taproom that left her uncomfortably wishing she had a maid after all. She ordered her meals brought up to her room and resigned herself to staying there until the next morning.

There was no noise. That's what she noticed first. No listening for cries or calls of "Mama," no smashes, crashes, or thuds. There might be a murmur from the common room, an occasional clink barely heard through the walls and doors, but no one was going to come looking for her. How was she expected to rest?

Graceanne decided to spend her solitary evening writing to Ware in case someone informed him of her doings. She supposed the steward at Ware Hold was in contact with his man of business in London, and she suspected that all of her bank transactions were reported back to His Grace as a matter of course. He'd wonder about her withdrawing all of her reserve and most of her March allowance. She'd left herself just enough for household expenses, unless she put some of Prudence's dressmakers' bills off till next month. Graceanne took the pins out of her hair and shook it loose, feeling some relief from the headache she was developing at thoughts of her budget. And here she'd felt rich for all of a month.

She wrote to Ware that there had been some unforeseen expenses in the family, nothing he should worry about. The boys were fine, learning their alphabets. They already knew *L* and *W*, and recognized *R*, *I*, and *P*. She wished him well and closed with another reassurance that she was not living above her means.

The next morning she rode home on a carter's wagon to save the cost of hiring a carriage. She was half frozen, but there were her twins shouting a welcome, the dog barking, and only one of the nursemaids crying. She was home.

The innkeeper at the Crown and Feather where Graceanne stayed got busy the next morning. Three carriages of sporting gentlemen pulled up, demanding accommodations for the mill to be held the next day outside of town. So he didn't put the widow's letter in the post that day. He put it in his pocket instead, where it stayed until his breeches were due to be cleaned. Which was after enough ale had been spilled on them that the local sot could get castaway on the fumes as mine host walked past. That's when Graceanne's letter got mailed.

The note went from Worcester to Ware's London house, where his secretary debated about the fate of such a scruffy letter. Should he consign it to the dustbin? Open it? Forward it, since the handwriting, as far as he could make out on the blurred address, was feminine? His Grace had no business dealings in Worcester, to his secretary's knowledge. For three days the letter sat on the man's desk with dubious charitable requests and questionable investment offerings. Then arrived a letter from His Grace's aunt, some correspondence from a university professor, and a ballot for a policy vote from one of the duke's clubs. The secretary gathered these and the waif from Worcester into a pouch to be sent to the Foreign Office for delivery via diplomatic couriers and embassy mailbags.

All in all, it was mid-April when Leland received Graceanne's note. By then he'd already had a message from his man of business that Mrs. Warrington had gone through her entire account for January, February, and March. He'd written back to increase the funds. She wasn't a henwit who would turn into a wastrel in two months. And he could afford the additional expense. Why, he'd won and lost more than her monthly income on one roll of the dice the previous night. He'd bought his current mistress, a highborn lady of the Austrian court, a diamond bracelet whose price would have fed and clothed the twins for a year. What he was spending on bribes to collect and dispense political information—his government's request, his pocketbook—didn't bear thinking about. And he was hating every minute of the whole thing.

The talks were going nowhere but from bedroom to ballroom. Any important decisions would be made quietly, privately, away from this circus. Vienna was London times two, wealthier and wickeder. In a word, decadent.

In the back of Leland's mind was the niggling worry that his life, this glittering world of power and money, was nothing but dross. And soon enough he'd have to select a wife from the haut monde, to perpetuate the race of hollow, empty people like himself.

He could have his pick of any of the women attending the Congress, but none appealed to him except for an evening or two of pleasure. He wanted an English wife, not one of the exotic foreign beauties who were weaned on intrigue. He didn't want anyone else's English wife, either, although bored British brides were waiting outside his apartments every night. There were more than a few beautiful widows on the prowl for a proposal or a protector. When Leland asked about their children, the Diamonds laughed and waved manicured fingers. Nannies, tutors, schools—la, who cared? A handful of debutantes fished the matrimonial waters of the peace talks. Sharks they were, smelling out titles and fortunes like blood on the water. The Duke of Ware was no one's supper.

Jupiter, he was getting too old for this life! Moreover, it was getting on toward spring, and he'd promised Willy and Les ponies and riding lessons. Let the diplomatic society swap lies with every handshake or kiss, Leland vowed to keep his word to two little boys. You couldn't trust a groom to do the thing properly, he was convinced, forgetting that it was John Groom who'd set him on his first pony and dusted off his breeches till he got the hang of the thing. No, servants didn't care enough. Then again, should he find one pony, because it would be easier to watch one child at a time, or two ponies so they could all ride together? He wondered if Graceanne rode. And did the ponies have to match?

The hell with the peace talks. With rumors of Napoleon's return flying around, any decisions would be moot anyway. Let the puffguts waste their efforts on these endless debates. They could dashed well do it without the Duke of Ware. Leland was determined to get home before someone else, some sap-skulled suitor of Tony's widow, made cow-handed riders out of the boys.

There were obligations, however, that not even the Duke of Ware could shunt aside, not without creating an international incident. While his departure was delayed, Leland notified his secretary, his steward, and his man of affairs to open his houses, send his yacht, and watch the horse sales for a pair of well-trained, even-tempered ponies.

He also wrote to tell Graceanne that he was coming home, that he was keeping his promise about the ponies. His letter was carried that same day to the British embassy, taken by special courier to London, and hand-delivered to the parsonage in Warefield. Where the vicar tore it up. Leland was too late; Graceanne was already gone.

Not quite by chance Graceanne picked up the post in the village one day. She'd been eagerly awaiting some word from her sister, word that her father would have read or ripped up, she knew, no matter who was the addressee.

Pru's letter did not relieve her trepidations. Prudence hated the trip. The carriage made her as ill as she knew it would, and the packet sail was positively hellish. She might never recover. Liam was hateful. He cared more for his precious horses than for her, which was no wonder, she was so ugly and bloated. And they hadn't found anyone to marry them, so they were staying at his father's horse farm, which was dirty and isolated. Liam was going to London on horse business, the letter went on, lines crossed and recrossed, and refused to take her. He lied to her about getting married, about his family's prosperity, and about the fun they'd have. Now he was leaving her alone with people who barely spoke English.

Prudence begged Graceanne to come rescue her. Or to send money so she could hire a maid. There went most of April's money.

Chapter Sixteen

Liam arrived almost in time with the May deposit. He was at his wit's end and had left his business at Tattersall's to come beg Graceanne for help. Pru was sickly. She wouldn't eat or leave her bed.

"And she says she hates the wee bairn."

"Never!" Graceanne couldn't begin to imagine such a thing. She remembered how she felt carrying the twins—a beached whale being the closest picture called to mind—but still exhilarated, gloriously enraptured of the new life she bore.

"Aye, she hates the babe," Liam repeated. "And Old Mara the midwife is that worried, she is." Liam shook his head, the red of his hair catching gold sparks from the sunshine. They were sitting outside the schoolhouse, in full view of the whole village. It wasn't Graceanne's choice, but there was no alternative.

There were other problems, too, Liam went on. No one would marry them. The Anglican curate wouldn't perform the ceremony because Prudence was underage; the Catholic priest asked Pru to adopt their ways and swear the babe would be raised a Catholic. She refused. Graceanne could hear the bitterness in Liam's voice when he told her this last; he'd been willing to renounce *his* church. They could have held an old Irish handfast ceremony, but Pru declared it wouldn't be recognized in England, and worse, Liam's father was saying that if they weren't married in a Catholic church, they weren't married in the eyes of God. So Prudence was a soiled dove in their town. None of the women but Old Mara called, not even to offer sorely needed advice. And Pru and Gilly Hallorahan, Liam's father, were constantly at daggers drawn.

"So you can see I have nary a choice but to leave me wee dearie there. She's too poorly to travel, and I made better time, just me and the horses I brought to auction, sleeping out in barns and such." He rubbed at a stain on his leather breeches. "I had to come away now, b'gosh. We need the money the sale will bring, and to keep abuilding on the reputation of the Hallorahan stud, don't you see."

Graceanne saw that they'd all be better off if the Hallorahans had stuck to breeding horses. She also saw that she had no choice but to give Liam what money she could, along with the address of His Grace's man of business in London, Mr. Olmstead. "He'll know how to go about getting a special license so an English priest will marry you. I'll write out a blank bank draft and request him to release whatever funds are necessary, as an advance on my income. We'll worry about making that child your lawful issue first, then worry about the eyes of God and your father later."

Liam stared at his work-roughened hands. "I don't know if Pru will wed with me anymore."

"That is *not* an option, either. The child's life shall not be ruined because Pru is in one of her takings, not if I have anything to say about it."

As she'd known all along, Graceanne was also out of options. She had no choice but to go to her sister, bringing aid, comfort, what assistance she could—and see the ninny-hammer married.

The vicar was no help, not that Graceanne had expected anything else. "If you leave my house," he fumed, "you leave forever. Don't come back. Both my daughters are as good as dead to me."

Graceanne turned to her mother, who was weeping into the handkerchief she clutched in trembling hands. "Mama," she said, "we are your daughters, too." Graceanne knew how she'd feel if anyone tried to keep her from her sons. "Mama?" Mrs. Beckwith cried harder. Graceanne went to start the packing.

Burning Beckwith bridges was one thing, defying the duke was another. He didn't want her to remove the twins from his domain. He'd be displeased if she took the boys away where he couldn't see them, he'd said.

Then he shouldn't have gone off to Austria having a high old time, Graceanne said to herself, tossing undergarments into a trunk. How much was he seeing Willy and Les from there? She read the London papers when they came her way, and couldn't help hearing as the residents of Warefield village kept track of "their" duke. She even knew the name of his Austrian mistress. A princess, no less. Graceanne wished her well. Just let the woman keep Ware happy and busy, she prayed, and out of the country.

She didn't think the duke would withhold her monthly funds on principle, not after he was reported to have bought the princess a bracelet worth a hundred widows' mites. And she refused to entertain the belief that the Duke of Ware, no matter how angry or imperious, would let his wards go hungry out of pique that his every want and wish wasn't being catered to. He was authoritative, not cruel.

There was no question of leaving the boys behind, of course. If the duke were home, with the estimable Mr. Milsom and that army of servants, an entire nursery wing, and extensive grounds, she might have considered parting with her cherubs for the duration. It was a measure of her confidence in His Grace's affection for the boys that she'd even entertain the notion of leaving the darlings behind. That and the dread of spending days or possibly weeks in a closed coach with her precious angels. Even a mother's love has its limits.

She and Liam hired the most comfortable carriage in Warefield, the most reliable driver, a footman who had young brothers of his own. Unfortunately the nursemaid Meg refused to leave the young man with whom she was keeping company; Susan was needed at home; Bertha was subject to travel sickness; and June was petrified of crossing the sea. In other words, they'd all rather go to Hell in a handcart than to Ireland in a rolling insane ward.

If no maid would travel with them, the dog would not be left behind. The moment Duke saw one box of the boys' clothing being packed, he was never out of sight. Besides, the vicar would have the collie tossed out on his silky ear the second Graceanne's carriage turned the corner. Then, too, Duke was the only loyal babysitter she had.

When they were ready, Graceanne withdrew the

rest of her account and wrote to the bank to forward her next deposits to the address Liam gave her, care of his father in Wicklow, Ireland.

They set out, then separated. Having seen Graceanne's party safely on the road, Liam was to ride as fast as possible to London to transact his own business. Then he had to see Mr. Olmstead, deliver Graceanne's letter for His Grace that explained her actions, get the special license, and meet her at the ferry dock in Cardigan Bay.

Graceanne packed puzzles and books and baskets of toys. That took care of the first morning.

The rest of the journey could not be described in polite conversation. Graceanne hoped the children liked Ireland: She'd set up housekeeping there for the next ten years rather than face another such expedition.

Once the carriage was unloaded, the driver and groom treated themselves to a two-day drunken celebration—after they'd put half a county between them and the Warrington ménage. Now it was just a matter of waiting at the inn Liam had recommended.

The rooms were clean, the food was adequate, and the staff there was friendly. Graceanne was learning to trust the boys with strangers more. She had no choice if she was to have a second to herself. Thank goodness for Duke, who always went along.

Days went by with no sign of Liam. No messenger, no mail. Graceanne was alone with two small boys, running through her money, with the staff at the inn growing less friendly by the hour. What could have happened to Liam? An accident, Graceanne supposed, but he would have sent word. Unless he was dead. No, a strong, healthy young man like Liam wouldn't just cock up his toes like that. The alternative was almost worse, that he'd taken her cash, her blank check, and the letter releasing her funds—and left for parts unknown.

Could she really be abandoned, stranded in Wales, where the people spoke an incomprehensible dialect? It certainly looked that way. *Now* Graceanne had a choice. She could take the boys home—not to the vicarage, for she had no home there—but home to England, to London. She could throw herself on the mercy of the duke's Mr. Olmstead, who would make some provision for her and the boys, she was sure, until Ware could be contacted and advised of her idiocy. Or she could continue without Liam across the channel to Ireland, where her next allotment of funds should be waiting, to save her sister from Mr. Gilly Hallorahan, who sounded as rigidly moralistic as their own father.

Ireland was closer.

"She did what?" The rafters of Ware House, Grosvenor Square, fairly shook with the roar of shattered illusions. Leland could hardly believe that Graceanne Warrington, that most virtuous of all widows, that female of hitherto Madonna-like purity, had run off with an Irish groom. Hell and damnation, she'd turned down his own amorous overtures! Such was the message from Ware Hold's steward, however, and here was her bank withdrawal of every last groat, confound it!

He could not even hare off to Warwick, not without duly presenting himself at Whitehall for interminable conferences about the course of the peace negotiations and rumors of the Corsican's return. By George, what was one more opinion about the future of European politics compared to the fate of two little boys? Ware's celebrated skills at diplomacy were sadly challenged over the next sennight, before he could order out his curricle and tear off to his country-seat.

What he found there challenged his composure even more. The steward swore he'd seen Mrs. Warrington and Liam Hallorahan together, cozylike, outside the schoolhouse.

His housekeeper, when called forth by Milsom, who had as usual accompanied his master into the country, reported that she'd seen the two of them kissing and hugging on the main street, bold as brass.

No, it was the younger sister, Prudence Beckwith, who was keeping company with Squire's Irish horseman, Leland swore.

The housekeeper swore right back that the whole village knew Miss Prudence had gone traveling with a wealthy lady companion well over a month earlier. She bought pretty new frocks right in Warefield, too. Word had it she was headed to Vienna and all the fancy parties. She'd be a great success, would Miss Prudence.

If Prudence was in Vienna, Leland thought, he was a monkey's uncle. The chit would have been hanging on his coattails from the minute her feet hit the ground. That or she'd be the latest comet of the demimonde.

Milsom was sniffing his disapproval of His Grace's gossiping with the servants, so Leland took himself off to Squire's. Hallorahan had left, all right, Maxton confirmed, and he was sorry to see the lad go. "Dab hand with the horses, don't you know." Of course, Squire was also glad his Lucy was promised to a respectable young gent, else he would have had to send the boy packing ages before. "Dab hand with the ladies, too, don't you know. Why, the pretty little sister leaves town, doesn't the chap take up with the widow. Not that Gracie's not a beauty in her way, but it's Pru who's the real dazzler."

The man's eyesight and intellect were so deficient, Leland decided, his comments could be dismissed. Not so Vicar Beckwith's.

"I neither know nor care," the man snarled when pressed for the whereabouts of Prudence and Grace-anne. "Fancy clothes, fancy men, fancy ideas in their heads. All of my teachings gone for naught, and their mother here weeping herself into an early grave while the household is going to rack and ruin. No, I do not want to speak of those wanton jades. I have no more daughters."

Leland slapped his riding crop against his booted leg. "And your grandsons?"

"Hah! Taking those fiends from Hell with her and the Irishman was the only decent thing the strumpet did. I have no more grandsons."

"Then perhaps you'll have no more position as vicar here, if you cannot show more generosity of spirit and forgiveness. I thought that was what you were supposed to preach, Beckwith, not vituperation and scandal-mongering."

The duke took himself back to Ware Hold, ordered his bags packed and his curricle brought around. He set out on the main road, but turned back toward the castle after a quarter of a mile or so, at the first intersection. Returned to the Hold's drive, he threw the reins to his tiger, stomped up the steps, and pounded on the door.

"Milsom!" he shouted when a surprised footman opened the heavy portals. "Where the devil is my yacht anchored anyway?"

Chapter Seventeen

At least there were ponies.

Hallorahan's stud farm was a green gem where Thoroughbred mares and their foals pranced between neat fence lines on a sunlit hillside. It was everything Liam had boasted about.

The Hallorahans' house was everything Pru had complained about. It was dark and dirty and hadn't seen a woman's touch since Liam's mother's death, eight years before. Unfortunately, it hadn't seen Liam since he set out for London, either.

His father, Gilly, was more concerned with the missing money from the Tattersall's sale than with his missing son. His quarterly rent to Lord Asquith was nearly due, and that English dastard would use any excuse to seize the farm now that he saw how successful Gilly and Liam had made it.

Besides, as he made plain when he grudgingly carted in Graceanne's boxes and trunks, the last thing he needed was to be saddled with another useless, hoity-toity English female. And this one had brats to be fed.

"Ye let 'em go next or nigh me horses, the plaguey little vermin, an' I'll feed 'em to the wolves. Didn't know Ireland had wolves yet, did ye? Aye, great hairy droolly beasties what chew on English bairns for breakfast. For dessert they nibble on fluffy dogs."

The boys ran shrieking behind Graceanne's skirts, dragging Duke with them. Welcome to Ireland, Mrs. Warrington.

Liam's father might have been labeled an old curmudgeon had he been old. Gilly couldn't be more than forty-five, and in fine condition from working with the horses. Graceanne saw a lot of Liam in the older man's face, but with more weathered lines, fewer smiles.

"Can you cook, girl? T'other one's about as useful as tits on a bull."

On the plus side, a check had arrived from Mr. Olmstead with a generous increase in her June allowance, to offset the costs of travel. Part of the boys' education, the man's note said, since travel was known to be a learning experience. Graceanne was certainly finding it so.

With the money she was able to soothe Gilly and, more important, hire a maid and a housekeeper so she could see less of housework and more of Prudence, who was indeed doing poorly. Pru's already low spirits were not raised by Liam's desertion, either.

"It's because I'm ugly," Pru cried, and she was. One look at her sister and Graceanne knew something was wrong. A further outlay of money brought a real doctor, who was no more encouraging than Old Mara. He had serious doubts of a happy outcome, he confided to Graceanne, or of Pru carrying the babe to term. Old Mara's herbs being as good a prescription as any he knew, his only suggestion was to keep Pru quiet and off her feet.

Gilly snorted when Graceanne told him. "An' ye needed to spend yer blunt to hear that? This female ain't done nary a lick o' work since she got here. Won't be no hardship keepin' 'er at rest."

Graceanne and the new maid helped Pru wash her hair, then they braided the long blond curls and got her into an attractive gown whose fullness concealed some of Pru's ungainliness. Pru felt so much better that she permitted them to help her to a sofa in the parlor, which had been tidied and brightened with new curtains and pillows. She even smiled and co-quetted with Lord Asquith when he came to see if Liam was back with the money. The English landlord would be put off only a bit longer, he wanted this all settled so he could summer in Scotland for the hunting and fishing. Meanwhile, he didn't mind the flattering attention of a little English strumpet.

Gilly spat tobacco juice out the window when Asquith left. "Too bad ye're breedin'. Looks like his highness'd take t'rent money out in trade."

Pru glowered at the crudity and began to cry. Scowling at both of them, Graceanne had to help her sister back to bed, then go stop her sons from practicing spitting out the window.

At least there were ponies for the boys, and lots of children for them to play with, red-haired, freckled children who rode bareback on sturdy little cobs, and stablehands galore standing around to watch out for them. For every maid missing in the house, there were two brawny lads to muck out the stalls. No wonder there was not enough money to pay the landlord. By dint of careful reasoning, then shouting, which he seemed to respect more, Graceanne made Gilly aware of his extravagant overhead.

"I never did have a head for figures," Gilly admitted, " 'cept th' female one, a' course." Graceanne accepted the first, ignored the second, and started helping with the bookkeeping in exchange for Gilly teaching the boys to ride properly, so they'd be safe. Duke stayed with them, thank goodness, for Graceanne was afraid to leave her sister for long. Prudence grew restless and weepy if left to her own devices, remembering every tale of death in childbirth she'd ever heard.

"That's nonsense, Pru," Graceanne tried to reassure the younger girl. "If I had no trouble giving birth to twins, you should do fine with just one baby. And whatever pain I had was worth it to have my precious boys."

Prudence moaned and cried some more.

Willy and Les, meanwhile, were growing tanned and strong, like farm children frolicking in the hayloft. Graceanne hardly saw them except for meals and bedtime and an hour or two in the morning, when she herded them and whatever other children were around into the parlor for lessons. She was not going to give Lord Ware the opportunity to accuse her of neglecting their education, in addition to whatever other grievances he held against her. She thought he'd be pleased to see the children so much less dependent on their mother, learning a rough-and-tumble, boyish life of horses and dogs, fishing and swimming. She hated it and missed her babies.

They did have a bedroom where she could stand up, she reminded herself, looking for silver linings. They'd never bump their heads on this roof no matter how fast they were growing. Of course, it was thatched, and she could hear mice scurrying in it sometimes, but she wouldn't think about that, nor the bruised elbows, the scratches from berry picking, the wet, ruined clothes. The boys seemed happy.

Not so Prudence. As the weather grew warmer, she grew more uncomfortable and more demanding. With no word of Liam, she became angrier at him, at his father, at the baby she carried. And her anger seemed to sap what little strength she had.

Then Tattersall's sent a bank draft to Gilly. They'd held a successful auction, the note said, but no one had come to collect the earnings, minus the fee, of course. Graceanne insisted that Mr. Hallorahan use some of the money left after paying Lord Asquith to hire a Bow Street runner to find Liam. Liam wouldn't run off without that money even if, as Gilly claimed, he had gotten cold feet about marrying Pru.

"B'gad and that horse money would have bought a lot o' warm socks," Gilly allowed, relieved now that his stud farm was safe for another quarter.

Graceanne wrote to Mr. Olmstead in London as soon as Gilly agreed to send the funds. She promised to add to the price if necessary from her next month's income if that would help. The boys could go barefoot all summer; Prudence's baby wasn't going to wait that long before needing a father.

Having ascertained that his yacht was in Portsmouth having its sails refitted, His Grace took himself off to London to wait, with Milsom's blessing. The butler chose to stay on in Warwick for the nonce, overseeing the spring-cleaning and underseeing His Grace's foul temper.

Leland decided that he'd meet the yacht in Bristol in a few weeks rather than face countless nights at indifferent inns, and endure the hired horses and wretched roads of a drive. Going by sea would get him to Ireland soon enough. Well, not soon enough, since he was already too late, but in plenty of time to fetch the boys back before they were ruined entirely. He thought the novelty of a boat ride might console Willy and Les at the separation from their mother if Graceanne decided to stay with her lover, damn her doxy's heart.

A visit from Olmstead revealed that the Irishman had called on Ware's own solicitor some time ago, bringing Graceanne's request that her money be sent to Hallorahan's place in Ireland and asking about a special license. That confirmed the rumors, and changed matters. If Graceanne married the man, could Leland really call her an unfit mother and take the boys away? Blast it, an Irish horse trainer raising his heirs! He went to Gentleman Jackson's parlor to polish his boxing science. Every sparring partner seemed to have red hair, the only thing that saved them from having their freckled heads knocked off was the fact that Hallorahan hadn't come back to get the license. The only reason Leland didn't set off for Ireland on horseback that same day was a raging storm that was reported to have washed away whole roads.

The same storm kept his yacht in Portsmouth an additional sennight. So Ware was still in London when Graceanne's latest letter to Olmstead arrived after a long, weather-related delay. This time she wanted to hire a Bow Street runner to find the Irishman. The bastard had shabbed off on her? After sending her to Ireland? Ware didn't bother going back to Gentleman Jackson's. He went straight to Manton's shooting gallery.

A report came directly from Bow Street. Mr. Liam Hallorahan was easy to trace, having last been seen leaving Tattersall's on his way to his hotel. He wasn't staying in one of the better lodgings, naturally, but had taken a room in a respectable inn which was, unfortunately, in a less than respectable neighborhood. Said neighborhood was visited that very evening, it happened, by a press gang for His Majesty's Navy. Liam Hallorahan, the report concluded, was now en route to the Americas, protecting His Majesty's foreign interests.

Prudence went into labor the day after the letter came, at least a month earlier than anyone predicted. It was an easy birthing by most standards, if you discounted the mother's screams. To Prudence it was the most painful, disgusting event in her entire life, and she wanted only to have it over and done. She refused to look at the child.

Old Mara whispered at Graceanne not to insist, for the babe hadn't a chance of surviving. Why break the poor lassie's heart by showing her that pitiful scrap? Mara had to blow into its mouth just to make the infant let out a thin, feeble wail. It was as if all of Prudence's screams had used up the baby's voice, too.

The child was bluish and tiny, as scrawny as a baby bird. Graceanne had never seen so small an infant, and she marveled as she wrapped her new niece in the softest blankets, holding her to keep her warm, comforting the tiny body so she wouldn't use up her tenuous hold on life in crying.

"It's a beautiful, perfect little girl, Pru," Graceanne lied. Or perhaps she meant it, her heart having gone out to the fragile infant the moment she took her from Old Mara, and love being notoriously blind. "What shall you name her?"

Prudence turned her face to the wall.

"Best to hurry, missus, an' have in Father to get her blessed," Old Mara warned. "Th' wee bairn's too frail to make it through till morning, I reck."

"Not the Catholic priest, Gracie," Pru insisted, but Old Mara took another look at that tiny pinched face and said she didn't think there'd be time to fetch in the Anglican minister. Then Gilly swore he'd have only the Catholic priest in his house, and Prudence started screaming again.

How could they be arguing over which church should baptize the baby? Graceanne wondered. Didn't any of them care that the infant might—no, most likely would—die? Was she the only one to sorrow for this pitiful little rag fighting so hard for every breath?

"Gilly, fetch your Father Padraic. He's closest. If God wants another angel, He won't care who sends her. Pru, stop that carrying on. You'll only weaken yourself further. Tell me what you want to call the baby."

"I told you, I don't want the thing! I was going to send it to the orphanage anyway. Let them name it, if it lives long enough."

"Prudence! You cannot mean such a thing." Even for Prudence, that was a shockingly heartless thought. "You're just overwrought from the birthing. You couldn't give away your own flesh and blood!"

"No? Watch me, Gracie. Father Padraic runs the orphanage. He'll take the brat if it's still alive."

Tears running down her face, whether for her new niece in her arms or for her sister, Graceanne swore, "I'll never let you."

"Fine, then you keep it. You name it. The brat is yours if it lives. Have someone get you legal papers if you want, Gracie, and hurry, for as soon as I can get out of this bed, I'm leaving here—without a sickly little Irish bastard."

The priest came, and Graceanne tried again to make Prudence give her child a name.

"I won't! Just give it something pretty, something silly, not like Prudence or Grace."

Father Padraic was waiting, the baby trembling in his arms.

"Antonia," Graceanne choked out, giving this infant the name she had selected for Tony's daughter. "Antonia Faith."

"Antonia Faith Warrington," Pru called.

Graceanne gulped and nodded. She'd do it. She had to. Prudence wasn't going to change her selfish mind, and Graceanne wasn't nodcock enough to believe she would. Even if Pru did have a change of heart—or any kind of heart—and decided to keep the babe, where could they go? How could they live? No, Antonia would be better with an aunt who already loved her. And no one—well, almost no one— knew when Tony had died. She'd claim little Nina as her own, his posthumous child, so there'd be no scandal. Pru could have her own life back to make of it what she could, and Graceanne would have the girl child she always wanted. If she could keep her alive.

Chapter Eighteen

Wet nurses didn't come cheap, not even in Ireland, where children died at an appalling rate. Father Padraic found Shanna McBride for Graceanne in the workhouse, where the poor girl would never be able to work off her debts. Tossed out on the street from her indentured position in an alehouse when she was found to be breeding, Shanna had begged and wandered homeless until her time. Her impoverished family couldn't take her back; they'd had to put her into bond-servitude in the first place just to feed the younger children. So Graceanne paid off the indentures, then the poorhouse costs, and what the parish had outlaid to bury Shanna's stillborn infant. Feeling dirty, like she'd just purchased a slave, Graceanne watched the magistrate filling out forms making Shanna her property. But Antonia had to be fed.

Pru almost laughed when Graceanne suggested she try nursing the infant. "What? And never get my figure back?"

Graceanne laid out more money for a solicitor to draw up papers, making everything legal. Prudence gladly signed, although she kept swearing there was no need; she was never going to try to reclaim such a sorry specimen. Why Graceanne wanted to go to all the fuss and bother was beyond her anyway, for the child couldn't live out the first fever or influenza.

Gilly also had to sign. He was all too happy to put his signature on the papers if it meant he'd never have to pay out good blunt to support the pawky bastard. "Never sure it were me boy's in t'first place," he muttered with a sour look at Prudence, who was smiling at the middle-aged solicitor. Pru slammed a book down on top of Gilly's favorite clay pipe. The noise woke the infant, who set off a feeble wail.

"Hush, *cara mia*, hush, *niña*." Graceanne cuddled the infant, rocking her back to sleep while she scowled at the others.

Antonia was now Graceanne's, hers and Tony's. She'd simply move the date of his death forward a month or two, if anyone asked, and wear her blacks a month or so longer. She was sick of them, but there was no money for a whole new wardrobe anyway. Antonia would need dresses and sweaters and caps and more blankets to keep her warm, even in the Irish summer.

And Antonia, little Nina, was another day old. She was not thriving, hardly suckling according to Shanna, but alive. If a heart could be kept beating on strength of will and prayer, Nina had Graceanne's. And Willy's and Les's, who thought she was the best thing they'd ever seen, uglier even than the pink baby mice that fell through the roof last week. And a sister might be nice, they allowed, for when they played knights and dragons. Duke never liked being the captive maiden waiting to be saved. He never wanted to wear a hat.

Every day the baby gained a bit. Her breathing was still ragged, her lips were still blue, and she was taking so little nourishment, Shanna was afraid her milk would dry. Then they'd just have to get a goat, Graceanne declared, not giving up. She held the baby as if her body warmth would keep her with them. She talked to Nina constantly, promising a world of wonders, pretty gowns she was even now embroidering, doting brothers, dolls.

If the baby was slow to gain, Pru was quick to lose. She dropped the extra pounds as fast as she could, almost overnight, and with them the drained, pulled look. She started eating decent meals, taking walks in the fresh air, and sleeping as much as she thought she needed, which was, of course, twice as much as Gilly thought any female needed.

One day Pru begged a wagon ride to the little village to buy a new hat, which she charged to Graceanne without a by-your-leave when Lord Asquith told her the bonnet was a perfect companion to her beauty. Graceanne was too busy with the fussing baby to argue, and too relieved to have Pru out of the house and out of Gilly's way. For the most part, Prudence spent her time reworking her gowns, taking them in, adding new trimmings. Not even she dared to ask Graceanne for money to hire a seamstress.

Lord Asquith took to calling, and Graceanne was happy enough when Prudence acted as hostess in her stead, pouring the tea, making conversation about people she never met. Graceanne had enough to do between the boys' lessons, the new baby, the household, and trying to keep some peace between Gilly and Pru.

One month after Nina's birth, the baby was almost as big as a normal newborn and almost healthy in color and breathing. Graceanne was almost ready to stop worrying that every time Nina went to sleep she might not awaken. And Prudence was almost ready to leave.

"Lord Asquith is going to Scotland for the rest of the summer," Prudence announced one day. "He's asked me to accompany him."

"To accompany him? That's an odd synonym for marry, Pru."

The younger girl brushed her sister's qualms aside. "Perhaps he'll come around by the time we get to Scotland." She didn't seem concerned. "He owns property in Jamaica, too, and says he'll take me in the fall."

"Oh, Pru, that's not the way it should be. It's wrong!"

"What's right, then? For me to go back to the vicarage and sing in the choir? Even if Papa would let me, that's not what I want—that's not what I've ever wanted. Besides, Gracie, not even you with your rosy outlook can have forgotten that I am already ruined. I can't make my reputation any worse. Instead of putting on sackcloth and ashes, I may as well wear silk."

After Prudence left, Graceanne had a lot to think about, although not much spare time to do it in. What about her own life? And the boys' and Nina's? It was time she thought of their futures, too. The twins were content enough, but they were nearly savages except for their two-hour lessons. How could they learn to be proper English gentlemen fit for polite drawing rooms if they were running wild in the hills? If, Heaven forbid, Willy got to be duke, he'd need to know more than how to tickle fish out of streams. And Nina would always be a by-blow of

Liam Hallorahan and an English doxy around here, no matter what name she bore. The country people had long memories, besides every superstition and prejudice Graceanne could name.

No, they shouldn't stay there. Gilly wasn't even family. And he was beginning to look at her in a way she did not like.

Things came to a head one day when she was sitting in the sun next to the kitchen garden behind the house. She was watching the twins gather peas, Nina on a blanket next to her.

Gilly stepped out of the kitchen door, pipe in hand, and sat next to her on the ground, too close for comfort. She pretended to fuss with Nina's blanket, as an excuse to put more inches between them.

"Ye know, ye could do worse'n settle here," Gilly started to say. "Ye seem to fit in the way of life hereabout. None o' them prettified ways about ye." He nodded. "That's good."

Well, it wasn't much of a compliment, but Graceanne bowed her head and murmured a thank-you.

"No telling if Liam'll ever get back, I be thinking," he went on. "An' I need brawny sons to help run th' place. Your two ain't fallen off th' roof recently, nor tried to burn th' barn down but that onct."

"It was an accident! And they're just babies, not the stablehands you keep trying to make them into."

"They'll grow," was all Gilly said. "An' I'm not too old to have more sons meself. A man needs a woman. Been a long time without." He let the implication drift off, that while she was there, he couldn't entertain another.

"Does this mean that you are asking me to . . . marry you?"

"Aye, ye're a bonny enough lass, for an Englishwoman. Good mother, hard worker . . ."

Graceanne said she needed time to think about it.

Gilly did offer security, and he was decent enough in his way. She'd seen him in his cups only twice, once when the letter came saying Liam was impressed, and the other time when Pru had given birth to the only grandchild he was liable to have, and that one a sickly female. Gilly already treated the boys with casual affection and her with a modicum of respect. She supposed Willy and Les could learn the ways of a gentleman when they went off to school. And she could convince Gilly to install a real roof as a wedding present.

But was a real roof over her head enough? Here was another man who wanted her sons and her warm woman's body. Gilly was more honorable than the duke, but the whole came down to the same: Graceanne was a commodity, not a person wanted for her own self, not a woman to be cherished. She couldn't do it. And if she was going to reject Gilly's offer, she definitely couldn't stay.

She couldn't face the return trip on her own either, not with the addition of a fragile infant, a young wet nurse, and an uncertain welcome in England. She almost wished the duke were back in London. He'd know what was best to do. Surely he had a small bit of property where she and her family could settle for a new start. Somewhere he wouldn't visit too often, with his too-tempting importunities. No, Graceanne told herself, she did not need any more complications, only an escort. She recalled how Tony's batman Rawley had seen her and the boys home from Portugal, taking care of their every need despite his injury. She'd had one letter from him after Christmas, thanking her for the gift. And no, he hadn't found work by then except helping out in his brother-in-law's apothecary. There wasn't much call for a one-armed veteran, he'd written.

Graceanne sat down and wrote to Rawley that very day. A one-armed veteran was precisely what she needed as pathfinder, protector, and provider of a male influence for the twins. Tony's cousin Ware was being generous, she wrote, so she could hire Rawley's services as equerry if he was still free. She enclosed a check for his expenses and asked him to hurry, since she found herself in a rather uncomfortable position in Ireland. She didn't mention the new baby; Pru's lapse was better explained in person.

Graceanne didn't get her knight in sergeant's uniform quickly enough. She got an escort fit for a princess instead, and she only wished the princess had managed to keep him.

His Grace finally got under way. Dead calms turned into thunderstorms which turned into gales. This was a boneheaded notion in the first place, taking the yacht to Ireland. What if the twins got seasick? What if they fell overboard? Grace would never forgive him. Besides, he could have been there ages ago if he'd driven. What if she needed help, with Liam taken up by the press gang? All in all, Lord Ware had too much time on his hands and too many worries on his mind. If not for the handsome wages he paid, the duke's crew would have jumped ship the third day out. By the time the Emerald Isle hove into view, they were considering tossing him off the side of the yacht, the salaries bedamned.

Totally unaware that his foul temper had nearly

caused a mutiny, Leland hailed the first fisherman he saw on the docks at Wicklow Head and asked for directions to Hallorahan's stud farm. Then he asked again at the livery stable, where he hired the likeliest-looking beast. And again from a shepherd at an unmarked crossroads. The deuce take it if he could understand a word these people spoke. So what the hell was Graceanne doing here, especially if Liam wasn't?

He got his answer soon enough, when Graceanne, looking more beautiful than he remembered despite the blacks she still wore, with a warm sun-glow to her skin and paler golden highlights to her hair, introduced him to Gilly Hallorahan. Liam's father refused to leave her side, even when Leland suggested they had private matters to discuss.

"Reckon ye do, but not in my house. High-nosed English toffs ben't in such high odor, Duke."

So that was the way of it. She'd left with the son, then took up with the older man—not too old; Leland noted the strong forearms and well-muscled thighs—when Liam involuntarily deserted her. Leland sat stiffly, his face a rigid mask of controlled fury.

At first Graceanne was delighted to see Ware, even allowing herself a moment to believe he cared enough about her to come fetch her home. Not with that aristocratic disapproval writ on his stony countenance, he didn't. She quickly realized he wanted the boys, that was all. Chiding herself for being a peagoose, she called them in and took up her sewing.

Watching Leland with the twins was like watching an iceberg melt. They threw themselves at him in an ecstasy of welcomes, raining hugs and wet kisses and shouts about their ponies and their friends and the mice in the roof all at once, while Duke pranced in circles, adding to the noise with excited barks. The twins wanted to show Collie their swimming pool and the foals and the barn cat's kittens and the new baby and their ponies.

"Whoa, bantlings," he told them, tossing one after the other up in the air and pretending to stagger when he caught them, so big had they grown. "Let me talk to your mother, then you can show me all your marvels."

When Willy and Les rushed out to tell the stablehands that their cousin Collie, who was really a duke, was really here, Leland straightened his clothes. He brushed a smudge of dirt off his fawn breeches. "The boys look well, sturdy and solid. They've lost some of the baby roundness, and their voices have deepened. They speak much better, too, even if they still both talk at the same time." And he still couldn't tell one from the other. "And Duke has turned into a handsome animal."

Graceanne was wishing they hadn't stormed in like unmannerly urchins, dressed like ragamuffins and climbing all over the immaculate nobleman. Even Duke had forgotten his training. "They're still young," she said by way of an excuse—for the boys, not the dog. "Only four."

"Are they?" They'd been three at Christmas. Leland felt a pang for the changes he'd missed seeing, the birthday he hadn't acknowledged with gifts, the blasted ponies some jumped-up horse coper was providing! He addressed the older man, still hovering behind Graceanne: "I heard about your son's impressment. I'm sorry."

Gilly barely nodded, so Leland turned back to Tony's widow. "As soon as I heard, I started arrangements to have him brought home."

"How generous of you. Isn't that kind, Gilly?" Gilly grunted.

Ware said, "Yes, well, I'm sure you'll be glad to see him."

Graceanne wasn't sure at all, not if she had to explain about Pru traipsing off with Liam's landlord, and not if Liam was going to cause trouble about the baby.

She must have murmured something suitable, for the duke went on. "Of course, it may take some time. Meanwhile"—he cleared his throat; confound it, there was no polite way of putting this—"I'd like to take the boys back to England on my yacht. And you, too, naturally, if you wish to come. I, ah, believe the twins belong in their own country."

Graceanne studied the tiny cap she was embroidering. "Yes, I have been thinking it was time we returned home."

"Here now," Gilly put in, "I thought ye've been thinking on my offer." He turned to Ware, fists clenched at his sides. "An' an honorable offer it do be, too, Duke. Ye've got yer yacht an' yer mansions an' yer piles of blunt, but I've got a wedding ring to put on her finger. Can ye match that, Duke?"

Something inside Leland turned to ash. It was true, then. Grace and this rough countryman had an understanding. And with the boys so obviously flourishing, Leland knew he couldn't take them away from her.

Graceanne died a little in the awkward silence after Gilly's question. Then, "Don't be a fool, Gilly," she said. "His Grace is only showing proper concern for his wards' welfare. He has always been a most excellent guardian."

Gilly spat out the window. Graceanne suddenly

wondered what he did in the winter, with the windows shut. With any luck, she wouldn't be here to find out. Setting aside the sewing she was too nervous to stitch properly, she asked Gilly to check on the boys while she and His Grace continued their conversation.

"I cannot return to my parents' home, Your Grace."

"Leland. And I should hope not. There are a few extra rooms at Ware Hold," he teased, inordinately relieved that she was considering coming away with him. "Just a few. And Ware House in London is almost as empty. On the boat ride home we can discuss where you'd like to live."

"I have other reservations, Your—Cousin." He gestured for her to continue, schooling himself not to grin, not to show he was willing to agree to almost anything. "At first you wished to have only Willy, your heir, come to you. I need to know that you'd not favor him over Les."

"Confound it, Grace, that was before I met either boy. You must know I'd not love one more than the other, or make them compete with each other for my regard."

"And you'll not establish Willy as your heir, confer titles and such on him, while you are still in your prime? I'd not have him disappointed later."

He nodded, liking that she thought him still young. Compared to Liam's father, Gilly, he was practically a lad. "I shan't dub him viscount until I'm at least fifty, and without male issue. Will that do?"

Graceanne thought the duke would be virile well into his seventies, but she didn't say so. She was thinking how best to put her most pressing concern. He was so good with the boys and would be such a loving father. She had no real cause to distrust him, yet his world did not accept children like Nina. The members of the *ton* kept their dirty linen hidden in the deepest closets. Hers was going aboard that yacht, first class, or none of them were going. "So you'll care for all my children, be a fair and even-handed guardian?"

"I said so, didn't I?"

"I would have your handshake, Leland. It's that important to me."

This was not time to quibble about a man's word, not when he was so close to filling that gaping hole in his life. Leland stood and took her hand in his. "I solemnly swear to love both your children the same, with no favoritism."

"*All* my children," she corrected him.

He shrugged. "All."

Chapter Nineteen

The duke returned to his yacht. He wouldn't have accepted Gilly's hospitality, nor was it offered. Furthermore, he had to alert the crew and rearrange the bunks in the cabins, since Graceanne insisted the children needed their nursemaid Shanna. Leland couldn't but think the Irish girl would be miserable away from home and family, but the chit convinced him she'd never leave Mrs. Grace, not after all she'd done for her. So be it. Shanna could sleep with the boys, leaving the widow's wide bed half empty. And his own the same, of course, if by any stroke of Gallic magic she preferred to sleep there.

He did not see much of Graceanne the next day, since she was busy with the packing, so he went with the boys on their farewell rounds of stalls and paddocks. He wondered if Graceanne knew that their favorite activity at the horse farm was watching the stallion perform. They were too excited at the prospect of a boat ride to worry about the horses left behind, especially when the duke described the ponies he had waiting for them at Ware.

Leland hired a wagon to transport the trunks, bags, and boxes to the dock, and a carriage for Graceanne, the nursemaid, and the boys. Willy and Les wanted to ride on the wagon with the dog, though, so he tossed them up, with firm instructions to stay seated and hold on tightly over bumps, while the widow and the maid settled themselves in the coach.

As he walked back to the carriage, Leland heard an odd sound. He looked under the wheel to see if a spring was damaged. No, it wasn't that kind of noise. His brows lowered, the duke pulled open the carriage door, then shut it quickly, backing out. The nursemaid was holding an infant to her breast.

Graceanne opened the door again and stepped down, but she stayed close to the carriage. "I should have told you."

"You should have told me?" he thundered. "You bloody well should have mentioned that you were bringing an unwed girl and her baby aboard my boat! And why the devil would you hire a—"

Before he could go any further with that thought, Graceanne quietly said, "It's not Shanna's baby."

If it wasn't the nursemaid's baby . . . Dear God, he thought, a baby. He staggered back from the carriage.

Graceanne reached in and lifted out a small blanket-wrapped bundle. She cuddled it, gazing down in such tenderness, his heart gave a lurch. My God, a baby.

Still staring at the infant, she told him, "I should have told you, but I was afraid you wouldn't want to travel with an infant. She won't be any problem, I swear."

Leland wasn't listening. He was calculating. The bundle was so tiny, what was nine months back from yesterday? He couldn't think. Could she have been breeding over Christmas? He recalled the velvet gown she wore, oh, so well, but it was cut in the latest style, with the waistline under the bosom. But Tony'd already been dead for months by then. Too many months.

"By all that's holy, woman, how could you?" His well-bred, aristocratic indifference gave way to abject anguish.

Graceanne didn't notice. What, did he think she should have tossed Pru's baby in the dust heap? "How could I not?" She looked up and read disgust on his handsome face. She held the baby closer to her breast. "She's mine, so speak now if you will not acknowledge her. But I swear to you, the boys and I will go elsewhere if you cannot accept Nina."

Still reeling, he automatically said, "I could force you, or take the twins. The laws—"

"But you said you would not. I hold you to your word. Nina is part of our family."

"Nina?" It was the gasp of a dying man.

"Antonia Faith. Little girl, *niña*. Nina."

"You named the bas—er, baby—after Tony? Tarnation, woman, does your boldness know no bounds? The gall, the absolute nerve!"

Her shoulders went back. "Tony would understand. He had a generous heart." Not like some others she could mention but didn't.

A generous heart, Tony Warrington? Ware was positive his hotheaded cousin would kill her, Liam, Gilly, and every horse on the farm. Leland wanted to himself. It was all he could do not to strangle the jade.

"And you hope to pass the child off as Tony's?"

"No one has to know the exact date of his death. It's not as if he died in a specific battle or anything.

And the timing is not that many months far from possible. Nina deserves that, Your Grace. She fought so hard."

"What? Is she sickly besides?"

"She's just delicate." Graceanne uncovered the infant's head and held her out toward him to see. "She won't be any problem."

All he saw was a pinkish red tinge to the downy hair on the infant's head. Like Liam's. Or Gilly's. That was problem enough. He turned away. "And you don't feed her yourself?" He jerked his head toward the carriage and the waiting maid. No, she wouldn't let a nursing babe interfere with her finding a new protector.

"Of course not. How could I? Why, you think . . ."

She was too late. Leland had already climbed aboard the wagon with the boys and given the driver the office to start.

Graceanne carried the baby back into the carriage, and the groom raised the steps. They were off. Graceanne sank back on the cushions, shaking. He thought that little of her? She knew he'd never seen her as a lady of his own class, but to think she'd fallen so low? And he'd never even asked, he just assumed she was Nina's true mother from the beginning, she realized now. Well, let him, then, she thought, her chin coming up despite the tears that threatened. Let him think the worst since he was determined to anyway. Graceanne Beckwith Warrington, vicar's daughter and soldier's widow, was not about to go begging his priggish lordship's pardon.

Perhaps traveling by sea was not such a good idea. If the crew was ready to keelhaul their captain before, now they were ready to abandon ship altogether. The twins were just a bit hard to keep out of trouble among the ropes and sails and masts, hammocks, longboats, and oilskins. Leland didn't dare take his eyes off them for a moment, lest one or the other decide to go swimming or fishing or repeating the sailors' expletives when they found the boys underfoot.

The nursemaid was no assistance. When she wasn't feeding the infant, she was cowering in her bunk, leaving Graceanne to deal with the baby instead of the boys. The superstitious chit heard one of the sailors say that now he understood why it was such bad luck having women on board, and she was positive they were going to sink. And the dog was even less of a help. Duke never found his sea legs and was sick as a pup—all over the *Silver Lady's* teak decks. Furthermore, the dog could not be trained to use a chamber pot or the buckets provided for such a purpose, so yet another section of teak decking had to be designated as the dog's necessary. The twins, on the other hand, delighted in aiming their spigots between the railings, especially when they sailed close to shore or another vessel.

The sleeping arrangements were also less than satisfactory. Mrs. Warrington insisted on having the baby in with her, since Shanna was a heavy sleeper and might not hear her cries. After the first night Leland didn't believe a deaf man could sleep through the infant's bawling. He didn't, nor any of the crew. And she was so small! With Shanna awakened to tend to that scourge, the twins could not be left alone in case one woke up and wandered to the deck. So the widow shared her lovely bed with a mewling infant, and the Duke of Ware in the captain's luxurious quarters was lumped in bed with two little boys who wriggled all night. The wet nurse, the blasted wet nurse, was the only one to have a cabin to herself.

The other thing Leland was finding awkward about shipboard travel was how hard it was to avoid his passenger. If they'd gone by carriage, he could have ridden alongside, or taken up the ribbons. Even a good-sized yacht like the *Silver Lady* did not offer a great deal of privacy. But the duke did his best, since seeing her—especially seeing her with that infant in her arms—made his stomach turn, and he was never seasick. Luckily she didn't like taking the infant on deck because of the wind and the sun, so Graceanne stayed mostly in the elegantly appointed stateroom. Leland stayed mostly outside on the deck.

There was one blessing to the boat trip: On the first day out Les fell and cut his chin on a cleat. Now Leland could tell his wards apart.

Graceanne was enjoying herself enormously. The duke was keeping such careful eye on the boys that she did not have to worry about their safety, and he was keeping so consistently out of her company that she could rejoice. He was uncomfortable in her presence? Good. The less she saw of that blackguard the better.

And for once she didn't have to see to the cooking or cleaning. The cook almost had a seizure when Graceanne stepped into the cramped little galley and offered to help. There was a steward whose sole job was to attend the needs of the passengers, and a cabin boy for everything else. Best of all, Nina was getting stronger. Even her complaints were growing louder than whimpers. Never had an infant's crying sounded so sweet. Graceanne was content to hold her and sing to her and plan their future. She wasn't quite sure where they'd live, Graceanne crooned to the infant, but she promised they'd live happily ever after, just like in fairy tales.

"Life is not make-believe, madam, and you do the child a disservice by teaching her otherwise." Leland took off his oilskin coat and sat as far as possible from Graceanne and the baby in the stateroom. The twins were in his cabin napping at last—he'd insist they have an afternoon rest until they were fourteen at least—with the cabin boy guarding the door. With a summer rain squall raging on deck, Ware had no place else to go. "Perhaps we should now discuss where you and the children will live."

"Yes, you said we could decide it aboard the yacht. The boys have been asking."

He got up and began pacing. "There is nothing to discuss. We go to London." At first, on his outward journey, Ware had pictured an idyllic family summer in Warwick, with picnics and simple country pleasures. Then, he'd planned, they'd all go to town for the fall Little Season. The twins would have nannies and tutors, and Grace would have a new wardrobe. Once she was out of mourning, he'd see she was eased into the life of the beau monde. Then, if she could find her place in his world . . .

Leland had never let his planning go beyond convincing himself that Tony's widow deserved pretty gowns and parties.

But now? Summer was nearly over and the villagers in Warefield would never accept soiled goods. And there was no telling whom she'd run off with next. In London he could keep a closer watch on the widow, and since she was keeping up this perverse pretense of mourning, he wouldn't have to introduce her to the *ton*, which could be even more morally narrow-minded.

"I prefer the country, Your Grace. It will be healthier for Nina."

"Why? You said she wasn't sickly."

"She's better, merely delicate."

Something in her voice made Leland pause in his pacing and take his first good look at the infant. "Gads, if that's delicate, I'd hate to see what you call ailing." The child had a pinched look to her face and a bluish cast to her complexion. She trembled and jerked her hands around spasmodically. "By Jupiter, we should have gone by carriage."

"No, I think that would have been worse, with the dust and the drafts and the jouncing around. The yacht is better appointed than many an inn we'd have to patronize."

He nodded and resumed his pacing. "Ware House in London is even more comfortable. It will be easier to put it about that the child is Tony's post-obit."

Graceanne insisted. "The children and I will be happier in the country."

"But I have business I need to attend to in London and duties at the Foreign Office, so that is where we are going." He pounded on the chart table for emphasis, sending maps rolling in every direction.

"I know what it is," Graceanne accused him. "You are making the trip longer, hoping Nina dies before you have to acknowledge her!"

"My God, woman, what you must think of me!"

"No worse than you think of me, I'm sure," she shouted back.

"I never wished a child dead! How dare you accuse me of such a thing!"

"Then why won't you ever look at her?"

"I just did! And if I hadn't already decided to go to London, I'd change my mind. There are better physicians there."

"Nina doesn't need a physician; she just needs time and love. You never even bothered to look at her before. How can you know what she needs?" Now Graceanne was up and pacing to calm the baby's fretfulness at the angry voices.

"That's because all I ever saw was her red hair."

"My mother had red hair. Everyone in Warefield will remember that."

"I still have business in London."

"Gammon, I can just imagine your business. What is it this time, an Oriental empress? Let us go on without you. If not to Warefield, then some other quiet place. You cannot want a houseful of children interfering with your 'business' in the city."

"No!" he shouted, setting the infant to wailing again. "My wards stay with me."

"Then, here," she yelled, thrusting the red-faced bundle into his unsuspecting arms and heading for the door, "here's your latest ward. Get used to her."

Sergeant Rawley arrived in Wicklow, Ireland, a few weeks later. What he heard about Mrs. Warrington sent him riding neck-or-nothing back to England without a day of rest. According to Hallorahan, that "generous" duke had come claiming the major's widow, along with a baby Rawley knew nothing about, except that it sure as hell couldn't be the major's. Major Warrington hadn't been next or nigh his sweet young wife for over six months before taking that fever what killed him. Hadn't Rawley been a-nagging at him the whole time to go visit the missus? That little darling wasn't increasing then, and she sure as bedamned didn't get in an interesting condition on the way home from Portugal. It sounded to Rawley like his lady needed more than an escort.

He'd taken the King's shilling and given his arm; even without Mrs. Warrington's blunt, he'd give that duke what-for.

———

Chapter Twenty

*E*ven the longest journey comes to an end except, perhaps, the journey to self-awareness. By the time they reached London, Lord Ware had devised a story to tell Aunt Eudora, and thus all of town. Milsom would see it reached the servants' grapevine, and hence to Warefield.

Despondent after Christmas, so Leland related, Mrs. Warrington fell into a decline because Tony would never see his new child. Her megrims were worsened by the offer to go traveling from a fellow officer's widow, an offer she had to refuse because of her condition, but which she was happy to have her sister accept in her stead. Prudence's departure made life at the vicarage more dreary, with more chores and less time to spend with her sons or resting for the baby's sake. With Ware's active encouragement from abroad, therefore, and his man of business's contrivance from London, Mrs. Warrington was sent to Ware's old retired nanny for her confinement. Liam Hallorahan was good enough to escort her on his way home; the duke left the peace negotiations to bring his cousins back with him.

"Humph!" Aunt Eudora snorted. "If you weren't a duke, my friends would laugh in my face."

"But I am a duke, Aunt, so they shall smile and nod politely and congratulate you on your new grandniece, as long as you accept Antonia as your kin."

"I don't doubt she's my kin, boy. It's which side of the blanket she was born on that has me flummoxed."

"What? You think the infant is mine?"

"I ain't blind, boy. I saw how you panted after the widow last Christmas." She pounded her cane on the floor for emphasis. "And you better not be acting like a stag in rut unless you want everyone else to think so, too."

Having carefully inspected the new arrival, Milsom drew his own conclusions, which he was certainly too well trained to discuss with his employer, or anyone else for that matter. "Very good, Your Grace," he said after being spoonfed a bowl of hogwash if ever he saw one. "Major Warrington would be proud of his wife and new daughter."

Leland swallowed his own retort and dismissed the butler to spread the word.

Ware's friend Crow Fanshaw needed a bit more convincing. He'd stopped by when he heard Leland was back in town, and the duke was forced to introduce him to Graceanne. Ware knew he couldn't keep her hidden away like the family skeleton, not if he wanted the *ton* to accept his story, but did she have to tote that blasted infant around with her like an extra shawl? Having the boys down to tea was one thing; let Crow see that not all children were barbarians, like his sister's tribe. It was bad enough that Les—or Will—asked his Tulip friend how Crow turned his head without poking out an eye on the high shirt collars he wore, but did Grace have to show off the half-pint Hallorahan?

Crow was polishing his quizzing glass later at White's when the inevitable came. "I say, Tony's boys couldn't be more alike if you held a mirror to 'em. Of course, the younger one—Leslie, was it?—is going to be the better dresser. You can tell."

"You can tell which is Leslie?" Now that Les's chin was healed, Leland hadn't a clue which twin was which. He was ashamed to admit it to a man-milliner like Crow, however. "That is, you can tell which has better taste?"

"Of course. And deuce take it if they aren't little Tony Warringtons come to life. Ah, can't say the same for the infant."

There, the question everyone was going to be asking, but not out loud. There was only one answer: "Mrs. Warrington's mother was a redhead."

Crow nodded and replaced his glass in its special pocket. "That explains it, then. Lovely female, Tony's widow. Too bad she's still in mourning."

Too bad he couldn't plant his best friend a facer, but Leland sipped his wine and smiled his agreement.

"She didn't seem too in alt about being in London. Not like m'sister, anyway, who can't wait to leave the country no matter if she has to drag the brats along with her. I mean, even if Mrs. Tony can't do the fall Season because she's in mourning, there are still the shops."

There had been words spoken over Graceanne's refusal to have the duke pay her modistes' bills.

Ware was not willing to trust her with more than pin money, so she still wore her country-made gowns. Not that he'd wash the family linen for Crow's ears. "Mrs. Warrington is used to a quieter life, and you must have seen she is a devoted mother."

Crow didn't know if it was devotion or being dicked in the nob, letting those rug rats climb all over her. He did know that he'd not be taking tea again at Ware House anytime soon.

Leland was going on: "She's concerned about the children here in London. I found an excellent tutor, a university student on convalescent leave, but that's only an hour or two a day, the boys are so young." And the tutor so weak. "But we cannot seem to find a suitable nanny, so Graceanne has the full burden of their care most times, in addition to the infant."

Actually they'd found three suitable nannies on three successive days. None of them lasted through the night. The employment agency was referring Milsom to their competitors down the block.

Crow was shaking his head knowledgeably. "Finding a decent nanny is the devil of a job." He spoke from his sister's experience. "You want one that'll keep the brats out of your hair, without worrying if she's got them chained in irons. M'sister finally found one who actually seems to like the little beasts, and they like her back. At least they pay attention to her. First time I ever saw them not trying to murder each other. Nanny Sprockett's almost got them civilized, by George."

So by ten o'clock the next morning, Milsom had bribed Nanny Sprockett to Ware House. In two days she had the boys eating out of her hand—sugarplums and ginger nuts—and the fussy baby eating some kind of pap to make her grow. She even convinced the Irish wet nurse to stop putting milk out for the little people—and every stray cat in the neighborhood. Then she threatened to slap Aunt Eudora's hand if she dealt from the bottom again.

Graceanne was pleased with the new nanny, except that suddenly she had too much time on her hands. She had no chores and no one on whom to pay calls. She had no money to visit the shops unless she was willing to have all her purchases, from toys to tooth powder, from bonnets to bonbons, credited to the duke's account. She wasn't.

She was amazed how the lack of funds made her feel so defenseless, especially since she hadn't had money in her own hands for all that long. For those years before, she'd never realized the helplessness of her position. Now she did. She didn't feel quite like a servant, since she had nothing to do in the vast, well-run mansion, but more like a poor relation. It didn't help when Mr. Milsom deferred to her in household matters he could have handled in his sleep, after she asked to be of assistance.

No, she had to have this situation out with Ware. Graceanne's pride wouldn't let her tell him the truth about Nina; neither would it let her be a nonentity the rest of her life. Ware was used to giving orders and expecting them to be obeyed, but Graceanne's days of "Yes, Papa" and "No, Papa" were over.

"Your Grace, a moment of your time?" She had to disturb him in his library, a room she'd never entered lest she meet him there. He'd been avoiding her assiduously, so this was her only opportunity. Bearding the lion in his den seemed to fit her mood.

Leland gestured her to the seat facing his desk. She was not going to start this conversation being dwarfed by the wide leather chair or being intimidated by the expanse of polished wood between them. "I prefer to stand," she said, "but you may sit, of course."

He could do no such thing, of course. He did lean his tall frame against the desk, though, managing to look relaxed and confident, blast him.

"About my bills," she began.

Leland held up his hand. "All of your expenses are being paid, Mrs. Warrington. No reasonable requests will be denied, I promise you. Every shopkeeper in town knows the address, so you merely have to place your order and give your direction." He crossed his arms across his chest, satisfied.

Graceanne wasn't, and was determined to make him understand. "But I don't have any accounting, whether I am overspending my allowance or not. And I have to ask Mr. Milsom every time I need to tip a footman or a delivery boy. I don't even have pin money to put in the poor box at church without asking Mr. Olmstead. It is degrading."

"So is having to chase you to Ireland."

Graceanne blushed, but managed to say, "I never asked you to come after me."

"And I never asked you to account for every pound and shilling."

"Your generosity is not in question, Your Grace. It's a matter of trust that you won't grant me the wherewithal to take a hackney across town, much less across the continent. And I am not permitted to hire my own servants."

"I thought you liked Nanny Sprockett."

"I did *not* like the dresser you hired for me."

Leland shuffled some papers on his desk. "I admit the first choice was not felicitous." He hadn't stolen that one from Crow's sister, but from his sister-in-law, who was always turned out in the height of fashion. "How was I supposed to know she did not like children?"

"And the second one? She took one look at my wardrobe and announced she wouldn't be seen dead in my castoffs."

He tried to hide a smile. "I daresay she was dressed better than you."

"Immeasurably, I'm sure. Now that Nanny Sprockett is here I might take the time to do some shopping, if you will show me an accounting of my bills, but that's not the point. The point is, I do not need you or one of your handpicked watchdogs overseeing my every move. I never had a dresser before in my life, and I do not require one now."

"Oh, you know the right shops to patronize, do you? Fair prices so no one overcharges you? Unsavory neighborhoods to avoid?"—Graceanne had to admit that she didn't.

"Furthermore," he went on, on the attack, "a lady is never—I repeat, never—seen abroad without escort in London."

"Are you implying that I am not a lady?" It was a good thing she wasn't sitting at the desk; the letter opener was a safe distance away.

"I am implying that without a maid in attendance, you are subject to worse insults than that."

"They couldn't be any worse than the way your aunt looks at me." Or the way he did, like she'd crawled out from under a rock. With Nina in tow.

"You are not that naive, Grace. There are a great many indignities you'd find more offensive than Aunt Eudora's disapproval. If it's any consolation, she is more incensed with me than with you." He tidied another pile of documents. "She, ah, believes me to be the infant's father."

"You?" And she laughed, which was possibly the worst insult to Ware's pride of all.

"Is that all?" he asked, taking up his pen to signal the end of the conversation. "See Mr. Olmstead about an accounting and an allowance if that's what you wish, but for your personal needs only. The boys' expenses are part of my household. And hire your own abigail, if you want to be bothered with references and such. Hire any blasted servants you want, as long as you don't go out of this house without one of them. And," he added without looking up from his papers, "as long as you aren't using them and my blunt to ship off again. Believe me, the consequences of another runaway liaison will be far worse than having to suffer Aunt Eudora's lectures."

Graceanne wasn't sure, but she thought she'd just won the battle yet lost the war. He was never going to trust her, and she was never going to be more than a prisoner in his house; a prisoner whose every want and need was met, who was treated with distant courtesy, but a captive all the same.

As for the duke, he was grimly satisfied that he'd made his points: His wards' mother was going to behave with propriety, and he wasn't financing another tryst. "Good day, Mrs. Warrington."

The words still left a bitter taste in his mouth when he returned with the boys after their riding lesson at an indoor rink. Lesson, hell, Hallorahan had made the twins into regular Lilliputian centaurs, although the Warrington blood had to get some credit. He had only to stand back and watch, and make sure they didn't attempt any jumps higher than their ponies could take. They'd be ready for Hyde Park any day now—any day he wouldn't be embarrassed to be seen bear-leading his little cubs. He was already a laughingstock at White's, having been caught teaching them to roll hoops in Grosvenor Square. Then there was all the time he devoted to their riding and taking them places. Boys new to London had to go to Astley's and the menagerie at the Tower and Gunter's for ices, didn't they? He couldn't very well entrust them to that weak-kneed tutor, no matter how his friends chuckled behind his back. Besides, the twins were better company than those rashers of wind at the Parliamentary sessions he was missing these days. His business ventures were also suffering, and his social life, too.

He couldn't seem to enjoy himself at the rounds of routs and ridottos now that summer was over and the *ton* was coming back to town. He'd think of Graceanne sitting in the house every evening with her endless sewing, or being fleeced by Aunt Eudora at cards, and the champagne would seem flat, the conversations insipid. More often than not, he just spent the nights at his clubs. Drat the woman, she was cutting up his peace more every day!

Then Sergeant Rawley got to town. The first jarvey he asked directed him right to Ware House. The door was opened by the starchiest butler Rawley'd ever seen. Why, if the fellow hadn't been wearing an old-fashioned wig, Rawley'd think he was the duke himself. The chap took his blessed time fetching Mrs. Warrington, too.

Graceanne came flying down the stairs, baby and all, shouting his name when she got the message.

She pushed the infant into Milsom's arms, then threw herself at Rawley's massive chest, weeping her happiness into his shirtfront.

Leland stepped out of his library to see what the commotion was in the hall, and did not like what he saw at all, Graceanne in the embrace of a large, rough-looking individual.

Rawley didn't like what he saw any better. Crying, was she? So was the infant. And that toff in the niffy-naffy pantaloons was looking as jealous as a ram with one ewe. So Rawley planted him a flush one, right-handed.

Now Ware didn't have to worry about any bitter taste in his mouth or any champagne going flat. He wasn't going to be able to eat anything for a week. And he wasn't going to have to fret over spending so much time with the twins, either, for Graceanne hired the man while His Grace was unconscious, to be the boys' mentor and her personal servant.

She also explained to Rawley about the baby and her sister, and how the duke didn't trust her. Rawley wished he'd hit the makebait harder.

So Graceanne had a loyal friend, and Ware had a malevolent giant on his payroll, one who was idolized by the duke's own wards. Resting in bed with an ice pack on his jaw, Leland decided he really had to do something about finding himself a life. A wife, he meant, a wife.

Chapter Twenty-one

They said Miss Eleanor Ridgemont had three offers her first season, two her second. This was her third, however, and if she didn't settle soon, the gossip went, she'd be on the shelf, Diamond of the first water or not. They said she was holding out for a better offer, a higher title, a heavier purse . . . or true love. They shook their heads.

The reigning Toast was certainly exquisite, tall and stately, raven-haired and alabaster-skinned. She was the daughter of an earl, an heiress in her own right, a talented watercolorist, and a graceful dancer. In other words, she'd make the Duke of Ware a perfect duchess. She'd not find a higher title, since Prinny preferred older women, and few unwed gentlemen in town had deeper pockets. As for true love . . . Leland shook his head. If she was that much of a peagoose, he didn't want to marry her anyway.

As September gave way to the opening of Almack's, the galas at the theater, and the endless private balls of the fall Season, His Grace had given serious consideration to finding himself a wife.

Between Rawley, Nanny, and Grace, he hardly got to spend time with the twins. He got reports from their tutor, of course, and brief onslaughts of boyish enthusiasm when the twins were between jaunts with their uncle Rawley, or when the sergeant was temporarily out of the gruesome war stories on which Willy and Les seemed to thrive. And Leland did make a practice of visiting the nursery after the children's supper when his schedule permitted, after Rawley was gone for the day and before Graceanne came to read stories and tuck them in. Nanny Sprockett smiled over her knitting as the boys related the tricks Uncle Rawley was helping them teach the ponies, and the steam engine Uncle Rawley had taken them to see, the battles he reenacted for them with the tin soldiers. Leland wasn't smiling. He may be spending more time with the twins than the average father of the haut monde, but by no stretch of the imagination could he convince himself he was actually raising them.

Not that he was complaining about their upbringing, and not that his complaining would do much good, after he'd promised Grace she could hire her own servants. It was natural Tony's children should be army mad, especially with a bigger-than-life warrior in their midst. After all, Leland couldn't expect them to be interested in land management or the workings of Parliament, things his own sons would need to know. When he had sons of his own.

The widow was finding her feet, too. She'd hired a middle-aged abigail, unexceptional according to Milsom, and was dressing more like a comfortably circumstanced officer's relict and less like a rag-picker, although still in those infernal, hypocritical blacks. She was going about with Aunt Eudora to afternoon teas, musicales, and the like, nothing out of keeping with her mourning period, but she was getting to meet society's old tabbies. She was passing their inspection, too, Aunt Eudora reported, except for a few raised eyebrows when the infant was brought forth at Ware House at-home days.

She was back to doing charitable work, he heard from Olmstead. Milsom and Nanny Sprockett had dissuaded her from volunteering at the foundling home, where she was too liable to bring infectious diseases back to the children. So Grace and Rawley and her abigail visited a veterans' hospital mornings when the boys were at their lessons. She wrote letters for the men or read to them, while her abigail did their mending and Rawley gleaned more barbaric tales to fill the twins' heads with gore. "An estimable female," Mr. Olmstead declared, which was high praise indeed from that noted misogynist.

So it was Leland who found himself at loose ends in his own venue. The parties were stale, his friends' conversations flat, the wagers and dares puerile, and the current crop of birds of paradise held all the appeal of plucked chickens. Every time he thought of taking one of the actresses or opera dancers back to her rooms, he saw Graceanne's lovely, sad face. She might have a child out of wedlock, that look seemed to say, but she was still a vicar's daughter. The rumors and gossip of his every move still shocked her, confound the woman.

Then, too, he heard some of the whispers. Not to his face, of course, but when his back was turned at a race meet or in a theater box. It seemed Aunt Eudora wasn't the only one to suppose a reputed rakehell like Ware was dallying with his cousin's pretty widow. See how he doted on those twins? There was even a bet on the books at White's that a certain duke would be pushing a perambulator in the park next. When hell froze over!

He kept even more distance between himself, the widow, and the infant, to dilute the scandal broth. He did it for her sake, Leland convinced himself, and his wards', so they wouldn't grow up having to defend their mother's honor. That was another reason for him to marry, if he needed another one: to end the rumor-mongering about Mrs. Warrington.

So he watched and he listened. He spent all of October propping up columns at debutante balls, playing whist for chicken stakes at Almack's, meanwhile scrutinizing the current harvest of Quality daughters. Miss Eleanor Ridgemont was definitely the cream of that crop.

Leland wasn't about to rush his fences, however, not after the disasters of his first two marriages. He wanted to know Miss Ridgemont's attitude toward child-rearing, child bearing, and country living. Even Willy could have told him what a clunch he was being. Miss Ridgemont felt just as she ought, which was however the rich, handsome Duke of Ware wanted her to feel. Until she snabbled him, at least.

In an effort to get to know the black-haired beauty better, Ware invited her for a drive in the park. In order to get the duke to come up to scratch, Miss Ridgemont was dressed in her most becoming day gown, which was too thin for a brisk afternoon in an open carriage even if it was only early November, too narrow in the skirt to allow her a graceful ascent and descent, and too low cut to permit Ware's eyes to wander toward any other female.

Ware was indeed absorbed between watching his mettlesome cattle and watching her chest take on a bluish tinge. He did manage to spot two small figures in the distance, though.

"My wards," he told her, happy that she'd get to meet them so soon. The boys were on their ponies, with Rawley right behind them on a huge rawboned gray, the dog trailing behind. Leland turned his pair in their direction.

"Oh, but we mustn't leave the carriageway," Miss Ridgemont protested. "My reputation, you know." She batted her long black eyelashes, all but daring him to sweep her behind a bush and steal a kiss.

Instead, he told her not to worry, his tiger was up behind them for propriety. He did notice that at least the chit didn't seem averse to lovemaking. A cold wife would not suit his purposes at all. A shawl, he was pleased to note, would fix Miss Ridgemont's temporary discomfort. He offered the carriage blanket in the meantime. Eleanor gritted her teeth and declined.

When the boys saw him, they waved and shouted for Cousin Leland to come watch them put their ponies through their paces. How could he refuse? He pulled up next to the sergeant, and his tiger jumped down to go to the horses' heads.

"Will you get down, Miss Ridgemont?" the duke offered, climbing out of the curricle before she could protest.

Eleanor hadn't come to the park to be ogled by a hulking manservant and a grinning tiger. She'd accepted Ware's invitation so everyone could see she was fair on her way to making the match of the Season. "It really is quite chilly, Your Grace. I don't know what I was thinking when I chose this gown." She tugged the neckline a smidgen higher.

So he shrugged off his greatcoat and tossed it over

her shoulders. Then the duke left her alone in the carriage to go watch some children ride in circles. Worse, she wasn't alone for long when the dog decided to join her, to make friends. The coziest Eleanor Ridgemont ever got with an animal was when she wore furs. She screamed, which caused one of the ponies to miss its footing. Luckily no harm befell Les, though Leland was there in a flash, ready to catch him. Rawley had more confidence in his lads, so when he came to order the dog out of the curricle, he just frowned in disgust at the bit of fluff His Grace was driving about.

The children had to go, Eleanor decided. This fascination Ware had with the infantry was unbecoming. In truth, identical twins might make charming pageboys, quite the amusing novelty, but as the duke's wards? She'd have them sent away to school before they could spell Jack Rabbit. As for the servant, it was the outside of enough for Miss Ridgemont to be scowled at by a great lunk of a lackey—and a repulsive cripple to boot. She'd get rid of him quickly enough, as soon as Ware returned to the curricle and took up the ribbons, in fact.

First she had to suffer an introduction to the brats. Ware led them over on their ponies. "Miss Ridgemont, may I present my wards. This is Wellesley, and the other handsome chap is Leslie."

She nodded her head fractionally, but the children nearly fell off their ponies, laughing. Ware looked confused; there was Willy up on his Patches, Les on his Peaches. Anyone could tell the ponies apart.

"A good rider has to sit more'n one horse," Rawley explained with a sly grin at Ware's discomfiture in front of his ladybird, "so I switch 'em off, Your Grace. Do you mean you couldn't tell?"

"Insolent bastard," Ware muttered as he gave his tiger the nod to release the horses.

That was just the opening Eleanor needed. "Precisely, Your Grace. That man insulted me with an insolent look."

Leland rubbed his oft-aching jaw. "Be happy a look was all he gave you."

"And he should have kept better care of that vicious dog."

"Duke? There's never been a sweeter-natured dog, unless you threaten the children. It was my fault for not warning you. I beg your pardon, my dear, that you were frightened."

Only partially mollified by his handsome apology, Eleanor persisted: "But the man has one hand!"

"Yes, otherwise he'd still be with the army, so I suppose we are lucky. He was the boys' father's batman, you see." He rubbed his jaw again. "Almost fanatical in his devotion, actually."

Eleanor was nothing if not determined. "But he obviously cannot manage two active children with that . . . that hook."

"Oh, he threatens to disembowel them with it if they misbehave. Works every time."

Now Miss Ridgemont's alabaster skin took on a greenish cast instead of blue. Leland wondered if she was sensitive or merely squeamish. He couldn't help but compare her attitude to Graceanne's, who spent her free time visiting wounded and maimed soldiers.

He didn't want a Lady Bountiful, Leland told himself; he wanted a duchess, an aristocrat. Miss Ridgemont was definitely that.

So His Grace was courting Eleanor the Iceberg, was he? If that was the type of woman Ware was going to install as his wife, Graceanne wanted to be elsewhere. She refused to contemplate why the thought of his bringing home a wife, any wife, gave her the dismals. But *this* prospective duchess was known to be particular in the extreme. And Graceanne had another bone to pick with the nodcock who put on his own blinders.

Once more she knocked on his library's door. This time she carried ammunition. Nina.

"Your Grace, you have not fulfilled our agreement."

Eyeing the bundle in her arms with misgivings, Leland put down his newspaper. "What agreement was that, Mrs. Warrington?"

"You swore to treat all my children equally."

He frowned. A lesser person would have fled. "A cheap trick, ma'am. A vow gained by dishonorable means is worthless."

"And is it worthless to Antonia to know some love and affection when she sees her brothers receiving it? Is she supposed to grow up thinking she is inferior because you are too enamored of your own deluded sense of honor to accept her as a person in her own right? I do not wish her to grow up in a cold, unloving household."

"What are you suggesting?"

"That you let us, the boys and Nina and myself, find a cottage in the country somewhere on our own, where you won't have to be reminded of us and our supposed sins."

"No!" he shouted. That was all.

That was it? No explanation? He was even more pigheaded than Graceanne thought. "May I remind you that your actions—or nonactions—toward Nina are branding this innocent child precisely what we have been at pains to avoid. The servants are talking that you don't treat her as a beloved cousin. Soon the *ton* will be spreading their gossip. Then what?"

Blast it, she was right, Leland acknowledged. "If I let you run off to the country, the rumors will have you exiled from polite company. So what am I supposed to do?"

"You could try being the doting guardian to Nina that you are to the boys. Here."

What he knew was coming came: an armful, nay, a handful, of wriggling infant. Confound the woman. "It's been months since you've so much as held her." Graceanne folded back a corner of the blanket so he could see the child better. "See how far she's come?"

Reluctantly he looked down, straight into blue eyes the color of tropical seas, Graceanne's blue eyes. And a smile. Wet and gummy, but a smile for all that. Lud, he must have traded his soul to win a smile like that, for he had no will of his own. "Do you think she'll be happier in the country, then?"

"I think the air is cleaner and the food is fresher. And I'd like to show her to my mother."

Who had red hair once, Leland reminded himself. By George, the infant—no, he had to start calling her by name—Nina was going to be a beauty. She was still tiny, but now she was rounded, with dimples. She even had dimples on those tiny hands reaching out to grab his neckcloth and put it in her mouth. He'd be fighting off her suitors with an ax. No, pistols. One in each hand. Just let some bounder try to get near her.

Of course, she still wasn't the sturdiest-looking thing he'd ever seen. Maybe the London fog was affecting her lungs.

"Actually," he said, "I have been thinking about a house party at Warefield over the holidays." He'd been thinking for about twenty seconds.

Chapter Twenty-two

Actually, a house party was not such a bad idea. Leland could invite Miss Ridgemont and see how she got on with the children, the countryside, and him. In the city there were too many social boundaries to keep them from getting to know each other well enough for such an important decision. One dance an evening—two would have shown too much particularity—did not reveal their compatibility, or lack thereof. At Ware Hold they could easily find themselves apart from others to carry on real conversations instead of the polite chitchat. And the mistletoe was a perfect excuse to find if they'd be compatible otherwise. Begetting his sons was his duty; he didn't intend it to be a chore. If all the dibs were in tune, then a New Year's announcement of the engagement would be in order.

He could not invite solely Miss Ridgemont and her companion, of course. That would be tantamount to a declaration he wasn't prepared to make without further deliberation. He needed some other young, marriageable females to throw dust in the eyes of the rumor-mongers, and so as not to raise false hopes. Then he'd need young, marriageable gentlemen to keep the chits happy and occupied so he could pursue Miss Ridgemont. Unattached females always came with mothers, fathers, chaperones, and maids. Then there were the valets and grooms and drivers from their carriages. Suddenly his little house party was taking on the proportions of a Carlton House fete. Milsom could handle it, of course, but was it fair to Graceanne to pitchfork her into a *ton*ish celebration when she was looking forward to a quiet country Christmas like last year's?

He consulted his friend Crow.

"Don't see why you think you have to make excuses for the widow," the baronet told him over dinner at White's. "I've seen her doing the rounds with your aunt. Good-looking female, pleasant manners. Even m'sister-in-law says so, and you know how starchy she is."

"Still, it's such a different way of life."

"From a vicarage perhaps, but didn't you say Wellington was your heir's godfather? If Mrs. Warrington was on such terms with Old Hokey, she can't be that much of a turnip."

"Tony did install her at the embassy," Leland reflected.

"There. Give over and tell me how goes the courtship of the ravishing Miss Ridgemont."

The duke was still pondering a flock of harpies alighting at Ware, getting their talons into Graceanne's history, shredding her reputation and her composure. "I don't know. She comes from a different world."

"Miss Ridgemont? Born and bred right here in

London, old chap. Father was an earl, don't you know. Silver spoons and all that tripe, same as you."

"No, Mrs. Warrington." Ware had barely touched the roast capon in chestnut sauce.

"Seems to me if a pleasant female like the widow can't fit into your world, maybe it's your world at fault." Crow took a mouthful of escalloped veal while the duke digested that bit of wisdom. "Besides, you've got the widow on your mind more than's healthy if you're pursuing another female altogether, especially the elusive Eleanor. Why don't you marry Mrs. Warrington and be done with it if all you want out of the match is sons? Lud knows she's fertile enough."

Ware couldn't tell Crow that was part of the problem: He'd never know if he was the father of his sons or not. No, he had to get over this fixation with Tony's wayward widow. Miss Ridgemont was the best alternative. "But you don't think a house party is a bad idea? You'll come? Or are you promised to your family?"

"Not in good odor with m'sister these days, don't you know. Not after telling you about that nanny. Uh, you wouldn't have your eye on my valet, would you?"

Ware surveyed his friend through his own quizzing glass, the hair à la Brutus, the neckcloth à la Polyphemus. "Devil a bit, my friend, devil a bit. Your man is safe from my evil designs. So you'll come help entertain the debs and do the pretty with their mamas?"

"I wouldn't miss this chance to watch you make a cake of yourself for the world. Not every day a fellow gets to see his best friend stick his own neck into parson's noose, don't you know?"

* * *

Aunt Eudora wouldn't travel with the twins. The boys wouldn't leave their ponies behind. Shanna wouldn't travel on the thirteenth of the month, Graceanne didn't want to be traveling toward her father's vicarage on a Sunday. The baby and Nanny had to be kept warm; Milsom's imported delicacies had to be kept cool. And the duke didn't want to have to rely on Warefield or even Oxford to do his Christmas shopping. This year he was getting to buy dolls and wanted to make sure he had the best selection. While he was at the toy shop, of course, there were a few other incidentals he thought might suit the boys and Nina. No matter the company, he vowed, the children were to have a fine Christmas, better than last year, even if it had to be a private celebration upstairs in the nursery.

The Three Kings might have managed a smaller caravan. And made better time.

And that fire at the last inn had nothing whatsoever to do with the duke's explaining to the twins the advantages of the modern sulfur matches over an old-fashioned flint box. Graceanne did make His Grace promise there would be no candlelit Christmas trees in the nursery.

By the time they reached Warefield, unpacked, and got everyone settled, there was no time to decorate the castle before the company was due to appear. Milsom came to Graceanne for advice, to her gratification, and she suggested that they leave the gathering of greenery to the young guests when they got there. Otherwise, she feared, they'd find Warefield dreadfully thin of entertainment. Before the Londoners' arrival, though, Graceanne had to call at the vicarage.

*   *   *

"There will be no scandal, Papa, unless you make one. Ware has been more than understanding," she lied, "and you can do no less. After all, Nina is your granddaughter."

Mrs. Beckwith was already christening the infant with her tears.

"If you don't accept Nina into the family and get over this foolishness of saying I am no longer your daughter, then I cannot come to church or bring the boys. Ware will hire a chaplain of his own, I'm sure, rather than see his wards snubbed. How will you explain that to your parishioners when they are looking forward to glimpsing the London nobs? Or to the bishop? Come, Papa, it's Christmas."

Beckwith hemmed and hawed a bit, then allowed as how he'd not turn a Christian away from his church doors. "But I won't have any of that wicked pageantry folderol like last year. You see where that led."

"Oh, but little Antonia will make a perfect baby Jesus," Mrs. Beckwith cooed.

"And the boys will be so disappointed if they can't be the cow. His Grace did mention he'd purchase new pews for the church, since he was inviting so many guests to see his wards perform."

So Graceanne had the pageant to organize, too. Luckily her angel, shepherd, and three Wise Men were still available, the costumes preserved. The Bindle brothers happily agreed to take over the sheep roles instead of the cow. Mary and Joseph were harder to find. Heaven alone knew where last year's players were.

Graceanne enlisted Shanna for Mary. If they could have a red-haired, Irish Joseph one year, they could have a red-haired, Irish Mary this one. Surprisingly, Rawley volunteered to play Mary's husband, giving rise to much speculation upstairs and down. At least he'd keep the barnyard animals under control while Shanna managed the baby. Satisfied, Graceanne was ready to greet the duke's guests. She even put on one of her new gowns, having decided to use Christmas as an excuse to come out of mourning, finally.

She donned colors—mostly darker ones rather than pastels—for the children's sake, she told herself, not to impress anyone or to feel more on a par with the London guests. The boys never noticed and Nina cried until she recognized her mother under the curled hair and russet velvet. Leland noticed and heartily approved, if his smile was any judge. Then he remembered himself and put on his forbidding ducal disapproval, but she'd seen the light in his eyes, and that was enough. She was finding it hard to hate him when he was so kind to the boys and now Nina; she hoped he was finding it as hard to hate her.

The first guests to arrive were Sir Crosby Fanshaw, escorting Miss Eleanor Ridgemont and her companion. Graceanne had been up in the nursery trying to calm some of the twins' Christmas fever by reading from a storybook, when they heard the carriage approach. She left them with the book to make her way down the staircase to the Great Hall, where Leland and his aunt waited. She wasn't putting herself forward; the duke had requested her presence to show they were all one family. Furthermore, she'd been helping Milsom and the housekeeper assign bedchambers, almost as if she were the hostess here.

Wraps were taken, hands were kissed, introductions were made. In fact, Miss Pettibone, the companion, was the only person not at least casually acquainted. Graceanne had met both Miss Ridgemont and Sir Crosby over various teas. Poor Miss Pettibone blushed and tried to hide behind one of the suits of armor when she was made the center of attention. She alone was relieved when a noise from the upper story made everyone crane their necks up the stairs.

"My God, no," prayed Graceanne.

"Heaven help us!" swore Ware.

"Disgraceful!" thumped Aunt Eudora.

"By George, look at them go!" enthused Crow.

"I'm going to faint," threatened Miss Ridgemont, but she didn't.

Miss Pettibone did, without saying a word, but taking the armored knight with her in a horrendous clatter.

Milsom was quiet, too, merely positioning himself at the bottom of the stairs and indicating to a footman to follow suit. Milsom plucked one small body out of the air as Willy soared off the waxed banister. The footman was not so deft with Leslie, who flew into the midst of the openmouthed company. Rather, he flew over Miss Pettibone's supine body and landed, splat, against Miss Ridgemont's chest.

The lady went down, shrieking.

Graceanne pulled Les off the hysterical woman and half hugged him, half shook him. "If you ever, *ever* do such a thing again, I'll—" She started to cry.

Leland had the other twin by the back of his collar, dangling. "Do you see what you've done to your mother? How you've upset everyone? I've a good mind to—"

Miss Ridgemont shrieked the louder for being ignored, and swatted away the hand Crow offered to assist her to her feet. She preferred the marble squares, it seemed, for she drummed her feet on them.

"Heaven help us," repeated Ware.

"Throw a bucket of water on her. It works on squalling cats," offered Aunt Eudora.

"I think Miss Pettibone needs smelling salts," said Graceanne from that lady's side, behind the fallen knight.

"M'sister uses burnt feathers," offered Crow, staring at Miss Ridgemont through his looking glass.

Milsom was, as ever, quietly efficient, signaling the gathered footmen to fetch wine, the housekeeper, Nanny Sprockett, and a vinaigrette. But the boys were trying to be helpful, to make amends. Willy grabbed up Miss Ridgemont's fallen shako-style bonnet with its towering plumes, and ran toward the massive fireplace to light the feathers. Les pulled the hothouse roses out of a Sèvres vase and was ready with the water, but he couldn't recall which lady Aunt Eudora said needed the bath, so he just tossed it between both of them. Which luckily put out Willy's burning hat.

Miss Pettibone was duly revived and guided to a chair by Nanny while the housekeeper made a special tisane, which was more tender attention than the companion was used to receiving. Miss Ridgemont was restored to order, more or less, with a glass of brandy provided by Milsom.

Then she demanded the children be beaten, birched, banished.

"I am dreadfully sorry, Miss Ridgemont," Graceanne began, "and the boys will certainly apologize. And they will never slide down the banister again, I swear."

"At least not until they are nine, I think." The duke

appeared to ponder the matter, his eyes twinkling. "Yes, I believe I was nine before I managed a creditable dismount. Tony didn't manage it till he was nearly eleven, if I recall. Do you remember that scar on his chin?"

Eleanor was still sputtering about boiling the boys in oil, and Graceanne was threatening to give the boys' ponies away to some deserving children who didn't scare their mothers out of their wits.

"Well, my buckos." The Duke of Ware knelt down in the wet and rose-strewn hall. "Which is it to be, boiling in oil, no ponies, or your promise not to slide down the banister until you are nine years of age?"

They solemnly chose to give their word to wait five years, holding out their hands to be shaken. Then they ran like hell, lest their cousin change his mind.

The duke watched them race up the stairs, still smiling. "I think the greenery should go up tomorrow just to be on the safe side," he told Graceanne and Milsom. "You know, garlands wrapped over the posts and the railing." Then he rubbed his chin, still looking up at that shiny banister. "But that's tomorrow, Crow. What say we give it a go tonight?"

"Are you daft?" Graceanne wanted to know, but Leland was grinning at his friend. "A friendly wager?"

Crow was torn. His clothes might be. On the other hand, a gentleman never turned down a bet, and the banister did look inviting, except for the newel post at the end. "I'm willing if you are, but you're the chap so desperate for an heir."

Aunt Eudora snorted. Graceanne bit her lip and told them they were acting worse than the little boys. And Miss Ridgemont, furious she was being disre-

garded, that her hat was ruined and the brats weren't
to be punished, stomped off to her room—right
through the wet, slippery roses. This time she slid
directly into the other suit of armor, which landed
atop her in a most suggestive pose. Miss Pettibone
fainted again.

Fanshaw put down his quizzing glass and patted
his friend's shoulder. "And here you were afraid the
house party might be dull."

Chapter Twenty-three

*H*ow could holding the wrong woman feel so right?

After Miss Ridgemont and her companion were carried off to their rooms by the housekeeper, the nanny, two footmen, and the butler, and after the Great Hall was mopped and restored to medieval splendor, Graceanne dissolved into tears. She just couldn't help herself.

And His Grace just couldn't help himself from gathering her into his arms to comfort her absurd blubbering about how she'd ruined his lovely house party. All she ever wanted was a little cottage somewhere for her and the children, she wept into his shirtfront while Crow studiously examined the slightly dented knights. She'd never wanted to associate with toplofty lords and lace-bedecked ladies, she cried. And look what happened when she did.

"What happened, Gracie, was two imps got up to mischief and two ladies' tender sensibilities were offended. That's all," he responded in his least toplofty voice. "They'll recover, and so will you, my girl.

Now, dry your eyes lest Crow here think I give every woman of my acquaintance the vapors.''

Graceanne accepted the handkerchief he held, although she had a perfectly good one in her own pocket, and made her excuses to Sir Crosby.

"The excitement, I don't doubt," he gallantly assured her. "Think nothing of it."

Graceanne left to make repairs to her appearance before any more guests arrived, and Leland took Crow off to the library for a sorely needed brandy.

Looking in her mirror upstairs, Graceanne realized she was more shaken by the duke's embrace and by his tender words than by the other events of the day. She'd felt so comfortable, so comforted in his arms— and he wasn't the least arrogant at all! She even thought he might—no, she was certain he did—like her! And oh, she was mortally afraid that she liked him back, despite his stiff-rumped pride, his autocratic intolerance, and his distrust of her.

Graceanne knew she'd have to tell him the truth about Prudence and Liam and Nina for the baby's sake, she told herself, but in all honesty she knew she'd have to tell him for her own sake. She'd have to swallow her own not inconsiderable pride, or regret for the rest of her life that she let him think the worst of her.

She'd tell him as soon as the guests left, she decided, if he hadn't already offered for Miss Ridgemont. But that was foolish. Once he offered for the lady, Graceanne's confession would be too late. She'd never know the answer to What if. . . . She owed it to them *both* to find out.

* * *

Leland was also shaken. Blast, once Grace was in his arms, he'd never wanted to let her go. If Crow hadn't been standing around, he'd have kissed her, stroked her, petted her, done his damnedest to get her upstairs to his room or to the bearskin rug there in the library. He hadn't cared. And it was more than lust, too. He'd seen enough women's tears in his lifetime to be inured, but Grace's nearly broke his heart. He'd have taken on the Mongolian hordes to keep her from crying anymore. Deuce take it, he must really care for the impossible chit!

How, he asked himself, how in bloody hell could he love a woman born to genteel poverty? True, she was a lady to her fingertips in most respects. But how could he love a female who turned down his carte blanche to bear an illegitimate child with a horse trainer? How could he think of making such a one his duchess? He couldn't. He wouldn't. He didn't.

He'd just have to give Miss Ridgemont more opportunities to show her better qualities.

Eleanor was at her finest that evening, sparkling like her diamonds among the other guests. She was stunning in a red satin gown, one long black curl draped over a pure white shoulder. She laughed. She flirted. She was a butterfly.

Graceanne was a moth in her quiet brown velvet and Tony's pearls. She sat with Miss Pettibone and the mamas of his other guests, Leland noticed. She was polite and friendly to the young bucks and Crow, without encouraging them to stay among the dowagers. Leland was glad she wasn't casting out lures to his friends, but why the devil did she con-

sider herself one of the chaperones? Dash it, Graceanne couldn't be much older than Eleanor. She
needed some gaiety in her life, too.

So he suggested dancing—informal, of course. Fortunately for his intentions toward Miss Ridgemont,
Graceanne volunteered to play the pianoforte for
them while the footmen rolled back the carpet. Unfortunately, Leland was aware of a sharp disappointment that he wouldn't get to hold the widow in his
arms again.

Eleanor was a superb dancer, light and lissome.
She was witty, too, chatting knowledgeably of the
latest books, poems, and theater productions when
the figures permitted. Yes, she'd do well as a social
hostess.

She wouldn't do quite as well as a country wife,
however. Before they parted for the night, Leland
invited the company to go out with him the follow-
ing morning to collect greens to decorate the Hold.
Miss Ridgemont gaily laughed and informed them
that she never left her bedchamber before noon, and
certainly not to go tromping through the woods, ru-
ining her boots and her complexion. And didn't holly
have prickers, anyway?

No one missed her, least of all Ware, who with the
others chased his wards and their dog from one end
of the estate to the other, followed by wagons and carts
to collect their armfuls of ivy and evergreen and mistletoe. Much giggling from the young ladies told him
he couldn't forget the mistletoe. They marked two
large firs as the Christmas trees for the estate woods-
men to chop down, and managed to locate a huge
fallen log that the twins were sure would burn for
the twelve days of Yuletide.

A laughing, happy, rosy-cheeked group arrived

back at the castle. Graceanne's face was glowing more than anyone else's, Ware observed as she skipped along, a twin's hand in each of hers, teaching them the words to a new carol.

But Miss Ridgemont was an enchanting picture, too, posed at the Adams room window with her lap easel and her watercolors. She was attempting the delightful view of the topiary gardens, she informed them all with a self-deprecating tinkle, as a present to their host. Miss Ridgemont was truly gifted, they all agreed, even the boys who crowded in to see the painting before they went up to the nursery for luncheon.

She could do another painting tomorrow, the duke insisted. Eleanor was so talented, he was positive the next would be better. As for his gift, it was the thought that counted. He'd pay for a new gown, of course.

After lunch everyone again gathered in the Great Hall to fashion the mounds of greens into wreaths and garlands and kissing boughs. Graceanne and Milsom returned from the attics with ribbons, bells, candleholders, and glass ornaments, and the footmen brought ladders, scissors, string, and hot punch.

The boys were taking a nap, thank goodness, exhausted from the morning's exertions. So Graceanne was able to devote her energies to persuading the dowagers that their weaving and sewing skills were crucial if they hoped to have enough garlands. She also had to convince the ladies that three kissing boughs were really enough, and Crow and the other gentlemen that emptying the punch bowl really wasn't part of their job so much as getting on those ladders and hanging the festoons and mistletoe. Which, of course, necessitated that same giggling among the young ladies.

The Great Hall resounded with Christmas cheer, except for Eleanor's corner, where she sat in state directing the Duke of Ware precisely how she wanted her kissing ball hung. No, the archway was too high, the mantel too low. Miss Ridgemont's creation was a massive affair of interwoven grapevines, ribbons, apples, and candles, which she'd shamelessly coerced Miss Pettibone into making. Ware put up with her dictatorial behavior as long as he could, in compensation for her lost painting, although he was itching to join the others as they laughed and sang. He could hear Grace's pretty voice again as she led off carol after carol. Of course, he thought, she was used to directing the church choir. He wondered if she missed that.

Soon Graceanne had them all singing, even Miss Ashton-Highet's deaf grandmother. His own voice wasn't quite that bad, Leland judged. Finally he gestured to Crosby Fanshaw. "Here, old man, you'll be better able to advise Miss Ridgemont in placing her decoration. I'm afraid I don't have the exquisite taste the two of you share."

He left the two most beautifully turned-out people in the room arguing over the location of that monstrosity while he breathed a sigh of relief. He should *not* be feeling relieved to leave his prospective bride's company, he reflected.

That evening the young ladies performed in the music room, the usual set pieces of German composers to the usual polite applause. Then Miss Ridgemont took her place at the front while two footmen dragged forth the harp. Leland groaned inwardly, but devil take it if the chit couldn't play divinely. And she'd come prepared to emulate the angels, in a white satin gown with a net overskirt. What a perfect picture she made! How long she played! His applause was entirely sincere at the completion of her piece.

Then he groaned again. Graceanne was the only female left to perform. She had a pleasant voice, he knew, and was competent at the instrument, but she couldn't have had any formal training like the others. Coming after Miss Ridgemont's superb recital, well, she'd look no account, like a poor vicar's daughter among these peers' progeny and earls' offsprings.

Graceanne seemed to know it and smiled self-consciously. "I cannot hope to emulate the superb performances we've heard tonight, but perhaps you might like to hear what our brave soldiers in the Peninsula heard at Christmastide." She picked up a Spanish *guitarra* from behind the pianoforte, tuned it, then began to sing a Spanish carol. Almost no one in the audience could understand the words, but they all heard the love and joy in the message as her voice sang with the glory of the season. Miss Pettibone wiped a tear from her eye. After another song Graceanne put the instrument down and switched to the pianoforte and "Adeste Fidelis," motioning them all to gather round and join in.

Leland swallowed the lump in his throat.

The next day he decided to give Miss Ridgemont's mothering aptitude another go. The twins could be a bit, well, boisterous, he admitted, so he went to the nursery after lunch to fetch Nina while the other young ladies went for a walk with Graceanne to the village shops. The gentlemen were content at billiards, and the older ladies were resting. Miss Ridgemont had stayed behind, claiming a headache, but actually disdaining rustic markets. She hoped to get some time alone with His Grace, besides.

He wasn't quite alone. Nanny warned that Miss

Nina was teething and apt to be fretful, but he ignored the advice. "My precious *niña*'s never been anything but a perfect lady for Cousin Leland, have you, sweet pea?" He chucked the infant under the chin and she smiled and blew bubbles.

She was still smiling when he handed her back to Nanny Sprockett, but not even the most devoted of guardians could claim she smelled anything like sweet. Another of Miss Ridgemont's dresses would have to be burned. Leland's ears burned with her recriminations.

Well, they weren't her children, Ware reflected. A woman couldn't be expected to take just any infants to her bosom, could she? And a lady like Eleanor shouldn't be supposed to have the familiarity with infants Graceanne did. Lud, he hoped not. Still, he remembered the widow last year, leading all the village children through their paces at the pageant, knitting those endless mittens. And she'd held every one of his tenants' infants last year at Boxing Day, he recalled, sharing their mothers' pride. Damn and blast, he hadn't been this confused since his salad days.

One last try, that was what he'd give Miss Ridgemont. The mistletoe test, he laughed to himself. She'd grow used to children once she had her own, he was convinced, but if she cringed from his kiss the way his first wife did, or stood passively like his second, he'd rather name Willy his heir and be done with it.

He caught Eleanor under the kissing bough when no one was around the next afternoon, not a difficult feat, as Miss Ridgemont seemed to station herself there whenever he was near.

He laughed about the joys of the season as he

placed a chaste kiss on her lips and then, when she did not draw back, deepened the embrace. She put her arms around his neck; he put his around her back. His lips teased and she answered with passion. She was everything he could have wanted: warm and responsive without being as bold as a lightskirt, and with a truly magnificent bosom pressed willingly against his chest.

And he felt—nothing. Nothing but her lips and her breasts. There was no stirring blood, no soaring senses, no raging need to throw her to the floor and make wild love in the daytime. He'd be hard pressed to get up the enthusiasm at candlelit night, he decided, between silken sheets on a feather mattress, after champagne and oysters. He felt nothing, nothing but the wish that she were someone else.

Chapter Twenty-four

*B*eing a gentleman had definite drawbacks. Lord Ware could not, for instance, tell Miss Ridgemont that they would not suit, not when he'd never made a formal address to her in the first place. Nor could he tell her and her giggly, gaudy friends to get the deuce out of his castle so he could enjoy the holiday season with his own family, not after inviting them to stay through the New Year.

And he certainly couldn't grab Mrs. Warrington and press heated kisses on her lips as he was aching to do with every ounce of fevered blood that pulsed through his body. But he could catch her under the mistletoe! He could steal a legitimate kiss, by Jupiter, if she stood still long enough. Between entertaining the oldest members of the party and keeping the youngest out of everyone else's way, Graceanne was busy conferring with Milsom and the housekeeper over meals, menus, and Boxing Day gifts for the tenants and the servants. She was rehearsing the pageant and making new costumes, and, yes, helping with choir practice. Leland hardly had a chance to see the elusive widow, much less entice her under the kissing bough.

He half feared that kiss, anyway. What if it branded him, seared her memory into his soul for all time? He was half afraid it was too late.

And he still had to play the host. The Duke of Ware was nothing if not a gentleman.

It was time to stir the pudding, Graceanne announced to the guests. Everyone was invited to the kitchen to make his or her Christmas wish, from the lowest potboy—in fair warning to those high-in-the-instep dowagers—to the youngest child—in fair warning to Miss Ridgemont. Eleanor went anyway rather than remain above stairs all by herself. She also wanted to keep an eye on that Mrs. Warrington; Ware was being altogether too watchful of the dowdy widow.

When they were all gathered in the kitchen—a ridiculous idea in the first place; ladies did not belong in hot, messy places—Miss Ridgemont found herself wedged between a footman and Miss Ashton-Highet's deaf grandmother, which served her notion of propriety even less well. "This is absurd," she muttered, "making wishes on a lump of potage."

The deaf ancient didn't hear her, but the twins did. They were waiting their turns with Shanna the nursemaid, and it would be hard to tell who of the three was the most excited.

"It is not!" piped up Willy.

Leslie added: "How else will Father Christmas know what to bring for Christmas?"

Eleanor was delighted to get revenge at last. "You poor, simple brats, don't you know there is no such thing as Father Christmas? I'm surprised, Mrs. Warrington, that you permit such outrageous mummery in a good Christian household."

So the boys started to cry.

"Why, next you'll teach them to believe in fairies and elves and leprechauns."

So Shanna started to cry.

"Enough!" shouted the duke in his most awesome voice. The pots and pans shook on their hooks on the walls, half the servants disappeared without making their wishes, wishing to keep their positions more than anything else. "In this house," he thundered, "pudding wishes come true. And Father Christmas is real, Miss Ridgemont, because I say he is. And finally, if the little people talk to Shanna, perhaps she is more fortunate than the rest of us."

"Well, I never—" Eleanor began.

"No, and you damned well never will!" the Duke of Ware forgot his gallantry enough to say.

So Miss Ridgemont started to cry.

The next day Miss Ridgemont received an urgent summons, which never passed through Milsom's hands, to attend a sick relative. She begged her friends to bear her company in this time of woe, which was due to last until they reached the Earl of Cranshaw's house party.

Crow brought the lady to Warwick, so he was honor bound to escort her to her destination. He stopped to have a last toast with his friend while his valet was packing, a time-consuming task. Ware was worried that he'd placed a heavy burden on Crow's padded shoulders, but the baronet reassured him that it was no such thing. "In fact, Lee, I came to ask if you'd mind me cutting you out with the lady."

"I'll hand you the saber, my best of good friends," the duke replied. "Good luck to you. But are you sure? I mean . . ."

"Oh, I know the chit's rep, how she's hanging out for title and fortune, but we're well matched. Same interests, don't you know. Everyone says we make a handsome couple. She'll run out of dukes and earls soon, and I'll be waiting."

Ware shook his friend's hand, careful not to crush the fingers between the rings Crosby wore. "Then I'll wish you luck, Crow, and my best wishes."

By the time the company had all departed, some in better cheer than others, the afternoon of Christmas Eve had arrived. Graceanne decided she had to tell Leland now about Pru and the baby, before attending the holiest of church services with lies and distrust between them. She was well aware they'd never be social equals, but the hurtfulness had to end. And after all, Miss Ridgemont was gone; half of Graceanne's Christmas wish had already come true. She sought his direction from Milsom.

Ware was determined to get her alone at last. He asked the butler where she might be found.

Milsom *almost* said, "Waiting for you, you nodcock," but he hadn't had quite that much of the lamb's wool yet.

They met in the Adams room, and were admiring the newly installed Christmas tree and discussing how many carriages were needed to transport their diminished group to church that evening, while they each tried to get up the courage to speak.

Milsom cleared his throat from the doorway. "A military man has called, Mrs. Warrington."

"Oh, one of Tony's friends, I suppose."

"No, madam, this is a naval gentleman, a Mr. Hallorahan. Are you at home?"

Not only was she at home, she was out of the parlor and into Liam's embrace in the Great Hall in a flash. Leland stayed where he was, staring into the fire.

The deuce take it, he thought, he'd even pulled strings to get the fellow sent back. Now she'd go off with him again, and he couldn't do a blasted thing about it. Leland wouldn't stop her, not if it meant Grace's happiness. He knew that now, that he could never be happy if she wasn't.

Then he heard her ask Milsom to send someone to fetch the baby downstairs. Of course, the duke despaired, it wanted only that. How could he go on without the children? Her children. Liam's child. His life.

He didn't know whether to go offer his felicitations, forbid her to take the boys, or beg her to stay. He couldn't just do nothing, he told himself. He had to move, to try. He went toward the open door and heard the Irishman's voice.

"Aye, e'en if she'll have me own carroty thatch, she's a bonny, bonny lassie. Just like her mum, b'gor."

"Yes, and she has the sweetness Pru used to possess before our father's meanness changed her."

"Ah, but she wanted only a bit of liveliness, did Pru. She was a good girl, I know. I could make her happy enow to bring back the sweetness."

Graceanne didn't want him to get his hopes up, when he kept swearing he was going to find Pru and marry her. "I'm afraid she's dreadfully spoiled. Your father's house on the farm . . ."

"Aye, and don't I know that cottage is no place for Pru? I don't intend to go back, and so I told my da. I liked the seafaring life, I did, and did well at it, too, after I found my way about. Saved the captain's life during an engagement and got promoted right on deck. Now I mean to take my prize money and buy into a shipping firm. I can take a wife to all those places Pru wanted to see, b'gad."

"That's no life for a baby, Liam."

"No, more's the pity," he said, looking down at the infant in his arms.

Graceanne sighed. "And I don't think I could part with her now."

"And I wouldn't ask it of you. I could never offer all this"—he waved his hand around the opulent hall—"and I can see how you love the wee girl as your own. She's yours, and God bless you for taking her in. The good Lord willing, there will be bairns aplenty for Pru and me when I find her, and after she grows up some. She's just a babe herself, is my Prudence."

"You are much too good for her, Liam Hallorahan, but I wish you Godspeed, that you might find her."

"Merry Christmas to you, Mrs. Warrington, and God bless you and keep you, my darling babe. Forgive me."

Liam left without looking back, not even seeing the duke standing in the hallway.

Leland wanted to rush in and gather Graceanne into his arms, but she already had a baby in hers, getting wet from her tears. He put his arms around both of them anyway. "I have been such a fool, Grace. It is I who has to beg for your forgiveness, for distrusting you even for an instant."

Graceanne smiled through her tears. "I've been stubborn and too prideful to tell you. Can you forgive me?"

Leland finally got his kiss with the infant between them. It was necessarily a chaste kind of kiss, a bit distanced and much too quick, but enough to set his heart singing. If Miss Ridgemont's fervent kiss was a pleasant jog in the park, this tender touching was winning the Breeders' Cup at Newmarket.

Graceanne handed him the baby, worrying that if her knees were weak, so might her arms be. Of course, then they still had Nina between them, stupidly. They shared one more awkward kiss, though, which started bells ringing. Actually, they were the church bells.

"Oh, dear, the pageant!" Graceanne left him with the baby and a volume of unspoken words, to rush off to make sure the boys were ready.

Leland looked down at the babe in his arms, who was staring anxiously after her disappearing mother. "Don't worry, precious," he told her. "She's coming back. And I've got you." He buried his face in Nina's soft talcum smell, making her chuckle again. "I've got all of you now."

The pageant went well. The cow mooed from both ends, but Joseph and Mary were properly reverent in their roles, and Nina in her swaddling didn't complain too much about the rough homespun next to her skin.

Afterward they went home to greet the carolers, to light the Yule log with great pomp and ceremony, Ware guiding Willy and Les's hands holding last year's burning sliver to the new log. It was amazing how much warmth the traditional fire put out when done the right way. Then they all toasted the season with wassail, even Nanny taking a sip.

Finally it was time for the boys to go to bed and for Graceanne to put out the last nursery decorations and the gifts for the twins to find in the morning. The duke had to go wrap the last of his presents and make sure those purchased in London were assembled just right under the tree in the parlor.

While he was gone, Graceanne slipped off to her own bedchamber, where she lay awake listening to the distant carolers, holding her Christmas wish to her heart. She wished by every good luck charm of Shanna's, and said a prayer or two of her own.

On the morning of Christmas Day, Graceanne brought the children down to the parlor before breakfast. She was wearing an emerald green velvet gown and the boys had matching green velvet coats and short pants. They wore brand-new caps they didn't want to take off, even to open the mounds of packages under the tree. Graceanne complained again that he was spoiling the children, but Leland was enjoying every minute of watching their delight, almost as much as he'd enjoyed shopping for the unicycles and croquet sets, the small-sized pocket watches and tiny high leather riding boots. There was even a huge wooden castle, complete with carved knights on chargers, to match Nina's new dollhouse. And there were dolls. At least six of them stood or sat around the base of the tree, from rag babies to porcelain-faced beauties to peddler dolls with trays of tiny wares.

Leland shrugged off Graceanne's "Six dolls? You bought a tiny infant six dolls? Why, some of them are bigger than she is!"

"I couldn't decide," was all he said.

"Silly, all Nina needs to make her happy is a simple teething ring." Then she called the boys to her side and whispered into their ears. "But we have a gift for you, too, don't we, my angels?"

"Another pen wipe?"

"Better." The twins giggled, then together took off their new caps. Where Leland was used to seeing the twins with brown tousled heads, the riotous curls were all trimmed off and their hair was neatly combed—with parts on different sides!

"Les on the left, Willy on the wight," they chanted merrily.

"That's the best present of all! It's one of my Christmas wishes come true! I do have to confess I cheated and made two. No, I cannot tell you what the other one is yet. I have a present for your mother first." He turned to Graceanne and took a small box out of his pocket. "I hope you'll be happy with a simple ring like your daughter."

It was no simple ring at all, not with diamonds and sapphires, to match her eyes, he said. Graceanne had a horrible moment of doubt, that the ring was too ornate to be anything honorable.

But Leland was quick to read her smile's disappearance. "No, no, the one that matches is the plain gold band, but you don't get that one until you marry me, dear heart. Will you, and make my other Christmas wish come true? Do say yes, darling, for I don't think I can live without you, I love you so much."

"Me or my children, Your Grace?" she had to know.

"All of you, each of you, but none more than you, my Grace."

"Then yes, Leland, for I love you just as much, and now my wish can come true, too."

"And ours!" chorused Willy and Les, jumping up and down.

No such thing as Father Christmas? Don't dare tell the Duke of Ware, or his duchess.

Merry Christmas!

Read on for a sneak peek of
Barbara Metzger's next delightful
Regency romance

THE WICKED WAYS OF
A TRUE HERO

Available wherever books are sold
and on www.penguin.com

$\mathcal{T}$he end was near, inevitable and inescapable. All men had to meet their fates. Like all men, Daniel Stamfield protested his imminent demise.

"Great gods, I'm not ready!" he shouted, his fist raised to the heavens.

The gods, great or small, did not answer, but his companion cringed farther back on her side of the bed.

Daniel did not notice. He leaped from the bed, bare as the day he was born, and charged to the dressing table. He grabbed up the bottle there—brandy or gin or spice-scented cologne; he didn't care which. He ignored the nearby glass, just as he ignored Miss White's mew of distress when he raised the bottle to his mouth and took a long swallow. Then another. The liquor could not change the outcome, nor delay it. Being dead drunk on judgment day wasn't such a wise act, either, he realized, which only reminded him.

"Dead. I'm a dead man." He went back to the bed, as if sinking into the downy mattress, pulling the covers over his head and Miss White closer to his cold body could save him. "I'm too young to die. Not even thirty. I thought I had more time."

Don't all men think that?

The note was still on the bed, though, where he'd tossed it after the manservant brought the damn thing. On a silver tray, no less. Daniel stared at it now, the expensive stationery, the flowing script, his name on the front of the folded sheet, the familiar seal on the back. His blue-eyed glare couldn't make the missive disappear, this death warrant, this end of his carefree days, this letter from his mother.

"They're in Town," he told Miss White, "expecting me to play the beau for my sister's come-out." He looked longingly back at the bottle on the table, then at the window overlooking the alley, as if escape lay in that direction. There was no escape, Daniel knew, not anywhere in London. "I wrote that Susanna was too young to make her curtsies at court. I said she and Mother should come to Town before next Christmas to shop, to take in the theater and visit the lending libraries. A few tea parties and morning calls to Mother's old friends, especially those with daughters Susanna's age. I'd take her to Astley's Amphitheater to see the trick riding. Susanna would like that. I did at her age."

Daniel still enjoyed visits to the Circus, but now he went more to admire the bareback riders in their tights and short spangled skirts. He groaned at the memory that would be just that—a fond, forlorn dream now that his family was in Town. "A short visit would have been fine—a chance for Susanna to see the metropolis and pick up a bit of Town bronze and perhaps make some new friends before facing the marriage mart next year. A week or two—that's what I told them. Did anyone listen to me, the head of the family? No, damn it. They are here now, here for the whole blasted spring Season. Weeks. Months. Maybe into summer. An eternity of balls and routs, masquerades and presentations and operas. Balls," he repeated, with a different meaning.

No more bachelor days, wagering and wenching and lying abed, when he found his way home at daybreak or later. No more race meets or prizefights or tavern brawls. No more comfortable clothes, either. He grimaced at the loose shirt he pulled over his head, the baggy Cossack trousers he dragged on. They'd soon be gone, along with the opera dancers and actresses and serving girls.

The spotted kerchief he knotted at his throat felt like a noose. "Gads, they'll expect me to wear satin knee breeches and starched neck cloths." He could feel the rash already. And that was the least of his itches.

Some men came home from war with wounds or scars or medals. Daniel Stamfield had come home with a rash. Like all the men of his family, Daniel had a gift—or curse, depending on how one felt. Somehow, they could all tell truth from lies. His uncle, the Earl of Royce, heard discordant notes. His cousin Rex, the Royce heir, saw scarlet. Harry, his other cousin, from the wrong side of the blanket, tasted bitter lies on his tongue. Daniel? His curse wasn't subtle or private. That would have been too easy, too comfortable for a man who already stuck out like a sore thumb because of his overlarge, ungainly size. A sore thumb? He'd be happy with that. Instead he got itchy toes, itchy ears, bright red splotches on his neck, his face, his hands. Worst of all, a lot of lies, continuous lies, blatant lies, gave him a rash on his private parts. That was how he'd been thrown out of Almack's his first time at the hallowed hall of propriety. He'd scratched his arse. What if Susanna was denied vouchers for that sacred altar to the matchmaking deities because of him?

Hell, he would die at the first Venetian breakfast from all the polite mistruths and insincere flatteries the beau monde mouthed. His mother and sister would die too, of embarrassment. Susanna's Season would be ruined, a debacle, a disgrace. No gentleman would marry her. Sweet little Sukey'd be an old maid at seventeen, all because of him and his sensitive skin. He should have stayed in the army, no matter the cost. Perhaps he had time to reenlist. So what if the war with France was over and that madman Napoleon was finally defeated? There was bound to be a battle somewhere, some way he could prove useful. More useful than he'd be to poor Susanna.

All the Royce descendants were invaluable to the government, in necessarily secret service to their country. They'd be burned as witches or warlocks if anyone suspected their hidden talent, or ostracized as charlatans. Mind readers? The devil! Truth knowers? Bosh. So they worked behind the scenes, disguising their gift as wisdom, wit, and uncanny luck.

Uncle Royce advised the courts. Harry used to run a spy network. Rex worked with Bow Street after he was wounded in the Peninsula war, after Daniel left the army. Together Rex and Daniel had been the dreaded Inquisitors, the intelligence officers in charge of gathering information from captured enemy officers. Daniel's size alone intimidated their prisoners. Their unfailing results terrified everyone else, even their superiors. Since only a select few could know of the family trait, the War Office let stand the rumors that the Inquisitors were torturers, immoral brutes. They were despised by friend and foe alike, despite the countless English lives they saved. Daniel had constant rashes.

He came home when his father died, relieved to have an excuse to leave the army and his ugly but important employment. The life of a country squire, or a town buck, was just as filled with falsehoods, though, and boredom to boot. Then came the guilt over leaving Rex to serve the country by himself, until the fool got shot.

Daniel had sworn to look after his cousin and best friend. He'd failed. He'd lied, which was the worst thing a Royce relative could do. When Rex turned into a morose, hermitlike cripple, Daniel turned into a libertine, a wastrel, a gambler, a drunk. He threw himself into whatever debauchery London offered, along with its other dregs and demimondaines. So what if his new companions lied and cheated? Their haunts were usually too dark for anyone to notice Daniel's spots, and half his neighbors itched just as badly, from lice or fleas or bedbugs. Women were paid to please, and paid more not to pretend any tender feelings or passion. His size and reputation protected him from the dangers of the night, and his mighty fists protected him from anyone stupid enough to try in the shadows.

Then Rex came to London as a favor to his father and got involved with solving crimes. The clunch almost got himself killed again, for his efforts, but he actually liked working with Bow Street's investigators. Rex tried to drag Daniel out of the gambling dens and into his detective work, but Daniel was having none of it. Damn, did they think the suspects were going to confess when they knew they'd be hanged or deported? No, the scum told lies on top of lies, and Daniel got more rashes.

Even Harry, the earl's illegitimate son, tried to enlist Daniel in his sanctioned skullduggery, uncovering blackmailers and traitors and revolutionaries in the government. Were there no honest politicians?

Both of his cousins wanted Daniel to continue their work in Parliament or the police precincts. Uncle Royce offered him a magistrate's position, so he could use his gift in the courts. England needed him, they all said. He should be working, they all said, for the good of King and country.

Daniel'd said no. He was not interested in their noble missions, their self-righteous sacrifices, not when he could enjoy a redheaded wench and a bottle of wine. He'd served his country; he'd done his share. So no, he would not mingle among the gentlemen who ruled the kingdom, listening for their lies. No, he would not preside over the courts where bewigged barristers spewed prevarications to save their clients. No, he would not sit at some battered desk to hear scurvy felons plead their nonexistent innocence. No, he would not need a tin of talcum powder on his posterior every day.

"No chance of saying no to my mother," he told Miss White, his voice full of regret and resignation. He might be brave, and full of brawn if not brains, but she was his mother. She was also Lady Cora Stamfield, née Royce, daughter of the former earl, sister to the current Lord Royce, widow of one of the largest landholders in the eastern shires. Formidable in her own right, she ran Stamfield Manor and the rest of the parish as well. Mostly, though, she'd asked nothing from Daniel but his happiness for years now. She was not one for rants and recriminations, only steadfast love and loyalty to her only son. He knew she worried while he was with the army, and more so while he wallowed in London's pleasures. Sowing his oats, she'd called it, and waited for him to reap his harvest and come home. He hadn't, except for short visits. So how could he refuse her request to join her and Susanna at Royce House?

"Now she remembers I am the man of the family, when she thinks she needs me."

Daniel wouldn't be the head of the household if the earl came to town, nor would his presence be required. Mother was staying at the earl's mansion in Mayfair, after all, and Lord and Lady Royce held enough power in London to oversee seven debutante balls. But the earl and his countess were recently reunited and enjoying their life in the country. Rex, Viscount Rexford, that was, had enough countenance and connections to aid Lady Cora and Susanna too, but he was the proud father of twins, with another child due soon. He would never leave his beloved Amanda and their brood to take over escort duties. Even Harry would have done in a pinch, now that he was recognized in Polite Society. The former master spy, though, was also deliriously happily wed, traveling on honeymoon, showing off his beautiful bride to relatives, inspecting his new estate, and awaiting his first child.

"Like rabbits, that's what they both are," Daniel said as he pulled on his scuffed boots. "And curse them all for not being here when I need them. I'd rather face the blasted French cannons on my own than the *ton* without a friend at my back."

Miss White made a soft sound of commiseration, or protest at being ignored. She was here, wasn't she? Daniel sat beside her on the bed, gathering her close. "I am sorry, puss. I know you'd stand by me, but it will never do. You wouldn't be welcome at Royce House, you know. You're a beauty, my pet, but not of their elevated, rarefied world. No more than I am, but I have no choice. You'll be happier here." He looked around at the comfortable rooms he'd taken over from Harry, above McCann's Club. No one cared what time he came or went, in what condition, or with which companion. The service was excellent, the food ample, and the company undemanding. He'd miss it: the freedom, the camaraderie, the easy acceptance of who and what he was, with no demands that he become anything else. But his mother wanted him to reside with the family, likely to be at their beck and call. "I'll miss you most of all, my dear, but you'll do. You already rule the kitchens here, so you won't go hungry, and Harry will return soon and take you up again."

He gave Miss White one last kiss on the top of her silky head, then stood and brushed her white cat hairs off his coat. That was the least he could do for his beloved mother, present a neat appearance on this first day. She'd be disappointed in him soon enough. Like everyone else in the family already was.

REGENCY CHRISTMAS WISHES

Five Holiday Tales
by Barbara Metzger,
Sandra Heath, Edith Layton,
Emma Jensen, and Carla Kelly

Celebrate the joys of Christmas in Regency England,
with five stories by some of the most beloved
Regency authors. Ringing in the season with fireside
warmth, holiday wishes, and Yuletide romance,
these stories capture the spirit of Christmas. A
sparkling collection, it is sure to delight readers all
year round, with warmth, cheer—and love.

**Available wherever books are sold or at
penguin.com**

From *New York Times*
bestselling author

Jo Beverley

WINTER FIRE

Jo Beverley returns to the Georgian period and
the irresistible Malloren clan in this sumptuous
historical novel of sizzling tension, powerful
attraction, a false and forced engagement—and
the lavish use of mistletoe and rather
well-spiked eggnog.

**Available wherever books are sold or at
penguin.com**

From *New York Times*
bestselling author

Mary Balogh

UNDER THE MISTLETOE

Old loves rekindled, new loves found, and family bonds
strengthened...from the beloved, multiple-award winning
author Mary Balogh comes this compilation of four classic
Christmas stories: *The Star of Bethlehem*, *The Best Gift*,
Playing House, and *No Room at the Inn*, and a new story
exclusive to this collection—*A Family Christmas*.

**Available wherever books are sold or at
penguin.com**